Royal Runaway's Holiday

Royal Runaway's Holiday

MANDY BOERMA

For those who feel unseen or overlooked.
May you always know that God knows you
and loves you.
He has called you by name.

The sheep hear his voice,
and he calls his own sheep by name

John 10:3

D esperate times called for spying. Evalina Rosalind Marie Bexley absolutely should not be in a secret room in the palace eavesdropping on Parliament, but there had been no other option.

As the heir apparent, she'd never before been blocked from attending a meeting. There hadn't been a single session of Parliament she'd missed in the past fifteen years.

Until today.

Rather than sitting next to her father, helping others solve any problems that arose in her country, she stood in a dark room lit by her flashlight, in her comfortable yoga pants, with her hair in a messy bun. No need to dress for the spiders in the corners watching her.

She checked her watch. Fifteen minutes late, but she'd had to be careful getting into the hidden room. No one outside a select few knew of its existence. She'd found it quite by accident playing hide-and-seek as a child.

Lifting the metal flap about halfway up the wall, Eva studied the men and women she'd known her entire life as they shifted uncomfortably in their seats, the room surprisingly quiet.

"I'm sorry." Her father's voice held an edge to it that could cut down the will of a weaker man. "You want to enact an ancient law on my daughter that hasn't been exercised in over a hundred years?"

Yikes. Something had happened.

"There has not been a female heir apparent in over one hundred years in order for the law to be addressed." Eva didn't recognize that voice, but the nasal overtone held its own edge.

"I was not married when I took the throne." Father's curt words caused a chill to run down Eva's spine, but his fierce support of her warmed her, helping to chase the chill of the room away. The secret room didn't have central heating and AC, since it wasn't on any blueprints and never saw any updates. And with snow on the ground outside, the cold November temperatures kept this room cool.

"You were not a princess."

Eva couldn't see the misogynistic pig who spoke, but it sounded like Lord Veelsh. She never had liked the greasy old guy with his thin, wiry mustache. Some people just shouldn't attempt facial hair.

Her father's face flushed. "You're saying that the chromosome differentiating me as a male makes me better suited to rule this kingdom than my daughter? The one who has been attending Parliament meetings since she was eleven? The one who just last month balanced our budget, so we could add extra funding for our military and infrastructure development? The woman who has worked to make our children's hospital the best and most advanced in the world? And she's only a month away from her twenty-sixth birthday. Can you imagine what she will accomplish as the ruling monarch when I retire and she's crowned this spring?"

Murmurs ran through the room, but no one responded. Heat rushed up her neck. Her father never held back praise, but she'd seldom heard him boast about her accomplishments in such a fashion. She had worked hard for the causes near and dear to her heart. That it benefited her people, and her entire kingdom, only made the causes that much more important.

Her father stood. "Princess Evalina has studied, not only graduating top of her class, but with us. You've seen her work since childhood for the betterment of our country. She loves Nevive more than anyone I've ever seen. Having a male by her side will not change her ability to rule this country well. In fact, forcing her hand may cause problems that we, as a country, don't want."

"No one is arguing that Princess Evalina isn't a dedicated princess, but tradition says a male is a better leader." This from Lady Galveston, the first female to hold a seat in the parliament. Something that Eva's father had petitioned for. Since Lady Galveston worked for equality, her words pierced Eva.

If the women of Parliament didn't support her, did she even stand a chance to ascend the throne?

"I'm sure Queen Elizabeth would be rolling over in her grave." Her father's quick quip had Eva biting back a chuckle. "Princess Evalina is next in line. There isn't even a male in the current line of succession."

"Except there is." Lord Veelsh had always been a bit of a viper, but to pull this? She couldn't fathom he would go this far. What was he up to? There was no male who could step up and take over the throne. She had the line of succession memorized. No men were in line. It was the first time in Nevive history that this had occurred.

Another low murmur broke through the room. But Lord Veelsh cleared his throat, effectively cutting off the chatter. "My cousin Alexander Moriffiti is the son of the late Duke of Lexington. He is ready and willing to step up as the next king of Nevive if your daughter does not meet the necessary qualifications to be our monarch. If, as you put it, she loves this country, she should be willing to adhere to our long-standing laws and traditions."

Father paused briefly, glancing at the prime minister before speaking. "This law is archaic and outdated. I move to have this law ab—"

The gavel came down on the desk in three loud thumps, stopping Father from saying more. He sat down, nodding to Lord Mast, the speaker of the parliament. The man had been like a grandfather to Eva through the years, always handing her a Werther's Original before the meetings started. "The law stands. Princess Evalina must be married by her twenty-sixth birthday in order to take the throne. It gives her time to settle into married life before her coronation in the spring."

Eva gasped and dropped the cover. The metal clanged against the air vent, but the room had erupted in conversation, hiding the sound.

Married? By her twenty-sixth birthday? In a month?

In. A. Month.

She'd never loved her Christmas birthday, but she hated it even more right now.

She wasn't dating anyone. Hadn't dated anyone. Ever.

Mainly because there was only one man she would consider, and he showed absolutely no interest in her.

Gordon Tarpen.

Her best friend since childhood. And while every sweet dream of happily ever after revolved around Gordon, it was impossible, because the monarch must marry a citizen or royalty—of which he was neither. Not to mention he'd practically ghosted her since her father's retirement had been announced a few months ago. Their regular communication had dwindled to practically nothing. She hadn't heard from him in a month. A very long and lonely month.

Eva turned the flashlight off as she stepped into the hallway and made her way back to her apartment. Her father would come find her as soon as the meeting ended. He no doubt knew she had been listening, and she didn't need to hear any more. She'd been the reason the meeting had been called, and it made sense why they didn't want her there. The cowards wouldn't face her while determining her future. Whatever else needed to be discussed could be dealt with later.

It took her father forty-five minutes to join her, and by that time, she'd showered, dressed in a suit, pulled her red hair up in a French twist, and looked like the princess she claimed to be.

"The one you are," Kendra, her friend and body double, insisted when Eva spoke her fears. Her friend lounged on the couch, wearing a solid navy blue dress with three-quarter length sleeves, her dark hair in a low ponytail.

"For a little bit longer. But if this Alexander of Lexington becomes the next king, I will no longer be Princess Evalina."

"Nonsense. He can't strip you of your title. Besides, you are going to beat this. You were created to be the next monarch." Kendra's words helped to soothe the ache in her heart.

"But I have a month to find someone, fall in love, and get married, or I won't be the next queen. Merry Christmas to me." She should write a letter to Santa.

Dear Santa,

If it's not too much trouble, I need a husband.

Sincerely,

Eva

A baby dinosaur or unicorn would be more likely to appear in her stocking than a husband.

A quick rhythm knocked at her door, one only her father used with her, before the door opened and her father walked in. Since it was the first time she'd seen him today, she curtsied. "Good morning, Father."

Kendra also curtsied before she excused herself. Once the door closed and they were left alone, the king's poised mask fell away, and Eva deflated into a chair, motioning to the couch.

"You heard." It wasn't really a question, but Eva nodded, and her father rested a hand on her shoulder before sitting. "I'm sorry."

"I know. I heard your defense. I appreciate your confidence in me." Eva gestured at the coffee on the serving tray she had ordered up, but her father declined. "I always hoped for a love match like you and Mom had. I still remember the way you would look at her."

"I always wanted you to have that kind of love story too. Your mother would be livid over this." Her father's eyes glazed over. A familiar look whenever he thought about her mother, who had died in a rock climbing accident when Eva was nine years old.

"It will be all right. I have thirty days." Except that wasn't very long to meet someone, fall in love, and get engaged. "Now that I think that over, how am I supposed to find someone and fall in love in a month?"

Eva stood and walked across the room. She turned on her heel. "I can't do that, can I? This will have to be an arrangement. Do people still do that today? Didn't that practice end hundreds of years ago?"

Her father set his elbows on his knees and ran a hand down his face. "I thought we'd moved past such archaic laws and that you would be able to marry for love. Would you like to fight for a certain young reporter?"

Her ears burned. Her father knew everything. She shouldn't be surprised he knew of her feelings for Gordon. "I won't force him. He deserves to find love."

Her father sighed. "You'd hardly need to use force. But if you are uninterested, I will continue to fight this law. There has to be a way around it."

If only her father could be right. "Not with Lord Mast supporting it. Let's start looking at my options. If I can't marry for love, let's hope I can find someone tolerable."

Tolerable...such a romantic word. Weren't princesses supposed to find their true love and live happily ever after? That must be just as much a myth as talking animals.

"If not, then we will let the throne go. We will not compromise your future for this kingdom." Her father stood at those words and walked to her and wrapped his arms around her.

She relaxed into his warmth, allowing his strength to hold her up. "Spoken like a father, not a king."

His chuckle rumbled under her cheek. "I am both."

"But you know I will give up anything for the kingdom. There is no doubt I would sacrifice that for the people I love. For my country." Eva buried her face into her father's chest. Strong words, strong conviction, but she relished his support. She wouldn't allow her family line to fall because she wasn't willing to conform to a law, archaic as it might be. "I will find someone."

Her father nodded. "I know. But that doesn't mean I like it. As your king, I agree with your sentiment. As your father, I wanted to pound all of those men."

"Just not Lady Galveston?" Eva giggled. Her father would never "pound" anyone. But she appreciated his fierce loyalty.

"I would never harm a lady, but she did irk me royally today. I never would have considered she'd give in to such chauvinistic thoughts."

Honestly, Eva had thought Lady Galveston would be the one to stand up for her. The rejection had stung. "We'll make it work."

They would, it's what they always did. Her father smiled half-heartedly. "Call Kendra. Let's start going through the lists of eligible bachelors. I'll compile some names too."

"We'll make it a party. Tonight?" Eva pulled out for her phone to check her calendar.

"I can't tonight. Dinner meeting with the prime minister." Father checked his schedule. "But I'm free tomorrow after five."

"How about we meet at six? I have a meeting with the head of the children's hospital at four. That gives me a little time to get back."

"Done." They both blocked their schedule off, and Eva sent an invite to Kendra. If she had to pick a man to marry, she wanted her friend's opinion. Since Kendra also lived at the palace,

Eva would be meeting up with her later to fill her in on all the details, but the electronic calendars made it so much easier to plan things.

"While this session of Parliament was closed, it's only a matter of time before this leaks to the press." Her father nodded at her before leaving her room.

She slumped back on the couch with a sigh. News of this would get out, and with Gordon's job as a TV news reporter, he would be one of the first to hear. She should reach out and tell him. She opened her phonebook, and her finger hovered over his name. Her thumb brushed the screen, and the call started.

Oh no!

That's not what she meant to do. What would she say? "Hey. I'm getting married." Talk about an ice breaker.

Not to mention, if she told him, it would be real. She ended the call before it could ring. Hopefully, it hadn't registered on his phone and he wouldn't even see that she'd called.

Eva tossed her phone on the couch and walked to the window, studying the town below. The streets were filled with cars and people as they moved around.

The Christmas Bazaar—consisting of several tents and food trucks, a large stage, and a dance floor for live music—sat in the town square. It had always been her desire to attend, but life kept her away. It would be amazing if she could do more than watch Gordon report on the festivities. Even better, if she could tag along while he worked.

Not that a princess ever tagged along. No, as a princess, she could attend and observe.

In the square, people scurried about, but Eva could imagine a camera set on a tripod trained on Gordon's lopsided, friendly smile and his dark, teasing eyes while he reported some fascinating story about the Christmas traditions of her beloved people.

What would they think when they discovered she had to marry for a law and not for love? Full of passion and compassion, would they fight for her future if they knew? Or would they, too, think she would serve better with a man by her side?

She'd always known she'd have to let go of her childhood dream of a happily ever after with Gordon. Too bad the day had finally arrived.

If only her heart would accept that this was for the best.

"Reporting from the streets of downtown Lesa, I'm Gordon Tarpen with KEVE-TV News. Back to you, Dana." Gordon stood in front of the camera, waiting for the cue that he was off camera.

Finally, Kevin, the news producer, spoke in his ear. "All clear. Great story, man. Pack up and bring it back to the studio. We've got an end of show wrap-up. Try and make it back since you're only a few blocks away. I'd like to talk to you afterward."

Gordon stepped out of the view from the camera and started to dismantle his setup. He'd hoped to call it a night. So much for that. "Will do."

Tucking his phone/video camera into his pocket, he folded his tripod, took off his mic, and checked his watch. He had twenty minutes until show's end—just enough time to grab apple ciders on his way to the station.

Once he'd stepped into the warmth of the station, he tugged off his winter cap and unwound his scarf while balancing two travel trays stacked on top of each other, filled with the apple ciders he'd bought.

He set his outerwear and gear on his desk, then carried the drinks into the conference room for the post show wrap-up. His phone buzzed once in his pocket, and he took it out to notice a missed call from Eva. Quickly, he shoved his phone back in his pocket. Hopefully, no one noticed his phone screen. He couldn't let them know about that connection.

The anchors and director had already assembled, and Gordon closed the door to the hustle of the writers and technical people as they scurried to leave before a new story broke. Not that it happened often, but at the end of the day, everyone wanted to head home.

Kevin sat down, grabbed an apple cider, and lifted it to Gordon. "Okay, folks. I'm going to get to the point. Ratings are down. KAT-TV is inching into the top news spot, and we need something to pick things up. An investigation. Breaking news. Something. What do you have?"

Kevin sipped his cider. This was how he worked. He'd state the problem, tell people what he wanted, and let them brainstorm ideas. According to Kevin, there were no bad ideas during a brainstorming session.

Gordon seldom attended these aftershow meetings, but normally brainstorming happened at the start of the day, and post-show meetings were for wrap-ups.

"It's time Gordon pulled his connections at the castle. We haven't had a good royal scandal in ages." Dana pinned him in his chair with her piercing expression. She must be a mom.

Gordon shifted in his seat. Had she seen his missed call from Eva? "Sorry. I don't report on the royals."

"You know them. You're in and out of the palace." Dana pointed her pen at him.

"My uncle's the head chef. I visit him occasionally, not the royals. If you want to talk about the royals' dietary habits…" The change in topic had Dana wrinkling her nose and covered the fact that sometimes Gordon did visit Eva, just not as often as he'd like to. It had been far too long since he'd seen her. Not that he knew what often enough looked like. They could visit every day, and it might not be enough. Besides, he'd been the one to force some distance and slow their correspondence to a trickle of anything.

Growing up, she'd been his best friend, his only friend after his parents passed away and his uncle adopted him sixteen years ago.

Gordon had loved her the moment he first saw her, when she'd brought him a slice of cake. Her simple "desserts make everything better" attitude had them sharing sugary delights through the years.

Since that first meeting, they'd grown up and once college started, they had gone their separate ways. It happened naturally since he'd returned to the United States and she'd stayed for the local university. They'd exchanged messages and phone calls, but between Gordon's jobs to pay for his education and Eva's royal responsibilities, there hadn't been much extra time in their schedules. Now their communication had dwindled down. Especially since he'd had to get a full-time job and try and settle into a country that he couldn't really call his own because he still wasn't a citizen. Even though Nevive had been home for the past sixteen years, his requests for citizenship the past four years have been denied by the immigration office for various reasons.

"No one is interested in what they eat. But we need something. Is the princess seeing someone? Or the king? Perhaps he's ready to enter the dating field again," Dana pressed. She opened her computer.

Gordon scoffed. The king might consider dating when he retired, but the man wouldn't while he kept so busy. Plus, the maids all said he had a thing for his assistant, Renee. Not that Gordon would report that bit of gossip.

Kevin lifted an eyebrow and gazed at Gordon like he might have a story. "Do you know something?"

Oops. Had he let his face speak for him? "Hardly. But I doubt the king has time to date."

"And Princess Goody Two-Shoes has never dated." Liam tapped his pen on the desk. "But we could report on the children's hospital."

Eva loved to spotlight the work done there. Gordon took every opportunity he could to highlight the positive influence she had at the hospital. "There's a concert there this weekend. Johnny Rocco will be there. And he's also preforming at the bazaar this year. Maybe we could investigate why Johnny is doing so many concerts locally this season?"

"No more fluff news. We could go undercover. Is the hospital misrepresenting funds? Perhaps they aren't caring for the children properly?"

Gordon clenched his jaw. Yes, those topics sold news. No one could deny that, but people liked to hear good news too. "I hardly think news about Johnny Rocco would be 'fluff.'"

Liam closed his eyes and mocked a snore. "Snooze alert. We're always reporting on the celebrities making an appearance at the children's hospital. It's time to dig in a little deeper. How much are we paying for these people to show up? Is that taxpayer dollars? That could be the story. Funds that could be allocated elsewhere are lining the pockets of the rich and famous."

"Cynical much?" Dana rolled her eyes. "There are plenty of celebrities who do things for no other reason than publicity. It pays off in the end."

Gordon sat forward, linking his fingers so he didn't shake a hand or fist at Liam. "We don't pay the stars, they come on their own. Dana's right. Publicity goes a long way in the draw for these events. Princess Evalina might have contacted a few to start, but now they volunteer on their own."

Liam scoffed. "We need hard news. Something cutting-edge and scandalous."

They wouldn't find that among the royals. And Gordon had several stories lined up around the Christmas Bazaar. Several booths sent their proceeds, or a portion of them, to help different charities or the children's hospital. Several of the booths had a long history—stories hidden in plain sight, ready for a willing person to discover and present to eager viewers. The downside of living in a country with a low crime rate, generally friendly people, and a clean-cut royal family? Hard news stories were difficult to come by. It forced reporters to dig in.

The meeting progressed in much the same way. Eventually Kevin cut in, telling them to sleep on some ideas. He dismissed them but made eye contact with Gordon in a silent reminder to stick around.

After the room emptied, Kevin closed the conference room door and sat down next to Gordon. "Liam turned in his notice today. He's moving on after Christmas, and we need a new evening anchor. I'd like to pull you into the studio, but I need you to show that you're willing to cover hard news too. Viewers love your stories. They love you. You are the most requested reporter we have, and that works to your benefit. But I need to convince the higher-ups that you aren't a one-trick pony."

Gordon didn't like to dwell on the hard news, but for a chance to finally get a leg up, to sit at the desk? He might not like to cover the nitty-gritty, but he'd do it. Especially since it came with a bigger paycheck. He barely made ends meet now. Thankfully, his landlord was...lenient...when it came to paying. It helped that they'd been friends since college.

"I might be onto something." He had no idea what, but he had to throw Kevin some hope. Besides, everything he saw became a potential story. Reporters were always onto something.

"Anything you want to share?" Kevin tapped the table to a rhythm only he understood.

"I'm still ironing out the details. Give me a little time to make sure it's really there." Or find a story worth reporting.

Kevin stood and crossed the room. Before he left, he turned back. "I look forward to seeing your work."

Gordon relaxed into his chair. This changed things. Being an anchor might help him get his citizenship. It would certainly help him renew his work visa by showing he was committed to his job. Perhaps he should look into the immigration department that processed his papers. A more unorganized system would be hard to come by. There could be some kind of hard news story there.

Gordon took out his phone to write some notes and again noticed that call from Eva earlier. It might be a little late to call back —the drawback of evening news. He finished work as most people turned in for the night.

Her phone call tonight had been their first blip of communication in a while. He'd been trying to lessen their communication. Eva would eventually meet a qualified bachelor, and their friendship wouldn't continue. It would hurt less if their relationship had become nothing more than a few texts every once in a while—at least that's what Gordon told himself.

He opened his message app, his fingers hesitating over the keyboard. He could reach out. Say hi. Start a conversation. He used to do it often, but when the king announced he planned to step down, he'd pulled back. Soon she would be queen, and he was a reporter who couldn't manage to gain citizenship. Eventually she would marry someone who met all the necessary qualifications—a royal or a citizen, and he didn't meet those qualifications. Was it worth it to reach out now? She could potentially have a tip for a story. He'd never before asked her for one, but desperate times and all, she would know of something.

Before he could second-guess himself, he started typing.

GORDON

Hey! Long time no chat. Sorry to miss your call tonight. How are you doing?

Gordon stared at the message, but her read receipt never flicked. She must be busy. Or asleep. Or had she turned off that feature?

Shoving the phone into his pocket, he stood up. He didn't need to dwell on what could never be.

He had an anchor position to win.

Two

The next day, Eva sat still in her chair, not daring to pick at her cuticles. Nerves never looked good on a princess, but manicured nails did.

"Your father won't suggest someone that he thinks would be a bad fit for you or the country." Kendra sat on the couch, flipping through the local *Nevive Weekly News* magazine and wearing fuzzy pajama pants and an oversized T-shirt.

Eva plucked a minuscule fuzz from her black yoga pants. If only she had a cat, she'd be happy to pick off cat hair for the warmth a pet would bring. They'd agreed for casual attire tonight, Father insisting they'd be more comfortable. "You're correct. But still. I always thought I'd fall in love. It's so unheard of for arranged marriages to occur in this day and age."

Father would select good men, but none of them would be Gordon. Far past the age to hold onto childhood dreams, she needed to let go of that one.

Though it proved more difficult than she thought it might be.

Yes, Gordon had messaged her last night. She still hadn't responded. It had been so long since he'd initiated a conversation.

He'd probably seen her call—dialed accidentally in a moment of weakness—and reached out.

Now she'd have to respond. Tell him what she faced. He needed to hear the news from her, not through the media. But how did she tell the man she'd always loved that she was getting married? Especially when she didn't know who the groom would be.

Kendra set the magazine aside, crossed to Eva and pulled her up.

"You will have a love match. It may take some time, but Eva, whoever you pick will fall in love with you. What's not to love? You're kind, generous, gracious, and you have excellent taste in friends." Kendra placed one hand on her chest and batted her brown eyes. Finding a body double that looked like Eva had been impossible. Instead, they'd picked someone with similar features. Wigs, contacts, and makeup made up the differences. Plus, when they traveled together, no one suspected they might occasionally switch places.

Letting out a big breath, she nodded. "Let's go see who Father's picked out."

Eva enjoyed the closeness of her friend as they slowly walked arm in arm to her father's apartment. *Please, Lord. May I find a man who will love me someday.*

Prayer came easily, and she liked the idea that the Creator of the universe heard. It just didn't always feel like He listened. Often it seemed her prayers hit the ceiling and bounced back. Did He take notice of her when no one else seemed to?

As they got closer, the welcome scent of bacon filled the air, and Kendra walked a little faster when her stomach let out a loud rumble. "It's so unusual for your father to offer his apartment as our meeting place. Normally, if there's food involved, we eat in the dining area."

"We wanted to keep this quiet for as long as possible. Plus, his meeting at lunch was pretty big, so a lighter meal was acceptable tonight. Orlin could use the kitchen in Father's apartment." Eva took a deep breath. Orlin, the palace chef and Gordon's uncle, had gone the extra mile to smoke their own bacon.

Kendra would be thrilled. Honestly, they all would. Who didn't love home-smoked bacon?

In addition to the mouthwatering scents of bacon, hints of fresh baked bread filled her father's apartment as they entered. The open floor plan allowed a clear view of the large sitting area, the kitchen to the left, and beyond that a hallway to the bedrooms and her father's private study.

Orlin washed his hands at the kitchen sink and then dried them on the towel hanging over his shoulder.

He bowed as Eva entered the kitchen. "Your Royal Highness."

"Orlin, this looks fantastic. Thank you for going through the extra work to make this for us." Eva bit back the question on the tip of her tongue. *How's Gordon?* His uncle would know.

Kendra bounced on her toes as she picked up a slice of bacon. "Orlin, your bacon is the best. Tonight's going to be a good one, I can already tell."

Orlin chuckled as he stepped out of the kitchen toward the door. "Glad you will enjoy. I'll let myself out. Just let me know when you want me to come clean up."

"You don't need to stay for that. Go on home and send someone else up. I'm not sure how long we'll be." Eva took a couple slices of bacon too. The salty goodness couldn't be ignored.

"I know, but you also know I will stay. I can always find something to organize or a new recipe to test." Orlin left. He always took his responsibilities seriously, very protective of the royal family. Tonight, more than ever before, Eva appreciated that.

A knock sounded, and Eva let Renee in as her father came out of his study.

Greetings were exchanged, a quick prayer for their meal offered up, and they filled their plates with bacon, veggies, fruit salad, quiche, and fresh baked sourdough bread. Then they sat around the round kitchen table next to a stack of manila folders.

Her father opened the top folder on his pile. "I took the liberty of compiling a list of eligible bachelors, but I'm not so far removed from society that I don't realize looks matter, so there is a picture in each folder."

Eva's stomach twisted, and the bacon didn't look as appealing as it had when she'd been speaking to Orlin. Pushing the plate away slightly, she opened the top folder. A handsome face of a middle-aged man stared back at her.

Father's deep voice rumbled through the room as Eva noted the man's kind eyes and the wrinkles that gathered around them. "This is the Duke of Angles. He's forty, plays polo, and coaches lacrosse at a local elementary school."

All good things. "A tad old for me. Fourteen years isn't the end of the world. Are there options a tad bit younger? I do like the fact that he's involved in the community, though."

"The children love him," Renee piped up next to Father.

"We'll keep him as a maybe." Father closed the folder and set it next to him.

The next folder contained a much older man. Renee filled in some details. "Lord Sumpter from Germany. Forty-four. Writer. Biker. Swimmer."

Eva closed the folder. These men were...much older than she had hoped for.

"Too old." Kendra shook her head. "Way too old."

Eva couldn't argue.

Father cleared this throat. He set the folder on a different pile than the Duke of Angles. "I agree. But he's single."

They continued to sort through the pile of potential candidates, making two piles. Maybe and no.

Eva studied the picture of James Duncan in front of her. Athletic. Handsome, except for maybe his nose which was all wrong for his face. "How am I supposed to meet these men and pick one so fast? It's the Christmas season and people are already busy."

"That's easy. Most of these men can be invited to the Christmas Ball." Renee held up her tablet and started doing whatever magic she did to make things happen.

"The one next week? Isn't that short notice?"

Renee lowered her tablet. "No. Most of the men have already been invited. The few that have not can easily be included."

"So, the Royal Christmas Ball will be turned into a speed dating ritual for unsuspecting men?" Eva rubbed the side of her face, as she took a deep breath. How embarrassing.

Her father picked up his plate, stood, and walked around the table, squeezing her shoulder. "Don't think of it that way. Think of it as a way to meet potential suitors."

Kendra snorted. "Now it sounds like a scene from *Pride and Prejudice*."

Renee made a tsking sound under her breath. "We still have several more potential candidates. Let's keep going. Perhaps one will stand out, and arrangements can be made before next week's ball, which would help expedite the schedule we're on."

Her father lifted the plate he was filling. "Anyone else want seconds?"

Eva nodded to her still full plate. "I'm okay."

"You need to eat, sweetheart. These are just options. Nothing is set in stone." Her father turned toward the counter and continued to load his plate a second time.

"It's okay. I ate earlier." Hours ago, but he didn't need to know that. Food would not settle now.

Her father chewed on a carrot as he opened the next folder while Renee spoke. "The Earl of Brighton. Twenty-eight. Retired soccer player. He likes to travel but mainly lives off his trust."

Kendra shook her head. "I think he recently received a citation for driving under the influence of alcohol."

"Doesn't sound like a winner." Father quickly dumped him on the no pile.

Finally, Eva opened the last folder. Inside, the picture of a handsome man caused her to pause.

Her father said his name with an edge to his voice. "Alexander Moriffiti."

Renee didn't read his stats, didn't say anything else about him. Oddly, Father stayed quiet as well.

Not recognizing him, Eva didn't know why they'd never met. Lean, but well built, like a runner. His black hair flopped over his forehead and his blue eyes sparkled with humor. His dimple didn't hurt anything. *The Little Mermaid's* Prince Eric personified. And Duke of Lexington.

"He looks like a dandy." Kendra leaned forward. "Why don't we know him?"

Father cleared his throat. "That seems to be the problem. I don't know him either. And until this week, I didn't realize he'd been adopted into the royal line. How this flew under the radar is being investigated. But Alexander Moriffiti, thirty-two, is the son of my first cousin and his wife, Henry and Sylvia Moriffiti. Also, the cousin of Lord Veelsh. If the investigation doesn't show any shady business, he is apparently the second in line to the throne. If you don't marry, Alexander will take the throne."

"Doesn't that make us related? Why include him?" Eva shifted in her seat to study her father.

"He's included for two reasons. One, we need to know who he is. And two? No. You're not technically related. Not by blood. He's adopted. But you know our royal law is unique in that it has always allowed adoption into the line of succession. It started when King Hubert married a young widow. He fell so much in love with her that he wrote her young son in as his heir. It worked out in the long run, because they didn't have any more children. But Hubert made it law that adopted children could be put into the line of succession. After your birth, when Henry had more freedom, he moved to the US and married an American. I never knew about the adoption. Alexander's parents passed away when he was seventeen while he was attending school in the US. The Veelshes became his guardians at that point but did not adopt him. Since I have no siblings, Henry, as my first cousin, was second in line until you were born. Lady Veelsh, as Henry's cousin on the other side of his family has no claim for the crown. If they would have adopted Alexander, it would have taken him out of the line of succession since he has no blood claim. Odd nuances to that adoption law."

"Why wouldn't Henry tell us about Alexander?" Eva studied his strong jaw line, the easy smile. He easily filled the picture frame with muscled stature and broad shoulders.

"I'm not sure." Father's voice strained and he cleared his throat. "Henry never wanted to be involved in politics. It's part of the reason he moved away as soon as he could. When the Veelshes became Alexander's guardians, they didn't add him to the line of succession immediately. Perhaps to make this surprise move for the crown? I can't help but feel like it's an attempt at a hostile takeover. They have always been interested in moving up, politically speaking."

Eva couldn't really argue with her father. This attempt by Lord Veelsh to sneak in a bid for the throne didn't sit right with her. What exactly did he want? Power? That tended to be the answer when these things happened. Men got drunk on power and did terrible things to gain more.

Except Alexander didn't look like the type to be climbing a political ladder for fun, with his playful smile and easy posture. Thank goodness. "He looks pleasant."

"He recently moved to Nevive, and he's been volunteering in the social services department. He's a doctor and extremely well liked. He's applied to work at the children's hospital."

Eva pulled out her phone and opened the last email from the head of the hospital. She didn't normally look over the applications or interfere in the hiring process. Although, she did appreciate seeing them occasionally. She had been involved as they tried to build up their program. But now that the hospital had become one of the best, she left the hiring to the professionals. "If he's vying for the throne, why include him?"

Father looked up from his application and Eva set her phone down. The look in his eye meant he had something important to say. "You know the old saying. Keep your enemies close. But he's not a bad option. If you were to team up, it would make Lord Veelsh happy, and Alexander seems like a nice enough fellow. It would also keep him involved in politics, but not officially give him the throne. He would be King Consort."

"Since he didn't grow up here and has only recently moved back, do you think he'd make a good king? Is he even a citizen?" No wonder he looked so casual in the picture. Americans were not known for being formal.

"That is something we are looking into." Renee tapped on her tablet some more. "But we do know he has applied for citizenship here."

A hard smile flashed across Eva's face, and she worked to loosen her jaw. "He's not a citizen? But he is a royal, so he's qualified to be a match. Still, how can a noncitizen rule?"

"They found a loophole. There's a lot of underhanded politicking going on. Alexander is American. And his parents never bothered to request citizenship for him here. He could easily have had dual citizenship. They also never registered him in the line of succession, which is why we didn't know he existed."

"And you never saw a picture of him growing up? Social media, a Christmas card? A visit back?" Eva pushed the issue.

The king shook his head. "You know I don't have social media. They didn't either. And their Christmas cards were always handwritten, never including a picture. When Henry did return for meetings, he always traveled alone."

"Well, I say let's meet him." Eva studied his picture. He might not be anything like Lord Veelsh, but he could solve all the problems. "If it will help smooth things over and calm Lord Veelsh, he might be the best option."

Father nodded. "Good choice. Renee will arrange a meeting."

News of Princess Evalina meeting potential suitors at the Royal Christmas Ball tonight filtered through the newsroom.

Gordon picked up his phone and checked his messages again. Still nothing from Eva. No word, no hint, no clue that she might be meeting men. Even though he'd been the one to reduce communication because he knew this would happen eventually, still it didn't hurt any less. If he hadn't cut off their regular communication, would he have known about her wanting to meet a suitor at the ball tonight? Or was she was finally ready to pursue a relationship because he'd let her go? If she moved on that quickly... Gordon rubbed his chest, trying to ease the ache that thought brought on.

That was how it should be, though. She was the princess. He was a news reporter. She didn't need to tell him about her life.

Except, he wanted her to. He wanted every little detail.

He stood back from his desk with a little too much force, sending his chair flying into the desk behind his.

"What's eating you?" Tabitha, a fellow reporter, glanced up from her computer to study him.

Gordon shoved his phone into his back pocket and picked up his notebook, tucking it inside his coat. "Nothing. Heading out to start on my story."

At least he could cut out early tonight. Once he finished up his live report for the five o'clock news, he could create a short package for the ten o'clock show and be done.

"Enjoy your afternoon. Some of us don't have the luxury of a shortened workday." Tabitha stood and reached for the black dress she had hanging on the coatrack. She'd been assigned the Christmas Ball. "Any insider tips for tonight?"

"If I had any, I'd have been invited." Gordon nodded and headed for the exit before Tabitha could respond. It had stung not to receive an invitation to the ball. He never had, but even so, it always hurt. Especially with the rumors that Eva had decided to start looking for a suitor.

Gordon quickly made his way to the Christmas Bazaar. He'd scheduled an interview with the Wilkins family. They'd had a booth at the bazaar for four generations, and their apple cider, hot cocoa, and coffee were popular items people looked forward to every year.

The story lacked any real hook, even to Gordon. No wonder Kevin wanted him to show that he could report some hard-hitting news stories. These fluff stories were not cutting it.

"Merry Christmas," a young child called as Gordon stepped out of his car. Of all the crummy things to have to force—a happy holiday spirit—when he wanted to race to the palace and find out what was really going on with Eva. Why hadn't she responded? The missed call haunted him like the Spirit of Christmas Past.

Gordon quickly made his way to the ice rink which sat next to the carousel. A long line of children and parents wrapped around the carousel, laughing and singing to the calliope Christmas music. As Gordon walked through the shopping area, booths lining both sides of the walkway, every snippet of conversation he heard focused on the royal ball and their beloved princess looking for a beau.

His jaw strained as he ground his teeth, forcing a cheery smile as he approached the booth of the Wilkins family. Almost a dozen people stood in line, and Gordon pulled out his camera to record some B-roll.

Somehow he managed to make it through the interview, cut a

package, and do his live shot with enough Christmas spirit to keep even Liam chuckling during the show.

Finally, he heard Kevin's all clear through his earpiece. Gordon stepped off camera to take a second to blow out his breath.

"You okay, Gordon?" Kevin's voice rang in his ear.

Ugh. He forgot to turn off his mic.

"Fine." Gordon started tearing down his setup.

"Heard that Princess Evalina is entertaining gentlemen tonight. Whole town's abuzz as royalty from all over the world arrive. I've got Tabitha up there, but she's stuck with the press. Know anything about tonight?"

Gordon froze. At some point Eva would get married. It shouldn't sting to know she had started looking for a partner. At least he could answer truthfully. "Nope. Not a thing."

"It would be great if we could break the news of the ice princess thawing. Since she's never had a relationship, spilling the news on one would be awesome. That kind of story would earn you big points around here. Might even earn you the desk. How's that lead you're working on?"

Gordon ran his hands through his hair. He'd not found a single lead for a potential hard news story. "I'm still digging. See you tomorrow."

He removed his earpiece before Kevin could say anything else and tucked it away.

Normally, he'd stick around and enjoy the atmosphere, but there was only one place he wanted to be. Settling into his car—well, the car he borrowed from his uncle on a long-term basis because he couldn't afford to purchase his own car—Gordon pulled out of his parking spot and eased into traffic.

The palace loomed in front of him, the front gates open as scores of vehicles moved in and out.

He pulled around to the back gate and into the employee parking lot, filled to the brim with the extra staff for the big party tonight. Gordon drove around, searching for an empty spot. The royal family's personal kitchen would be closed tonight. His uncle seldom ran the big events anymore, but he'd still be inside the closed kitchen prepping for tomorrow or trying a new recipe. The kitchen had practically become Orlin's home after Gordon moved out.

The phone pinged just as Gordon found an empty spot close to the kitchen door and parked. Staff moved about, and Gordon knew the event kitchen would be mayhem. His phone pinged again, and Gordon dug it out to see Mallory Fitzgerald's name. His landlord.

Gordon thumped his head on the steering wheel twice. This message would not bear good news.

MALLORY

Your rent is overdue. This is the third month. I need you to pay up.

Not this again. Between the loans he'd taken out for college, the unexpected trip he'd made to Florida for another uncle's funeral a few years back, and all the other bills piling up, his reporter's salary didn't stretch. The job appeared glamorous, the pay anything but.

MALLORY

I hate to say it, but it may be time to talk to your uncle. I wouldn't push but it's pressing.

Gordon deflated. Mallory wouldn't be hounding him if she didn't need it. Something was going on. She wouldn't bring up his uncle otherwise.

GORDON

I'll get it to you.

A second run today would be better than facing his uncle right now. He hated to ask his uncle for money, but other than illegal means, he didn't have any options. The number one rule of being a reporter—don't become the headline. If he wanted the seat behind the desk, he couldn't risk anything crazy.

His phone pinged again.

MALLORY

Also, can you stop by and see me sometime? I have something I want to talk to you about.

GORDON

I'll try.

Or not. He had no desire to face his friend when he couldn't even pay his rent without help. He'd find a way to slide the money under her door without seeing her. Tucking his phone away, he headed inside to the kitchen. Stomping his feet at the mat just inside the door, Gordon relaxed at the familiar scents of spices and sugar.

"Gordon, what brings you by?" His uncle crossed the room and embraced him, pounding him on his back before Gordon could even step into the room.

It didn't matter if it had been five hours or five months, Uncle Orlin always greeted Gordon like he couldn't be happier to see him.

Gordon shuffled his feet. He hated to ask for money, but his checking account had enough for food this week and nowhere near enough for the bills he'd accumulated. If he got the request out of the way, he could enjoy this visit.

His throat tightened and sweat ran down his back. His uncle could spare the money, but even if he couldn't, Gordon knew he'd share. The man was the picture of generosity.

"Ah. You need money."

How horrible was it that Uncle Orlin knew Gordon's needs before he could even voice it? That he couldn't manage to make it on his own? Had he become so predictably dependent? "It's not why I came. I actually came to see you, but Mallory just texted."

"I'm not sure why you don't go see the king? He's offered you an exclusive interview. Even a job on the palace's press team. They pay much more than TV stations. Either would up your salary."

The palace PR team did make good money. But if he accepted, he'd have to be at the palace all the time. That meant interacting with Eva, seeing her daily but never able to be the man he wanted to be for her. On one hand, he'd love to see her more often. On the other, it would be pure torture to watch her live without him.

"I'm sorry, Uncle. It's just that I want to try and make it on my own—my own merit, not because of the people I know."

Uncle Orlin returned to the counter he'd been wiping and pulled two coffee mugs from the cupboard. He moved to the coffeepot that brewed the perfect cup of frothy goodness at the touch of a button.

"No one is begrudging you that, son. Your work ethic precedes you. The king mentioned how proud he was of your determination to make it in the industry on your own without compromising your standards." As the second cup brewed, his uncle opened his wallet and pulled out a check. "Now how much do you need so we can enjoy our visit?"

Gordon swallowed his pride. "Just enough for rent."

Surprise lit his uncle's face. "You could live with me. I have plenty of room."

In his uncle's apartment above the kitchen at the palace? "I can't live at the palace. Kevin would never let me live it down that I had such access. I won't betray the king's trust in me. And I could never do what Maria Kopal does."

Maria Kopal, the royal reporter for the competition, reported anything and everything she could scrounge up. Too much of it turned out to be hearsay and a good bit of it untrue. Her gossip segment had big viewers, though, and she'd managed to land a column in the weekly news magazine and had her own podcast too.

Pride bloomed in his uncle's features, and he placed the check on the counter, preparing to fill it out.

Gordon hated to tell him how many months of rent he needed, let alone how much rent costs, but his uncle handed him the check, written for a year's worth of rent.

"I can't take this. It's way too much."

Uncle Orlin shook his head. "It's hardly anything. What do I spend money on? If I can help out in this small way, let an old man think he's still useful."

His uncle's thick gray hair still curled around his temples, although it was possible his wrinkles were a little more pronounced. Still, Gordon would hardly call his uncle an old man in his mid-forties. "Thank you."

Gordon tucked the check into his pocket, then took the mug his uncle handed to him.

"Tell me what's going on in your life." Uncle Orlin settled on the stool and motioned for Gordon to sit beside him. The outside lights shone in through the kitchen window, splashing over the sink and counters.

"There's a promotion at the news station. I could potentially move to the desk. Kevin says I need to report on a really great story to prove my chops. More than the light news I typically like."

"There's always the royal family. It could be time to pull out your connection. Interview the king."

"We've discussed that. I can't. I won't betray their trust." Gordon twisted the mug in his hand, then picked up the mug and took a sip.

"I understand what you're saying. But the king has offered you an interview. Most reporters can't say that. You wouldn't be betraying them, you would be accepting his offer and giving him a chance to trust a reporter not to butcher his words."

His uncle studied him until Gordon squirmed on his stool. He'd not thought about it like that. Still, it seemed like an advantage others didn't have. He wanted to earn the spot.

His uncle tapped the counter and walked to the large pantry. He came back carrying a Tupperware container. He pried the lid off and offered Gordon a scone from within. "I hear the Christmas Bazaar has a thief."

"I haven't heard about a thief, but that might be just the thing I need. There's so little crime in Nevive, so why a thief? And what is he or she stealing?" Gordon took one of the pastries and set it on the plate his uncle also offered him.

"He's stealing small sums from the venders. Several people are mentioning they're occasionally coming up between fifty and one hundred dollars short at the end of the night."

Gordon's hope sank. No story in that. "It's probably just an error in accounting."

"I'd agree, but Marjorie Wilkins said that several booth owners have said the same thing on a semi-regular basis. I don't think they'd all have the same glitch at the same time."

"Every night?"

"Well, it started as a sporadic thing, but the thief is getting more gutsy. It's pretty consistent. You could talk to Marge. She'd have more details."

Gordon would find Marge first thing in the morning. This could be the story he needed to take the desk—a little crime, a little mystery, a little investigative journalism. This story had promotion written all over it. Kevin would love it. "I can't believe I haven't heard about this. I interviewed Marge earlier today and she didn't mention anything about a thief. Not a peep about it."

His uncle sipped the last of his coffee while studying Gordon over the rim of his mug. "Now, is there anything else I can do for you? The night is ticking by."

Gordon took the mugs and placed them in the sink. "No. I'll head back to the bazaar. I could talk to Marge tonight rather than in the morning, if they're not too busy."

"You'll do no such thing. I have my suit, so why don't you head upstairs and join the ball."

Gordon whipped around. "I can't do that."

His uncle stood and walked to the coat closet, took out a

garment bag. "Sure, you can. The princess is dancing with all the eligible men tonight, and while I'm flattered, I think she would enjoy your company more."

"I'm not invited. I can't crash a royal ball."

"Ahh, but you are." Uncle Orlin unzipped the bag and pulled out a thick piece of cardstock. "Here's your invitation right here. You're young. You love her."

"We can't go there, Uncle. I'm not qualified. I'm not a citizen. I have no pedigree. And that invitation is for you."

"But you—"

"I have you. Yes. But that doesn't change the fact that I can't get citizenship. I've tried. Filled out the paperwork three times now."

Uncle Orlin shoved the suit into Gordon's hands. "Minor details. Now, go suit up. My name's not on that invitation, and you will use it to get in."

With reluctant fingers, Gordon accepted the bag, shaking his head. But his uncle would hear no arguments. No reason.

Good thing Tabitha had been barricaded with the press. The king did not allow them into the actual ballroom. If anyone caught him doing this, there'd be no promotion for him. He could not break the cardinal rule of reporters—never become the headline. Crashing a royal ball? That would certainly qualify as a news headline.

Peasant sneaks into palace to dance with princess.

While he needed a great story, that headline would most certainly not land him a seat at the desk but rather a full security escort from the palace.

Three

Soft string music filled the room as people dressed in all manner of finery milled about. If only Eva could find a comfortable seat and slip her shoes off. Would anyone notice if she went in her stockings? She'd already danced with half the eligible bachelors present. Still so many to go.

Even with all the men she'd been introduced to, she hadn't managed to meet Alexander. They'd been unable to coordinate their schedules before the ball, setting her timeline back. No one she'd spoken with tonight would be a good choice. If nothing else, at least she could rule them out. Her list of tolerable options grew shorter with every dance.

"Drink this." Kendra passed a tall thin glass flute into her hand. "It's the fruit punch."

She could eat a cheeseburger right now, with fries or onion rings, or both, but the juice would have to suffice. The sweet beverage cooled her parched throat.

"Any luck?" Eva stepped closer to her friend as they walked away from the crowd.

"There hasn't been any talk about the law tonight. Members of

Parliament have been silent on the issue. However, your willingness to dance with so many bachelors has been discussed." Kendra spoke quietly. Her long red ball gown swooshed as she turned, probably to block people from reading their lips. "Even the people in town have discussed it."

Great. Well, people were going to talk about her, and she'd always preferred to control the narrative. This just happened to be an uncomfortable subject no matter how it came up. "Let them talk."

Unfortunately, she hadn't even had a chance to tell Gordon. Sure, he'd messaged, but how could she bring up the subject? *FYI. I'm getting married.*

"Princess Evalina?" She turned as a tall, lanky man walked toward her. She hadn't even had a chance for a second sip, let alone a bite of food. Tomorrow she'd eat the cheeseburger, because there would be none served at the ball. And even if there was, there'd be no time to enjoy it.

Kendra stepped closer, taking Eva's drink and whispering in her ear. "Richard Lipsaksiv."

Without Kendra, Eva might just take off her shoes and run for the hills. Normally she didn't need the reminder of names, but with so many people—so many men—to meet, well, she'd make sure Kendra got a bonus after tonight.

Richard caught her hand and brought it to his mouth, leaving a sloppy kiss. No wonder women wore gloves in formal settings until recent years. Pulling her hand back, Eva refrained from wiping it on her dress—it might stain, and she rather liked this green gown. With her red hair, she loved to wear green, as it brought out her eyes.

"Would you care to dance?" His slightly nasal voice would be a nightmare to have to listen to for years to come.

No. Eva pushed her smile up and nodded. "Thank you, Richard. That would be lovely."

The rules didn't exactly say she had to dance with everyone

who asked, but she'd never turned down a dance at the Christmas Ball. It had become an expectation, and tonight rumors had spread that she had started hunting a more permanent partner.

Although she might start a dance with one man, she occasionally finished it with a second. She gave Kendra the signal to let someone cut in. Hopefully someone would. If not, wet-lipped Richard had better not think about pressing those things anywhere else.

Richard, a short man who ironically was a giant in the pharmaceutical industry, placed his hand on her back and drew her close. She straightened her arms and offered him a tight smile. No way would she allow this man an intimate hold.

"Ahh, perhaps the term 'ice princess' is deserved." Richard dipped his head low, his hot breath moist on her ear.

Eww. Rather than responding, she simply created a little more space between them.

Richard's face flushed, and they continued to move across the dance floor. Eva had lost the desire to fill the silence, and the man likely seethed under his mask of indifference to her.

What would these men think if they realized the "ice princess" had never been kissed? As a child, she'd fantasized that her first would be magical. Now, it would likely never happen in the way she imagined. With the man she imagined.

Someone cleared their throat—praise be!—and Richard sighed dramatically, stepping back.

There, in the middle of the dance floor, stood all six foot plus of her childhood friend Gordon Tarpen, looking absolutely delicious in a tux. His blond hair was a little disheveled in that perfectly styled and relaxed way guys could pull off, his dark brown eyes sparkling with friendly humor.

Richard slapped Gordon on the shoulder and shook his head. "Thank goodness. She's as icy as they say."

Gordon frowned and his hand flexed, forming a fist.

Eva rested her fingers on Gordon's arm. Although she didn't

appreciate Richard's crude words, she would much rather spend a song or two in Gordon's arms than trying to break up a fight.

His warm gaze flashed as he reached for her. She quickly placed her hand in his, and he pulled her much closer than necessary. For the first time that night, she allowed her dance partner to have the liberty of such an intimate embrace. Gordon turned to the slimy-lipped Richard, and Eva could feel the smirk that lit up Gordon's face. "Or it's just you."

Eva bit her lip to keep from laughing as Gordon led her away from Richard, their bodies moving perfectly in sync.

Eva melted into the firm and protective stance of her friend. "Thank you. Your timing was impeccable."

"I would have laid him flat." Gordon held her a little closer, erasing what distance remained between them. "Tell me all these peacocks haven't been speaking to you that way."

Gordon's spicy cologne filled her senses—warm, woodsy, and something wild. She leaned away from the irresistible draw of his scent.

"Not all these peacocks have spoken to me that way."

Gordon paused, then let out a sigh. "Eva."

"Don't stop dancing. Besides, I saved you from being tomorrow's headline. *Ballroom brawl breaks out over Ice Princess.*"

"It wouldn't be a brawl if I knocked him out without much effort."

"Details, details. Just keep moving, or else someone will cut in. And for the first time tonight, I would rather they didn't."

"I'll honor that request as best I can." Gordon expertly stepped around a man, making sure they were not interrupted. The music carried them away, and for a brief moment, Eva wondered if this was what Aurora felt like when she danced with Prince Phillip at the end of *Sleeping Beauty.* She could almost pretend they were dancing among the sunset-colored clouds.

Gordon's strong arms held her sure, his feet graceful, and she relaxed. For a few moments, she just wanted to enjoy her friend and not think about the future. Not think about the fact that she had to tell him she was getting married. And certainly not think about his nonchalant attitude. If he was chill about her marrying someone else, that would… Well, she didn't want to think about what that would be like. Instead, she just enjoyed the moment. The feel of his embrace. His excellent dance skills. The effortless way they moved together. It helped that they'd learned to dance together. More hours than she could count had been spent in this room practicing the waltz, the tango, and her favorite—swing dancing. Not that she'd use that particular style at a formal event, but she and Gordon had begged their instructor to teach them.

The song ended, and their surroundings returned.

She stepped back and applauded the musicians. Another song started, and when Gordon held out his hand, she willingly stepped into his embrace at the slower waltz. "Tell me about what's been keeping you busy."

Gordon drew her close to his chest. "News stories day in and day out. But you haven't been reported on lately. I expect that to change tonight."

An uncomfortable feeling settled in her gut. Of course, Gordon heard the rumors. She'd wanted to be the first to tell him. What could she say, even now, though? *I'm getting married. Yay me.* He'd been pulling back, so why tell him? Besides, he'd see all the speculation and would soon see the headlines about her speedy marriage. "But tell me more about you. I didn't know you'd be here tonight."

Gordon looked to his right and left. "I stopped by to see my uncle, and he insisted I take his invitation."

Eva stepped closer, letting his familiar scent wash over her again. "So, you snuck into the Christmas Ball?"

Gordon's head bent down, his cheek brushing hers, his breath on her ear. Goosebumps appeared on her neck when he spoke. "Are you going to call security?"

A delicious shiver ran down her spine at his nearness, at the warmth of his breath.

Eva tilted her head from side to side. "Since you saved me from that wet-lipped Richard, I believe I will give you a pass."

"I'm not sure I want to know the story behind that nickname."

"At least they didn't touch my lips." Eva chuckled, and Gordon's arms seemed to tighten around her.

"Probably for the best with such a nickname."

Couples clapped around them, signaling the end of the song. Eva hadn't noticed the music had stopped.

Gordon let go of her and bowed.

"Thank you, sir," she said loud enough for those around her to hear.

Gordon nodded toward the edge of the dance floor where Kendra stood making the slight signal that Eva needed to address something or someone. As much as Eva wanted to ignore her responsibilities, ignore the future, ignore everything and steal another dance with Gordon, duty called. She inclined her head to Gordon as he offered her his arm. Before she had to face reality and whatever Kendra needed.

"Thank you, Gordon. For sneaking in. For interrupting. Perhaps we can dance again later?"

"I'll keep my eye on you." He winked and bowed before leaving her next to Kendra, who handed her a punch glass.

This time, Eva didn't waste any time and took a few swallows of the sweet beverage.

"Your father is heading this way with Lord and Lady Veelsh. The Duke of Lexington is with them."

Eva carefully peaked over Kendra's shoulder as she sipped the punch again. A tall young man walked with them. Every bit as handsome as his picture, maybe more so.

Eva handed her glass back to Kendra. She'd really like to chug the entire glass, but she knew better. Someone would be watching her. The last thing she wanted was a picture of her guzzling her fruit punch on the front page of the paper in the morning. Even though the press didn't have access to the ballroom, it didn't take much effort to find someone willing to sell a picture.

"Evalina." Her father's deep rich voice held a slight edge to it, one only she'd pick up on. It was in the way he emphasized the *L* in her name. It helped her to know things were about to get sticky.

She nodded at him. Since she'd already seen him today, she didn't need to curtsy again. "Father."

"You know Lord Veelsh and his wife, Lady Veelsh." He gestured toward the older couple with him. Lord Veelsh came to Father's shoulder, his salt-and-pepper hair slicked to the side in a dramatic comb-over. His wiry mustache twitched, and he did not bow in greeting, as propriety dictated. His wife, a petite woman with an upturned pert nose, did not curtsy either.

Eva held out her hand and they both shook hers, only then offering a half bow or curtsy. Not what should be given from someone who knew the proper etiquette. Eva lifted an eyebrow but did not call them out on their rude behavior. However, her father's eye twitched. He'd had enough, and if she didn't diffuse the situation, he might cause a scene.

"So glad you could join us this evening. Would you care for a glass of—"

"We will toast when Alexander is king." Lord Veelsh gestured to the younger man beside her father.

Very few people had the lack of manners to cut her off. Yet again, instead of calling them out, she turned her attention to the attractive man next to them. His dark hair and blue eyes a breathtaking combination. He shook his head, a look of displeasure on his face as he studied his cousins.

"Evalina, I'd like you to meet Alexander Moriffiti, Duke of Lexington." Her father emphasized the *L* in her name again, and Eva caught his eye twitching again.

She extended her hand, and Alexander took it in a firm, yet

polite grip. He bowed deeply, and pressed a warm, dry kiss to the back of her hand. "It's a pleasure to meet you, Your Highness."

"The pleasure is all mine." And for the first time tonight, she meant every word. The song ended and people applauded. "Perhaps you would like to dance?"

Alexander's dimple appeared, and he offered her his elbow. "I'd like nothing more."

He led her to the dance floor and took her into a proper hold, his hands staying in place as he guided her across the floor in perfect time to the music. His movements were confident, as though he'd practiced them for years. He received extra marks for not pushing her outside her comfort zone.

While he moved with ease and held her within bounds of a proper hold, Eva couldn't help but compare him to Gordon. A little taller, a little leaner, but Eva preferred Gordon in every way.

She would not scrunch her nose. But she could also not allow such a side-by-side comparison to gain space in her mind or heart. No one could live up to Gordon.

"I'm sorry about my cousins. They have been a bit..." Alexander looked away to study them as they spoke alone. Her father had disappeared, leaving the couple standing on the side of the dance floor. Lady Veelsh turned away from her husband, almost like they'd been fighting.

"Insistent?" Eva offered.

"That's nicer than rude. I'm sorry they were so disrespectful just now." His voice was genuine. Something in his expression confirmed he could be trusted. "I know what they're trying to do, and I'm sorry for the problems they're causing for you. You're truly exquisite, Your Royal Highness." His face flamed red, and Eva couldn't help but feel her heart rate kick up.

Shock stiffened Eva's spine, but she forced herself to relax, not missing a step. She had not anticipated him to be so...human.

Alexander kept his hold perfectly proper, but he studied her with a kindness she hadn't seen tonight from other men. Where others had seen what she could offer them, something about the way Alexander studied her, despite his grab for the throne, didn't seem that way.

"I thought perhaps we could team up. Beat my cousins at their own game. I know they want me to take the throne and that you have to get married."

What was he proposing? Before she could question him about anything, he continued. "Perhaps if we get to know each other, I could be that person for you. You'd get to keep your throne, and I would get my cousin off my case."

"You do not want to rule?" Eva waited for something to flash across his face to show some sort of dishonesty, but his open expression, his consistent eye contact made her believe he spoke truth.

He quickly shook his head. "No. You are the rightful heir. And this trumped-up ancient law is ridiculous, not to mention archaic. I don't support it."

"You could simply take yourself out of the line of succession."

"It wouldn't solve your problem. My cousin is insistent on enforcing this law he dragged up. He would find another way to cause problems." Alexander spun them away from the direction they were going. Over Alexander's shoulder, Eva saw a man looking a little dejected. Well, at least Alexander could be considered obser-vant and had kept them from being interrupted.

"What exactly are you proposing?"

"That we team up. You could rule, and I could continue my work at the hospital. And get my cousin off my back. If you're married, the requirements for you to take the throne, however archaic, are met."

"And what do you get?"

"Freedom from my cousins."

"Why do you need that? You're a grown adult."

Alexander looked around the room. "I am. But they say this is what my parents wanted. Showed me some communication with my parents. I guess, I'd like the freedom to make my own choices. From the guilt of not living up to expectations. But I would like to honor my parents' memory. Do what they wanted me to do. I just wish they would have told me about this as well."

Eva tore her gaze away and glanced around the ballroom, looking for her father. What would he think of this conversation? A familiar figure caught her eye—Gordon stood next to Kendra.

Eva's heart stumbled, and her foot followed suit, landing on Alexander's toes. "Oh! I'm so sorry!"

Alexander didn't hesitate, keeping them moving as though nothing happened. "Please don't think anything of it. I was too forward in my thoughts."

Eva shook her head. Her father's words came rushing back. *Keep your enemies close.* "No. Not at all. In fact, I'd like you to come to lunch tomorrow, if you're available."

"For you?" Alexander's dimple appeared again. "I'll be here."

She stepped slightly closer to Alexander and glanced around the room, catching Gordon's eye. He lifted an eyebrow as if to ask if he should cut in.

Her heart broke. She'd love to spend all night dancing in his arms, but for her kingdom, for her future, she shook her head.

She may have found her lifelong partner.

THE HUSTLE AND BUSTLE OF THE NEWSROOM NORMALLY invigorated Gordon, but three days after the Royal Christmas Ball and the only thing anyone could talk about were the multiple dates Eva had been on with this new royal, Alexander Moriffiti, the surprise son of the Duke and Duchess of Lexington who were killed several years earlier in a freak accident in the United States.

After Eva had danced with Alexander the way she had, Gordon

shouldn't be surprised. The American had held her a little too close, and she'd allowed it, encouraged it even. But the emotions churning through his gut were ugly, and he'd rather not name them. Even after adding an extra couple of miles to his run each morning, he couldn't lose the feelings churning through him.

Eva and *Alexander* had been to a simple lunch, the ski slopes followed by a quiet dinner at a café at the ski lodge, a walking tour of the ports, and then they'd been to the children's hospital to deliver some holiday cheer to the children. Not to mention he'd taken her to the theater. Everyone loved the American, and if Gordon heard one more word about his "charming smile" or how "happy he made the princess," he might chuck something at someone.

It had to happen someday. Eva had to fall in love and get married. No matter how much he'd tried to prepare himself for it, hearing everyone talk about how happy Alexander made Eva stung.

They were wrong, though. Although he'd only seen one video of the couple—because it had been on right before his package— Eva didn't look happy. She appeared tense. Tired. Her posture was rigid, and the camera only caught her profile, which didn't scream happiness and love. The chemistry everyone clamored about was nonexistent. Proof people only saw what they wanted.

He had chemistry with the princess. If people had seen him dancing with Eva, they'd know what chemistry was. But perhaps he'd imagined it. It could have been entirely one-sided. Drinking sour milk would be more pleasant than these thoughts.

"The princess and the American are heading to the pier for a cruise today." Tabitha sighed and rested her chin on her hand.

"In this cold weather? She really is an ice princess." Caleb, one of the camera guys, scoffed.

"Oh, I'd go if that dreamy man would keep me warm."

Gordon turned his back on them. If he could put in his earbuds and listen to music, he'd do it. It wasn't like he'd gotten any leads about the thief, but Kevin would have his head if he saw.

Reporters were supposed to be observant and listening at all times. No earbuds allowed. Instead, he pulled out his phone and sent Eva a text.

GORDON

Looks like you've been busy.

To his surprise, three little dots appeared immediately, and Gordon squeezed his phone while he waited.

EVA

*gif of a woman shaking her head saying "you have no idea."

I'd give anything to visit the Christmas Bazaar you report on so regularly.

GORDON

Over all the dates you've been on? Why not arrange to visit the bazaar?

Petty? Yes, but he'd love to know what Eva was really doing.

EVA

If only it was that simple. How are you?

GORDON

*gif of Robert Downey Jr. shaking his head saying "Swell, it's fine."

EVA

*gif of Willy Wonka saying "really?"

Gordon set his phone down. Even without seeing him, she knew when he exaggerated, and she seldom let him get away with it. But if he told her the truth, that his request to become a citizen had been denied again, because they'd lost his birth certificate, then she might try to get involved. He didn't need that. He'd put in a request for a new one, but to have it shipped over from the States during the holidays would add another delay. He might not have enough time, and he might have to fight for his visa from Florida, where his cousins lived. Not to mention that hearing everyone talk about the princess falling in love made everything worse.

"Gordon, are you planning on being our man on the street at the Christmas Bazaar again tonight?" Kevin tapped on his desk, and Gordon realized the morning news brief had begun without him even noticing.

Liam chortled. "It's not like Gordon has any breaking news to share."

"The Christmas Bazaar stories are some of our most watched stories online. They may not be hard journalism, but they are what people like." Gordon leaned forward, ready to defend his work. "I had over fifty thousand views overnight on my 'fluffy' news."

Liam nodded. "Touché. But the princess and her beau got over a million, so tell me what the people really want."

Stories involving Eva always topped the watch list. The whole country, the world even, enjoyed watching the perfect princess. But Gordon would rather chop off his arm than report on Eva falling in love. Especially if it involved another man.

"I had planned on hanging around there tonight. With an interview lined up for a story about Johnny, the lead singer and a Nevive legend, I could turn it into a series if you'd like. *Home star hero returns to local stage.* He's doing a couple of concerts locally this season. Maybe there's more to the story."

Kevin nodded. "Johnny is always good to his roots. Let's do a series. Find out what's next for the local-turned-celebrity and why he's back for this holiday season. He could be touring, yet he's here giving free concerts? I'd like to know why."

Liam scoffed. "You could always bring his mommy into the interview."

Kevin shot him a sharp look. "That's actually not a bad idea, Liam. Gordon, look into it. Liam, I'd like you to talk to the high school principal. His hog won best in show in the country fair."

Gordon coughed to keep his chuckle in line. Kevin brooked no nonsense in his meetings, and as soon as he thought someone was not contributing, he'd pull out the strangest story to stick them with. Liam had reported on his fair share of unusual stories to placate Kevin. There would be no love lost when the anchor finally moved on.

Later at the bazaar, as Gordon set up for his live shot of the band, a commotion caught his attention near the south entrance across from the food truck setup. Perhaps the thief had struck again. Gordon grabbed his phone for his camera and headed toward the noise, only to discover Alexander standing next to Eva as they browsed the fair.

Her long red hair hung in soft curls down her back, and she had on earmuffs that matched her scarf and gloves. Gordon stood transfixed, his phone in his pocket. Kevin would kill him if he knew he could have gotten footage of the princess and hadn't. But when Eva turned, he caught her eye. Gordon's entire chest relaxed.

That wasn't Eva.

While most people couldn't tell Eva and Kendra apart, it only took one quick glance for Gordon to know. He'd know Eva anywhere.

Kendra nodded in greeting, but then turned back to Alexander, who played his part perfectly, touching his hand to her low back and talking to Marjorie as she handed them both a hot cocoa.

Kendra took a sip of the cocoa, careful not to allow any of the whipped cream to stick to her upper lip. Even so, Alexander cupped her chin as he ran his thumb over her cheek. She leaned in, and Gordon snapped a picture. They looked very much like a couple in love.

Gordon switched from photo to video and started recording. Knowing it wasn't Eva somehow made it easier. But why wasn't Eva at the festival?

This whole setup seemed odd. And it proved once again that people only saw what they wanted. Kendra wore a scarf wrapped around her neck that covered a good portion of her face when she wasn't drinking.

Eva had mentioned now several times how much she wanted to come to the bazaar. Why send the body double, when she could have come herself?

Gordon sent the footage to Kevin with a message.

GORDON

Surprise visitors at the bazaar tonight.

KEVIN

ARE YOU KIDDING ME? That's great. Grab more footage if possible. See if you can talk to them. Or is security too tight?

GORDON

Security is high.

Thankfully that meant Gordon wouldn't be able to get close enough to report on anything of substance. Gordon quickly opened his search engine and looked up Princess Evalina and Alexander. He looked at the pictures of their recent dates. Only their first lunch date had been Eva. The palace had done a bang-up job covering the fact that Kendra had gone with him.

He followed the couple around to gather video and pictures. No one seemed to notice that the real princess hadn't made an appearance. Did Alexander even know? Something had happened, and Gordon hated that he had no idea what. Thankfully, the couple left before his interview with Johnny Rocco.

After the "happy couple" left, Gordon talked with a few vendors about the thief, but there had been no activity in two days. His story lead had dried up.

However, the appearance of Alexander and Kendra tonight had given him a second news package. If he could have a few more days where he could present two stories instead of one, plus the series with Johnny Rocco, he might actually have a chance to make the promotion.

Four

E va watched the Christmas Bazaar from her balcony, wrapped in a muslin blanket, a hat on her head, and fuzzy socks on her feet. She'd give anything to be down there.

The music wafted up as Johnny Rocco sang. Wouldn't it be amazing to be in the middle of the crowd and listen to him? Sure, she'd met him and even had a private performance, but listening to him with the other people, sipping cocoa, or even dancing—what an incredible night it would have been.

Except she'd come down with a stuffy nose.

The doctor had called it an upper respiratory infection, but she didn't feel terrible. Anymore.

Even so, Kendra stepped in, again, because Eva had been 'under the weather.'

Apparently, a princess sneezing in public was taboo enough to call in the backups. Eva rolled her eyes and then sneezed. Ugh. It had been a mild fever, but even so, she'd missed her chance to attend the bazaar tonight. She hadn't even had a chance to develop a relationship with Alexander beyond their first lunch. They'd had full days planned together and she'd been unable to attend.

49

The worst thing about it, no one noticed the switch. Kendra did a great job, and Eva praised her for it. But just once she'd like someone to notice that she'd been replaced. Did Alexander even know?

They wouldn't tell him yet, but it hurt that he couldn't tell a difference. Most people didn't even notice when a switch had been made. Kendra's job as Eva's body double was a top-secret position. That's why Kendra had been trained from a young age. With the wig, colored contacts, and makeup, they did look almost identical. It helped that people only saw what they wanted to see, but still, it hurt.

No one ever saw her—Evalina Rosalind Marie Bexley. They simply saw Her Royal Highness, Princess Evalina.

She blew her nose and tossed the tissue into the nearby trash can. If she'd been able to go tonight, she might even have seen Gordon report live. Not that she should be thinking about him when she was practically engaged to another man.

She wiggled her empty left hand—practically, but not yet. It had only been a few days since the dance, even though Alexander and "Eva" had been on multiple dates since their lunch the day after the ball.

"Your Royal Highness, you're home because you're not feeling well. Please come in from outside." Beverly, Eva's childhood governess wrapped her arm around Eva and turned her toward the balcony door.

"I'm not really even that ill. My fever is gone. I feel fine." Eva rolled her shoulders, and Beverly dropped her arm.

"Be that as it may, you cannot overdo it and relapse." Beverly stepped forward and opened the door, and Eva kept from letting her feet drag in protest. At almost twenty-six she should be able to open a door for herself, at least in her own quarters. "I don't think an outing with my soon-to-be husband is overdoing it. How am I supposed to get to know him if I am unable to accompany him on outings?"

"Don't get worked up, darling. Have a seat and drink your tea."

Eva plopped down on her loveseat, and when Beverly handed her the tray with tea and cookies, Eva almost pushed it away. No need to act like a little girl throwing a tantrum, though. With a sigh she picked up the tea. The warm liquid soothed her sore throat and warmed her up.

"Here you go." Beverly handed her two pills, and Eva swallowed them. It didn't matter what they were—arguing with Beverly wouldn't change anything. Once Beverly made up her mind, no one could change it. Eva still chafed that Beverly had been called in for a minor and fleeting fever. She didn't need a nursemaid. She needed to be at the bazaar. Needed to get to know Alexander. Needed to save her throne. Her family. Her kingdom.

"What were those?" Eva stretched and yawned. Perhaps if she convinced Beverly she was tired, she'd leave for the night.

"Cold medicine. They should help you sleep too." Beverly sat down on the chair, as though she would settle in for a while.

Eva set her teacup down and stood. "I think I'll head to bed. Please don't stick around. I'm not good company tonight."

Beverly opened her large tote sitting next to her and retrieved out her knitting needles and her current project. It looked like a blue-and-white baby blanket. "I'll stay until you're asleep."

Nope. Absolutely not. "Thank you, but no. I can put myself to bed."

Beverly lifted one eyebrow and tilted her head. "If you are certain you are ready for bed, I can see you to it."

The sooner she agreed, the sooner Beverly would leave. She made her way to her bedroom and laid down pulling her covers up under her chin, but Beverly's knitting needles clicked together quietly. She should have closed her door, but she'd gotten used to leaving it open. Normally she was the only one in her suite. Eva inhaled deeply and studied the smooth ceiling, rather than watching Beverly through the door. A knock sounded at the door to her apartment, and Beverly set aside her knitting needles and went to answer.

Eva had barely sat up, resting her back on a pillow propped up by the headboard, when her father's voice thundered through the apartment. "I appreciate what you're doing, Beverly, but I think it's fine if I want to check on my sick daughter. You head home for the night."

Eva let herself relax. Beverly wouldn't dare argue with the king.

Her father walked into the room. "I hope I'm not waking you."

Eva coughed again. "As if I could sleep with Beverly hovering."

"She does mean well." Father settled on the edge of her bed, and Eva had memories of him tucking her in as a child. Her mother had died in a rock climbing accident with Orlin's wife when Eva was young, so most of her memories were surrounded by her father.

"Perhaps, but I didn't really need her called in for a minor cold." Eva worked to keep the pout from her voice. "I could have attended the Christmas Bazaar. Finally. I've never been."

"Never? Surely, you've been. You used to love to ride the carousel."

"I guess not never. But not since I was a child. You took me once. I don't remember riding the carousel at Christmas. But since then, there's always a reason why I can't go."

"Perhaps it's time you take matters into your own hands. Just go." Her father stood and straightened the blanket.

"Security would never let me." Eva scooted down into bed, as her father kissed her forehead.

"Then don't tell them." He winked. "Oh, I wanted to tell you, I've been looking into that law. Trying to find any kind of exception, historical reasoning...anything. So far, nothing has turned up."

"I found that Princess Marie had been forced to marry over a hundred years ago as well. She died mysteriously a few days after she gave birth to a son. Her husband, the King Consort, had been appointed regent until her son could take the throne."

"Yes. Your great-great-great grandmother. I read that too. Her son petitioned to have the law changed when he took the throne, but Parliament buried it. We will find a way." The king knocked on the wall before turning off the light and leaving.

Puzzled, Eva rubbed at a knot forming in her shoulder. They'd keep looking, and hopefully they could find a way to fight the law. If they couldn't, she had to be ready to marry.

As Eva rolled over to her side, her father's voice echoed in her head. Don't tell security.

Could he be serious? How would she manage that? Eva closed her eyes, and the next thing she knew, a knock sounded through her room. Beverly switched the light on and walked in, carrying breakfast on a tray, with Kendra following behind her.

Whatever medication Beverly had given Eva had knocked her out for the night.

"Good morning, Your Royal Highness." Beverly, ever the prim and proper companion, curtsied and then set the tray on the table. Eva stood and Beverly removed a silk robe out of Eva's closet.

Hadn't Eva burned all those? Or at least hidden them? She hated the feel of the fabric. A flannel or cotton robe was so much better.

Kendra sat in one of the two overstuffed chairs in the small seating area of the bedroom, but a knowing look crossed her face as she watched.

"I'd prefer not to wear the robe, thank you." Eva left Beverly by the bed and sat in the other chair next to the small table, without her robe.

Kendra lifted her teacup to hide her smile.

"It's improper to serve yourself before the princess has had her tea. Especially in her own room." Beverly set the floral silk robe that no one would ever wear on the foot of the bed and came over to pour Eva tea. Not coffee. Beverly always only offered tea, but first thing in the morning, a girl needed coffee.

Eva picked up the teapot before Beverly could serve her. Occasionally, and especially in the privacy of her own apartment, she enjoyed taking care of herself.

"Thank you, Beverly. I'm fine." Eva set the teapot down and turned toward the older woman. "I appreciate you coming when I was sick, but I am better now. I am sure your grandchildren will be happy to see you again. I am sorry you were called away from your family."

A small smile spread across Beverly's normally downturned mouth. Any mention of her grandchildren always softened her. "If you are sure you no longer need me."

"I'm much better this morning, Beverly. Thank you." Eva insisted and Beverly inclined her head. Before Beverly left, Eva stood and hugged the woman. Although Beverely tended to hover, she meant well. She'd always been kind and loving to Eva, even if a bit overbearing. Her lessons to Eva as a child were certainly ingrained, and Eva often thought of her governess fondly. As much as Eva loved Beverly, hopefully, she wouldn't be called out of retirement again for a while. A long while.

As soon as the door closed, Eva slumped back on her chair, tucked her feet up under her, and turned toward her friend. "Tell me about last night. How did it go?"

A strange look crossed Kendra's face. Her dark brown braid hung over her shoulder as she took a sip of her tea. "Perfect. No one questioned the switch, and Alexander played his part perfectly. A gentleman in every way. Funny, enjoyable, and handsome. We rode the carousel, which actually was quite fun with him."

Eva let her head rest against the back of the chair. "If I didn't know better, I'd think you liked him."

A flush crossed Kendra's pretty freckled face and she picked at one of her cuticles. She immediately stopped and pressed her hands flat. Kendra's cuticles would give her away if she wasn't careful.

Something must really be bothering her if she was fighting old habits. "He will be a good fit. He's faithful and loyal, and I believe he will make a good match."

"For who?" Eva chuckled.

"For you, of course." Kendra's serious response didn't go unnoticed.

Everyone had a good opinion of Alexander, but Eva had only had one meal with him since the dance. She'd been locked up instead of getting to know the man she was expected to marry, and Kendra had taken her place on the outings. Most of the official pictures released were taken at such a distance that the media would not notice the switch. It would likely be a big headline if they did, *Double the Princess, Double the Fun*. Even in unofficial pictures people didn't question the story. Eva couldn't quite understand how gullible people were. There had been one person who noticed the switch immediately—Gordon. They'd been young, and he'd almost blown Kendra's cover.

As far as Eva knew, he was the only person who had ever noticed a switch. Of course, some of the staff may have noticed, but they signed strict NDAs when they started working at the palace.

"Tell me about the bazaar." Eva picked up the tea cup, and swirled it around.

"Same as every year. Vendors selling Christmas goods, hand-made art, hot cocoa, apple cider, specialty coffee, baked goods, the ice skating rink. And the live music last night."

"And of course the carousel. It's like a Christmas movie. I wish I could find a way to go this year." Eva took a sip of her tea. "I would prefer coffee."

"I know." Kendra smirked as someone knocked on the door of Eva's apartment. "I'll grab that. I bet it's your coffee. I happened to be in the kitchen when Beverly placed your order. Orlin knew your preference and tried to tell her, but you know Beverly. I asked him to hold your normal order fifteen minutes and then send it up."

Kendra left the room to answer the door. The scent of coffee met Eva before Kendra came back in carrying a tray.

"Bless him. And you."

"And his nephew." Kendra set the tray down, but Eva moved to pour her coffee before Kendra could. Her hands shook slightly. Kendra had gone to the bazaar and seen Gordon. She had all the fun.

Eva sipped the rich, dark brew with a splash of heavy cream, trying not to seem too eager for news on Gordon. "You saw him last night too?"

"Him? Him who?" Kendra took a sip of her own coffee, hiding a teasing look.

Eva's heart skipped. "You know who. Gordon. Did you see him?"

"Of course. We didn't talk, but his eyes were brimming with jealousy until we made eye contact, and my cover was blown."

"He outed you?"

"No. But the relief on his face when he realized it wasn't you there last night would have been a giveaway to anyone who noticed." Kendra settled back into her seat, tucking her feet under her.

"He knows how much I've always wanted to attend the bazaar. He would have been thrilled I was there."

"Not with another man." Kendra picked up a scone, carefully catching any crumbs that fell when she bit into it before setting it back on her small plate.

"Whatever. He doesn't see me that way." Eva selected her own scone and a few strawberries, placing them on her plate.

Kendra took another bite and spoke around the food in her mouth. "If you say so."

It wouldn't do to argue over Gordon. She had to consider the future of her country, of her position, and no part of that included Gordon. "So, I was thinking...perhaps we could switch a little longer. I want to see the Christmas Bazaar, and I need to go before I can't."

"Can't?"

"Marriage will change things."

"Agreed. What do you have in mind?" Kendra sneezed.

"Please tell me you're not getting sick." Eva handed the box of tissues to her friend.

Kendra held up a hand to refuse. "Seriously? I'm fine. It's just a sneeze. Tell me your plan."

"What if I sneak out and go to the bazaar alone?"

"Yes. Do it. I have a wig...you'll need something to cover your red hair. I'll bring some extra clothes and give you my car. You can sneak out. No problem."

No push back, no hesitation. Everyone needed a friend like Kendra who jumped onboard with crazy plans, no questions asked. "You think it will work?"

"Yes. Let's pick a day that you won't be super busy. I can fill in, and you can disappear."

"You know as well as anyone, I'm busy every day." Eva stood and walked across the room to pick up her phone and opened her calendar app. "Tomorrow is swamped. I have a meeting with the historian to try and fight this law. I am also meeting with the head of the hospital and then have dinner with Alexander. But Thursday, the only thing on my schedule is an outing with Alexander."

Guilt ate at her. She'd already missed so many outings with him. "I shouldn't give up that time with him. I could go after that. I could at least see the festival at night. The music. The dancing. The ice skating."

"I don't mind going out with Alexander again. And it's a helicopter tour scheduled for that morning. No one would see 'you' up close." Kendra opened her phone. "You do have dinner with your father that day."

"I'll cancel. He won't mind." Eva sent Renee a message canceling the dinner with her father. She showed the message to

Kendra. "Easy-peasy. If you're sure you don't mind doing the heli-copter tour. Has Alexander noticed the switch yet?"

A look crossed Kendra's face. Eva knew that look, the one that said *no one sees me*. "I don't think he has noticed. Super nice guy, just not the most observant."

Eva shrugged. "In his defense, we've only met twice. You are a convincing double."

Kendra bit her lip then flipped her hair. "It doesn't matter. Let's do this. Thursday. It's the easiest day to make the switch. And it's your slowest day this month."

Two days. She'd be free to escape and visit the Christmas Bazaar in two days. Hot cocoa, shopping, food from local vendors —it couldn't come soon enough.

GORDON SAT AT HIS DESK IN THE NEWSROOM AND flipped through the pictures of "Eva" and Alexander again. If he hadn't seen Kendra last night, he'd probably be like the rest of the country, assuming the princess had a new beau.

But after looking at all the pictures—he realized the palace had released very strategic ones. Eva's face couldn't be clearly seen. The back of the princess and a smiling suitor stood atop a cliff, looking over the country. The profile of the princess, as she looked up at a doting Alexander. Walking together but at such a distance that when Gordon zoomed in, their faces were blurry.

He'd seen one video, had barely glanced at it, and assumed Eva was unhappy by the slant of her rigid posture. Today, he couldn't even find that video, but he found photo after photo of the "happy couple." Not one of the pictures included Eva.

One photograph showed a beautiful silhouette of the couple as they entered the theater. Romantic, yes. But it could be anyone in that photo.

Clever.

The more he studied the pictures, the more convinced he became. Princess Evalina had not been the one photographed with Alexander for a single outing. He'd seen her at the Christmas Ball—had something happened since then? Normally Kendra only stepped in during high-risk situations or when Eva was under the weather.

Kevin's voice interrupted Gordon's perusal of another picture. "Gordon, are you heading out to the bazaar again?"

Quickly closing his computer, Gordon stood up and put on his coat. "On my way now. I'm interviewing Marjorie in thirty minutes."

Tonight's story had the possibility of going big. He still hadn't told Kevin there was a suspected thief at the bazaar. But Marjorie had mentioned four booths around her had come up thirty dollars short last night.

"I'm not sure this story has the wow factor we're looking for. Marjorie has been around forever, don't get me wrong. But how many times will you interview her this season?" Kevin knocked on the desk. "Look for more diversity."

Gordon couldn't respond because Kevin had already moved on to another reporter's desk.

Gordon quickly left the newsroom and jogged across to the parking lot to climb into the station van. Inside, he pulled out his phone and opened his conversation with Eva on his message app. He scanned over their last message.

GORDON

Interesting pictures the palace has been releasing. You ok?

Gordon set his phone down, but then three little periods popped up.

Heat filled his chest. Did it give too much away to tell her he'd always notice?

Three little dots appeared again. And disappeared. Then reappeared. But another message never popped up.

Gordon set his phone back down and drove to the bazaar and parked near the entrance. Only a handful of people and booth clerks milled about, since most people came out after work hours. Gordon easily walked through the maze of booths.

A young teen girl caught his attention as she browsed. Her long dark hair was braided down her back, and she wore black leggings and a worn purple puffy jacket. She had on name-brand shoes that had obviously been well-loved because they sported a hole in the back.

Gordon watched as she browsed, keeping her head down. It was unusual to see children who obviously needed some clothing. Where were her parents? Why wasn't she in school?

He worked his way toward the Wilkins booth. Marjorie chatted easily with a middle-aged mom who held a toddler on her hip. Marjorie handed her a cup carrier and a small bag.

"Thank you," the woman said, as she moved toward a picnic table set up near Marjorie's food truck—if you could call it that. Even after multiple generations, Marjorie operated out of the back of her Ford pickup truck, a rectangular folding table in front of her. All the food was in plastic containers, and the beverage dispenser and small fridge were in the truck bed next to the picnic area. Above several tables, large Edison bulbs, which would light up the area at night.

Marjorie waved and then took off her apron and handed it to a younger version of herself.

"Gordon!" Marge walked around the table and opened her arms to him, embracing him with a maternal warmth, while her daughter continued to work. "You're looking rather skinny. Are you eating?"

She treated him a bit like a grandmother would—at least that's what he imagined. His grandparents had passed before he was born.

"More than I should." Gordon patted his belly, but Marge pushed his hand off and scoffed.

"If only my belly included a flat stomach and abs." She backtracked to the table and placed a large cinnamon roll on a paper plate. After pouring a cup of coffee, she brought both to Gordon.

"Eat first, then you can do your video thing." Marge pushed the items into Gordon's hands, and he had little choice but to take them or be covered in sticky icing and hot coffee. Gordon followed Marge and sat across from her at a picnic table, not far from the mom and toddler who had been talking with Marge when Gordon arrived.

They'd barely sat down when the teen girl Gordon had seen earlier walked up to the truck. Marge popped up and practically pushed her daughter aside to speak with the girl, who was sent off with a bag full of food and a cup carrier full of drinks.

Marge waved off payment, and the girl hurried away with her arms full. Gordon watched until she disappeared out the entrance of the bazaar.

"She's here so often, and she looks like a waif. I'm not sure about her family situation." Marge settled down across from Gordon again. "The first time she stopped by, she asked if we had any work. The girl should be in school. She doesn't look older than fourteen. When I questioned this, she shrugged and said she was homeschooled."

Gordon took a bite of his cinnamon roll, allowing the sugar

and butter to melt on his tongue. "It's a popular form of schooling today."

"I wouldn't think anything of it except she's so thin. I've never seen her eat, just carry food out. I asked around. No one hired her, but she's here regularly. Always offering to work. I load her up when I can. If I could hire her, I would."

Marge stared out the entrance where the girl had disappeared. "But with the money disappearing, I'm struggling this year."

"More money has gone missing?" Gordon shoved the last bite of the pastry into his mouth. This was the information he wanted.

"It's never much—twenty here. A hundred there. But it's become consistent. And it eats into what I could pay someone. And really, other than super busy evenings, Jamie and I can handle the truck just fine." Marge gestured toward her daughter, who spoke with a gray-haired man with a mustache.

Marge scanned over the entrance again. "I wonder..."

Gordon waited for her to fill in the words she was holding in, but she shifted in her seat, pointing at his empty plate. She stood and cleared his trash. "I guess you want to start. We could stand over there, so you could get Jamie and the truck in the background. You set up, I'll be back in a few."

Whatever else Marge had thought to say, she wouldn't now. But over his shoulder, Gordon caught a glimpse of the purple puffer coat weaving through booths the next aisle over. Why was she back? He followed quickly as the jacket moved in and out, until he lost track of it.

She had managed to slip his tail, but he had a mere hint for a bigger story.

His phone buzzed and he took it out of his pocket as he walked back to Marge's food truck. A message from his landlord. She'd asked him to stop by and talk, and he still hadn't. He'd paid what he owed plus December's rent. He'd put the rest his uncle gave him in the bank and used it to catch up on some other bills.

Just one more reason why he had to find an incredible story, land the anchor chair. New job, better pay. The purple puffer coat girl could potentially be the key to his success.

If he landed at the desk, surely he could find a way to renew his visa. Perhaps the notoriety of an anchor position could finally secure his citizenship.

Five

A once in a lifetime day.

Freedom loomed just beyond the castle walls.

All Eva had to do was escape.

Yesterday's dinner with Alexander had been everything Kendra said it would be. He had been thoughtful, polite, and considerate, but there were no sparks. And he didn't seem to notice that she was a different person than he'd been out with previously.

How could he not notice?

At some point he'd be brought in on that secret, but not yet. And it irked her a little that he couldn't discern the difference between herself and Kendra.

Gordon always knew. He hadn't been brought in on the secret, he'd discovered it. The first time they'd pulled the switch he'd almost blown Kendra's cover.

But for the future of her throne, her kingdom, her dreams...she had to keep her eyes on the prize. Even if it meant the man she would marry couldn't tell the difference between her and her body double.

Copious amounts of research and the meeting with the historian all pointed to having to comply with the marriage law. She had to prepare to marry a man who didn't notice a swap.

Except for today.

Today she could ignore her responsibilities. Forget the pressure of the future. Forget the stress of a forced marriage. Forget that the future of her kingdom rested on her ability to let go of her personal dreams of love and settle for an arrangement.

The woman in the mirror didn't look anything like Eva. The dark brown wig with caramel highlights had been styled in a low ponytail with a few strands left loose to frame Eva's face. Darker and more dramatic makeup to cover up her own freckles along with thicker lashes than Eva had ever worn added to the new look. It had taken several minutes to grow accustomed to the heavier lashes, but now, Eva could appreciate how they had changed her appearance.

Fleece-lined leggings and a long taupe tunic paired nicely with knee high boots. The final touches were a jaunty cream cap and scarf and a navy winter coat. She placed her gloves in her coat pocket for later.

Kendra stood dressed as Eva in a simple eggplant-colored dress and black stilettos, her red wig in place, and much less dramatic makeup than Eva currently wore. "This may be the craziest plan you've ever had, but it's going to be a blast."

"It's a terrible idea. But I've always wanted to see the plaza at Christmas up close and personal and attend the bazaar. I'll be back late tonight, so keep a watch out for me. I want to stay through the end of the concert."

"You have money?"

Eva opened the small purse she'd packed for the day. "Yes. And lipstick and some extra necessities in case I need to fix the wig. And my phone, but I turned it off."

"Good. Now, let's get you out of the castle. First challenge— get by the guard. I'll ask him to bring up coffee." Kendra crossed the room to the door.

Eva stopped her before she opened the door. "That will never do. Tell him you saw a dog in the garden and it looks like the gardeners need help."

"Brilliant. But I would like a cup of coffee. I'll just call the kitchen and have them send some up."

"After you send the guard on his way." Eva motioned toward the door, and Kendra stuck her head out to talk to the guard.

She ducked back in the room and closed the door. "Coast is clear. Now is the time to go. Make sure you hold the hand of a handsome man, okay?"

Heat rushed up Eva's neck. "I'm practically engaged."

"But you're not yet. Plus, you're incognito. So, go! And have some fun for once. If a handsome man asks you to dance, say yes." Kendra gestured for Eva to go.

Today she could be a normal girl and fly under the radar. She could walk in a crowd, drink coffee or cocoa—or a cup of each, no one would be there to judge. She could dance with strangers and talk to anyone she fancied. Tomorrow, she would return to being the perfect princess once again.

Eva stopped just before her apartment door. "This can never happen again. Do you think it's better not to go? To never experience the dream of today?"

Her boots had very little heel, and her wig felt all wrong. How did Kendra wear these things so often? Her clothes didn't feel right either. Leggings? In public? This was a mistake. This taste of freedom would make the coming restraints all the worse.

Would God ever hear her prayers? If He did, it seemed He always said no or just seemed to ignore her. Was she doomed to be a lonely prim-and-proper royal forever?

Father always said that the heart of the ruler was in God's hand, but did it mean her heart would be lonely and forgotten there? Did it matter to God if it was her or someone else? It could be anyone really. Easily interchangeable, even to God.

Kendra's soft voice invaded Eva's thoughts. "Don't second-guess yourself now. Go, Princess. Don't think about expectations. Don't think about the future. Don't think about the kingdom. Today is for you. Enjoy."

Kendra settled her hands on Eva's shoulders and forced Eva to look into her face. Their build and features similar. If Eva studied Kendra close enough though, she could see the colored contacts hiding her dark eyes. "I don't know."

"I do. Go. Have fun." Kendra opened the door again and looked both ways. "The coast is clear."

"What if we get caught?" Eva tentatively peered into the hallway, confirming that it was indeed empty. A deep blue runner stretched down the long hallway, with life-size portraits of past royals on one side and large arched windows on the other.

Kendra grabbed a laundry bag and shoved it into Eva's arms. "Take this and go. It's going to be fine. No one will question you while you carry dirty clothes. They'll assume your shift is over and you're taking them to the laundry on your way out."

"Wish me luck." Eva stepped into the hallway and took a deep breath. This was it. Her chance to be real. To be normal.

"It's going to be fine. Have fun, and don't do anything I wouldn't do." Kendra waved to Eva as she hurried down the hallway toward the stairway the staff used to access the kitchen.

Onions and oregano wafted from the loud and busy room. Eva held her breath as she walked past, keeping her head down.

No one called after her, and no one rushed out to stop her.

She slipped into the hallway that led to the laundry room. She dropped the bag on the floor where Kendra had instructed, then made sure the hallway was empty before heading toward the back exit of the palace. Sunlight shone in through the glass door, lighting the cream tile, like a beacon showing her the way to freedom.

Eva took a deep breath. She was going to make it. She set one foot in front of the other, until the door opened and a shadow cast down the hallway.

Eva froze.

Renee, her father's personal assistant, walked in.

She'd failed her mission.

She'd been caught before she ever stepped foot out of the castle.

Eva had to keep moving. She couldn't freeze up. Renee would definitely notice her then.

Lowering her head, her hand aching to hold something, anything that might give her a reason not to make eye contact with her father's personal assistant, she kept walking toward the exit.

"How do you do? I don't think we've met." A sweet voice stopped her in her tracks. There was no ignoring the king's assistant.

Eva was sunk.

She forced a smile and looked into Renee's familiar face. There wasn't a blink of recognition. Eva could play along. What did she have to lose? Lowering her voice, she responded. "How do you do?"

Renee opened her mouth, but she snapped it closed when her phone rang from her pocket. Eva recognized that tone—it was the king's. Everyone in the building used that tone for the king. Eva stepped to the side, and Renee waved as she strolled by with the phone pressed to her ear.

Close call. One Eva didn't want to chance again, so she hurried on to the back door and yanked it open. Once outside, she inhaled the cool fresh air and blew it out, letting go of the weight of her responsibilities.

Quickly looking over the cars in the parking lot, Eva found the black sedan Kendra had left for her. She unlocked the car and climbed in, half expecting a guard or staff member to stop her. Instead, no one seemed to pay any attention to her.

She quickly started the car and gripped the stirring wheel, tapping her thumbs on the wheel to the beat of "Frosty the Snowman" as it sang through the speakers. Of course, Kendra would have a Christmas station on in her car. Adventure lay just outside the palace gates. She'd never been more thankful that her father had insisted she learn to drive. Putting the car in reverse, she backed out of the space and drove to the gate.

She'd made it out.

Out of the palace, away from her obligations.

One entire day of freedom stretched before her and she wouldn't melt away like Frosty.

WHY SHOW UP AT THE CHRISTMAS BAZAAR ON HIS DAY off? Especially this early in the day? Perhaps it was the call of Marge's coffee or the hope of finding a lead on the thief. Or maybe he just didn't want to sit in his lonely apartment. Gordon really didn't have a clear answer.

He'd stopped by Mallory's unit last night, but she wasn't home. He'd texted and she'd responded, saying they needed to talk. She probably wanted to raise his rent, and he just didn't want to hear it, so he said they would. Soon. He just didn't commit to a time.

If his request for citizenship or a visa was denied again, the cost of rent would be the least of his concerns. He'd have to find a place in the US. Hopefully, close to his cousins in Florida.

Sipping his coffee, he walked the bazaar, studying each person that passed him. Three days ago, four booth owners had each said they lost fifteen dollars from their register. Minor mistakes...they'd probably consider it an error, except everyone couldn't be making the same mistake.

Why would a thief go to the effort to sneak in, steal sixty dollars —such a minimal amount—and leave? Who would do that?

A familiar laugh floated through the breeze, and Gordon zeroed in on a brunette woman as she took a cup from a vendor a few stalls over. He was a new guy who sold specialty coffee and candy. Though his coffee didn't compare to Marge's, he held his own and had some interesting flavor combinations. She lifted the steaming beverage to her face, her every move graceful and elegant. When she spoke to the vendor, the young man moved into her personal space with a cocky smirk and responded. Whatever he said had her tossing her head back laughing.

That laugh—Gordon would know it anywhere.

Drawn in by the mystery of the familiar laugh, he started walking toward her. The brunette turned, and as soon as they made eye contact, recognition flared in her eyes. She broke their connection and hurried away.

Her dark brown hair bounced in her low ponytail, but her steps, the way her hands moved, the smile that graced her lips up as she spoke with the guy who gave her coffee, she could have added a wig, changed her makeup. But Gordon was certain that woman was Princess Evalina, and she didn't want to be identified.

No security officers, even ones dressed in street clothes, wandered about. How had she managed to leave her guard behind? He'd never seen her without at least three security officers. Even in the palace, though they gave her space, they flanked her rooms and followed her.

He dropped back, hiding behind people and booths whenever he could. She cast a casual glance over her shoulder as she stepped into an artist's booth. Zadock painted Christmas scenes on polished wood and had become well known for his paintings of Nevive. Eva ran her fingers over one of his more detailed pieces. Probably one with the castle in the background. She carefully picked it up—yep, the picture of the castle. She spoke with Zadock and eventually exited the booth without the painting.

She glanced back again, giving a quick sweep of the people behind her. Gordon ducked behind a tall man, and her posture relaxed slightly. Was she looking for him? She should know by now, he'd never blow her cover.

He slowed his step. She obviously recognized him. Did she not want to talk to him?

Eva walked into the next open-air booth and browsed the jewelry that Julia made, picking up a long necklace with a pearl setting.

Either way, he had to talk to her. If he got the feeling she had been avoiding him because she didn't want to talk to him, he'd swallow that hurt.

Gordon stepped up behind her, brushing his arm against hers. "I'm so sorry. Please forgive me."

Eva's quiet intake of breath as she bit her bottom lip surprised him, because she normally didn't show emotions in public. She set the necklace down and turned to leave. "No harm."

With her actions so out of character, he had to stop her. If she had gotten out free of security for the day, he'd follow her high and low. It would make a fantastic news story, not that he'd ever use it. Her safety, though, was paramount. He had to make sure she'd be safe in the city without security. "You look familiar to me."

Her cheeks turned a lovely shade of pink, and she ducked her head. "I must have one of those faces, because I hear that a lot."

"Perhaps we went to school together." They didn't. He had been homeschooled until he'd come to live with his uncle, then he attended school with all of the other castle staff children. Eva knew that. She'd had a private tutor with Kendra until University. Though they did learn to dance together.

"That's highly unlikely. Private tutors." Eva turned from him and shrugged.

"University then?" Again, they hadn't. He'd gone back to the States to study, and she'd stayed in Nevive, attending their local university.

Eva walked to the next booth, but he stuck by her side. She picked up an orange bar of goat milk soap and brought the block to her nose. "I doubt it."

"Hmm. Weird." Gordon stuck out his hand. "I'm Gordon. Nice to meet you."

Her gloved hand slid into his, and he held on, forcing her to look up at him. Her cheeks flushed again, but she jaunted her hip to the side, a flirty lift to her eyebrow. "News Channel 4. I've seen you on TV."

"Then I'm at a disadvantage."

Glancing around, she gave him a name. "Rosy."

Gordon nodded. She'd pulled out one of her middle names and shortened it. Quick thinking. "Are you here with anyone?"

She shook her head. "Just browsing and enjoying the bazaar."

"Well, if you've seen me on TV, then you know I love this event. I could show you around."

Eva—Rosy—started to walk away from him. "I don't normally walk around with men I don't know."

"But you already admitted that you do know me. Gordon Tarpen, KEVE-TV News Channel 4." Gordon kept pace with her.

A soft chuckle escaped Eva—Rosy—and she tossed him a playful smile over her shoulder as she stepped to the side, allowing someone to walk between them. "Fair enough. But aren't you here to work?"

"It's my day off." Gordon easily maneuvered the light crowd to walk beside her again. He had been trying to find more information on the thief, but now he'd take this day off and enjoy every moment he could with Eva.

"Your day off, and you're still here, just to enjoy? You must really love it."

If they were playing like they didn't know each other, Gordon wanted to see where this would go. "Something like that. But walking around with you might make today even better. Would you care to ice skate?"

Eva's eyes lit up, and Gordon knew she wouldn't refuse. She took the last sip of her coffee and threw the cup into a nearby trash receptor. "Let's go."

He removed his glove and offered her his hand. He'd never dared to hold her hand, but he knew their hands fit together well after years of dancing instruction. She studied it briefly before pulling her own glove off and sliding her smooth skin across his palm. He linked their fingers together, and the sparks climbed his arm. Perfection. He knew it would be, but still, the thrill of holding her hand as they walked made him want to slow their steps and enjoy the moment for as long as he could.

Whatever Eva wanted, Gordon would be all in. He might be a scoundrel, not calling her on her falsehood, but he also didn't want anyone to know that the princess of Nevive walked about without security.

No matter what happened today, he'd forever be glad he'd given up the extra sleep to come to this bazaar. He might not find a lead story, but he'd enjoy every second with the princess.

And that was priceless.

Six

Two hours of freedom and already she'd run into Gordon. Today couldn't be any better if she'd dreamed a perfect day.

An entire day with Gordon.

Gordon!

Perhaps God had finally heard her prayer and answered with something other than no. Did He finally see her heart and desires? Why now? Whatever the answer, she'd take today as a gift, because that's exactly what time with Gordon was.

Even if Gordon hadn't recognized her and she'd been forced to come up with a fake name so she didn't reveal her identity where anyone could hear them, he'd flirted with her and asked her to go ice skating. Even held her hand.

Never before had she considered donning a pair of borrowed skates and gliding across the ice, but to continue to hold Gordon's hand, she'd do it. The rental skates didn't fit like her own, and she chuckled at what Beverly would say if she could see her. Her lips would turn down, and her eyebrows would scrunch together as she turned her nose up in the air. *"Ladies don't share foot germs."*

As she tucked her hand safely into Gordon's and he pulled her almost foolishly close for ice skating, she welcomed the bite of the cool air as it nipped at her warm cheeks. A rich tenor singing *It's a Marshmallow World* pipped through the local speakers, which helped to cover the noise of the crowd and the carousel that sat not too far away.

"So, Rosy." Hearing that name on his lips felt wrong somehow, yet the tone, so warm and friendly, made all the difference. "Tell me a little about yourself."

Yikes. Well, if she wanted to enjoy the day, she had to come up with something. But outright lying…it just wasn't something she wanted to do. Especially to Gordon. "I'm not sure there's much to tell."

"What do you do for work?"

Grasping for something that would be truthful, she finally said, "I work in the family business."

"What's that? Law? Manufacturing?"

"A little bit of organizational planning. I mainly work in human relations." Like fundraising and making sure people were cared for and running a country. Those kinds of relations. "Tell me about your job. Being a TV reporter must be exciting."

He shook his head, a shadow crossing his face. "It can be. I love telling people's stories."

"I sense a but." Eva squeezed Gordon's hand as he slowed his movements.

"There's a lot of pressure to tell different stories. More hard-core news. And I'm not sure how long I'll keep my position." Gordon looked up at the palace fleetingly but then back at her.

"But people love your stories. I always watch them." Eva bumped up against him.

He stopped and turned toward her, taking her other hand. "I didn't realize that."

Eva caught her breath as he studied her face. Did he suspect her? Had he seen through her disguise? "How could you, we just met?"

The grin he unleashed had her insides tumbling about. "Touché. But I like the idea of you watching them every day."

"I love your stories about the Christmas Bazaar. I've not been since I was a child, and your stories paint this place like a movie set. I've always wanted to come back. I'll be honest, this place does not disappoint."

"You've haven't been in years?" Gordon guided her around the curve of the rink, the sun shimmering off the ice ahead of them.

Oh, yikes. Talk about a giveaway. Gordon knew she didn't come to the bazaar. She had to be more careful, or she'd blow her cover. She shrugged, hoping it seemed nonchalant. "It's a busy time of year at work, and it's not easy to get away. Your job allows you to come regularly. What's your favorite part?"

Gordon shrugged. "I do spend more time here than most. It's hard to pick a favorite, though. You've already had coffee. But you didn't try Marjorie's. Her coffee and pastries are amazing. She also has a mean apple cider. Visiting with her each year is a highlight."

Dipping her chin, she recalled the young man who had handed her the fancy latte. His fingers had lingered on her hand, and he'd winked at her. Obviously, he knew how to work his patrons for a bigger tip. "I'd love to try her cider. Maybe we could stop by later today? You've interviewed Marjorie before. I'd love to see her setup."

Gordon chuckled dangerously low, and a strange feeling buzzed in her stomach. She'd given away a little too much in that one statement. Some people scrolled social media to kill time, but Eva? She rewatched Gordon's news stories. He didn't need to know that, though.

"She would be pleased to meet you." Gordon's smile had that buzzing creeping up to her chest, and he tugged her a little closer, letting his shoulder skim against hers before guiding her around a teenager trying to find his balance.

Warmth spread through her, and Eva almost regretted the layers she'd put on to stay warm. Something in the way he looked at her was too familiar. Too knowing. If anyone would see through her disguise, it would be Gordon. "Wait a second. How do you know I didn't try Marjorie's cider this morning?"

Gordon's nonchalant shrug made him seem confident and carefree. "I didn't really. I just assumed. But it didn't seem like you'd been at the bazaar for too long. Besides, I may have watched you for a bit."

He'd watched her before she'd noticed him? For how long? Did he suspect? "Stalker much?"

"Hopefully not. But a beautiful woman caught my eye. I had to make sure you didn't have an admirer with you."

Beautiful. Oh, goodness. She might melt into a puddle. "What do you recommend as a must-see?"

"Well, skating, coffee—those are musts. Also, the spiced nuts, the pastries, the cookies."

"Do you do anything else at the bazaar besides eat? I may not be able to walk home if I eat all that."

"You'll burn it off when we dance at the concert tonight." Gordon paused, pulling her to a stop on the ice. "If you'll go to the concert with me?"

She'd planned to stay for the concert and had already told Kendra she'd be out late. She'd never dreamed she'd find Gordon and dance the night away with him. "I'd love that. If you're sure you don't mind spending your whole day off with me?"

She started to skate again, looking ahead. Almost afraid he'd say no and withdraw his offer. Or that she'd wake up and realize this was all a dream. Instead, his warm breath swept her cheek, sending a shiver down her spine as he ducked closer to her and spoke into her ear. "I'd like nothing more."

Her inner teen wanted to squeal. Gordon Tarpen *wanted* to spend the day with her. He might not know her real identity, but at this moment in time, it didn't matter. It appeared that he *liked* her.

They started skating again, and Eva moved a little closer to Gordon, letting their arms brush. They went an entire lap in companionable silence, remaining close until a blur skated past Eva, bumping her leg. Gordon immediately responded by swiveling in front of her. His hands gripped her waist, stopping them abruptly. But between the force of whatever had bumped her and Gordon's abrupt stop, Eva couldn't find her balance. A child slammed into the wall, and pushed off again, rushing past them.

Eva's feet moved back and forth quickly between Gordon's legs as she tried to keep herself from falling, but she started toppling backward, bringing Gordon with her. As soon as Eva landed with a solid thump on her backside, Gordon's hands came around her head to keep it from hitting the ice as they continued to fall backward. His body pressed heavily against her, knocking the air out of her lungs.

No one came rushing over. No one pushed the crowd back because the princess lay on the ice. Instead, Eva's world shrank. Gordon's beautiful dark eyes roamed her face, settling on her mouth. His weight pressed against her, and his hands gently massaged her skull.

Gordon's face transformed into worry. He quickly placed his hands on either side of her head and pushed back, so his weight wasn't crushing her. "Are you okay?"

Not quite ready to speak, she nodded.

Gordon scanned her face, pausing again at her lips. He closed the space between them, his gaze locked on her mouth. "Please. I need to hear you say it."

Air rushed into her lungs quickly as his warm breath washed across her face. He came closer, closer. Was this it? Would this be her first kiss? In the middle of the ice rink, with borrowed shoes and the cold creeping into her bum? When he thought she was someone else?

Working to find her voice, she pushed out some words. "I'm fine."

Barely more than a whisper, it seemed to be enough to snap Gordon out of his trance. He immediately pushed off and stood, extending a hand to her and pulling her up.

A frazzled-looking mom skated up to them. "Are you okay? I'm so sorry. Teddy's just learning. I thought he had it under control... but then he got away from me, and he's like a speed demon on the ice. Are you hurt?"

The woman grabbed Eva and started brushing off her backside. Laughter bubbled up and spilled out from Eva. Never in all her days had someone manhandled her in such a fashion. Beverly would be appalled right now. Her security would have intervened had they been here.

Stepping away from the frantic woman, Eva glanced around for the child that caused such a fuss. He stood gripping the side of the ice rink across from them now. He pushed off the wall again, zooming past unsuspecting people before slamming into the wall farther down. "We're fine. No harm. Is Teddy all right?"

She waved a hand, glancing around the rink until she found the child and watched him slam into the wall yet again. "Boys bounce back quickly. He's already skated off. If I ever catch up, we'll have a chat about skating into people. Are you sure you're okay?"

After wondering if Gordon might kiss her? After his body had been pressed against hers? His warm breath puffing on her cheeks? She might never be okay again. She would dream about waking up to that, dream that she hadn't been incognito...at least until she had to marry for the country. Then she'd have to forget this moment and the feelings it had evoked.

The weight of what she had run from threatened to consume her. Gordon's hand on her back pulled her out of the trance. "Of course. I'm fine. Gordon is too."

The mom studied Gordon, and her face flushed. "Gordon Tarpen? News Channel 4? Oh, my word! My sister has the biggest crush on you. She will be so jelly that I met you. This won't end up on the news, will it? *Toddler Terrorizes Ice Rink*."

Eva chuckled, and Gordon placed his hand around her waist, pulling her closer, and used his free hand to draw an *X* on his chest. "I promise it won't be on the news. I'm off the clock today."

"Even worse. I ruined your date. I'm so sorry. You guys have fun. I have to find Teddy. And then tell my sister you're off the market." The mom glanced around, then hurried toward the young boy, probably five or six years old, who held the edge of the rink, only to push off and go speeding across the ice, his arms circling like propellers.

Gordon's arm was still around Eva's waist. "Well, I don't know about you, but I could go for a bite of lunch. And a chance to warm up." His breath tickled her ear as he spoke, and her skin tingled all the way to her toes.

He seemed to play up the date aspect. Could it really be one? As much of a date as she'd ever been on. Formal outings didn't count, and she certainly hadn't been interested in anyone romantically. "Rosy" seemed to have a knack for this easy-breezy-as-they-come date routine. Maybe she'd have to remember to be a little more like Rosy moving forward.

Eva turned in his arms, and to her great disappointment, he let go of her and scooted back slightly. A shiver ran down her spine as the chill from the ice finally sank in. "I wouldn't say no to that."

Gordon grinned, took her hand, and they headed to the exit. "I know the perfect place."

Never had Gordon considered a lunch alone with Eva at his favorite place to eat, Ria's Café. This wasn't her world or her circle, but now that he sat across from her, the sun filtering in through the window and lighting her hair, even if it was a wig, he couldn't imagine anything better.

She could go by any name she wanted, especially without security, because she needed to be safe. Even so, he knew her. He'd known Eva for years, might have loved her since he met her. His love had only grown through the years, but that didn't change that today was a lot like a first date.

There were no hidden cameras. No one had followed them, even at a distance, and he couldn't see any news reporters or cameramen. Nothing seemed out of place. He'd maneuvered her into a chair so he could watch for any suspicious behavior in the restaurant behind her.

"What's good here?" Eva studied the menu and bounced a little in her seat as she considered all her options.

"I like the soup and salad or sandwich." Opening his camera app, he framed her up. The lighting highlighted from behind, with her elbow on the table, her hand under her chin as she perused the menu. He preferred her red hair, but the dark wig framed her face, and her smile lit up the room far better than the sun could. She glanced up and caught him taking her picture. A flush brightened her cheeks.

"Could we take a selfie?" Eva bit her bottom lip. He scooted his chair closer and placed his arm around her, leaning in so their cheeks almost touched, her unique scent drawing him in. He'd long remember this moment.

Lowering the phone, he moved away slightly, so he could still see the people inside restaurant, but close enough that he could leave his arm around her. She didn't seem to mind and even gravitated toward him.

The waiter appeared, and they placed their orders. Eva turned her back to him, leaning into him as she glanced around the room.

The painted wood, the eclectic art, the lights strung across the ceiling—Gordon didn't need to see any of the familiar surroundings to appreciate Eva's wonder of them.

Soft music played in the background, and Eva sighed. "I bet you bring all your dates here."

Surprise filtered through Gordon. She knew. Of course, she had to know there had never been anyone. Did she not realize he'd seen past her disguise? If she wanted to play this game, he'd rise to the challenge. "Hardly. I'm not seeing anyone. Are you?"

She straightened and faced him, her eyes shuttered, and blocked him out. "It's complicated."

Gordon sat up, starting to pull his arm back. He shouldn't be taking such liberties. Especially with the pictures painting a love story between her and Alexander. Stupid Alexander. But her hand caught his, keeping him from removing his arm.

Eva bit her lip and held his gaze. "I've sort of been seeing someone, and it may turn serious, even if I don't want it to. However, in this situation, what I want is irrelevant. I can't promise anything more than today. But for right now, I am here. I'd like to enjoy the day with you."

He should move his chair back.

Run.

She had someone else.

"I—" A camera flashed across the restaurant. He removed his arm. He couldn't take a chance that someone would take a picture of him and Eva like this. It would ruin her reputation.

Gordon scanned the restaurant until he found the couple smiling for the picture. They weren't photographing Eva, but still —it would be risky to be so comfortable with her. To spill what he knew.

"I'm sorry. It's just..." Eva let her voice fade away.

Of course, he knew about Alexander. But why would she force a relationship she didn't want? "Why do you have to be in this relationship?"

Eva studied him, then broke eye contact. "There are some rules that may require I marry. Soon. But today, I have some freedom. And for this one brief moment in time, I'd like to just enjoy what comes my way without thought of tomorrow. Without promises. Can we do that? Live in the moment?"

Gordon's stomach and throat tightened. This wasn't the seventeen hundreds. How could someone force her to marry? Gordon set his hand on the table, palm up offering it to Eva, and she immediately took his hand and linked her fingers. He should put space between them. Even if she didn't want the relationship, she belonged to another man. But if he withdrew, if he left her here, he would always wonder what could have been. Yes, this bubble they found themselves wrapped in would only be for one day.

One beautiful, glorious, amazing day.

But could one day satisfy all his dreams? Could one day be enough?

No.

It would *never* be enough.

Not when he wanted a lifetime. If he passed up this opportunity, though, he'd regret it. Never again would he be able to spend time with her in public without security. He'd never be able to reach up and tap his finger under her chin, directing her gaze back to his. He'd never get to enjoy her fingers linked through his.

This might be a mistake, but he would regret walking away now.

Tomorrow he could worry about the heartbreak that would surely come. Today he would embrace the gift in front of him.

He nodded, and the smile that lit her face was worth of any pain he would feel in the future. "Carpe diem."

"Thank you." Her smile brightened and he longed to wrap his arm around her, draw her close once again. But for now, this was enough.

They sat that way in comfortable silence until the waiter arrived and set their soup and sandwiches on the table.

Eva did a small dance in her chair as she studied the sandwich, artfully arranged on the small plate with the frill of a large toothpick holding it all together. A swirl of cream topped her tomato soup, and the look of sheer delight on her face over the food amazed him.

Eva had once lamented that every outing was carefully curated down to what she ate. Security always went ahead to watch as it was prepared.

Gordon had picked this café for lunch not only because it was his favorite, but because the owners were extremely loyal to the crown. If anyone happened to recognize Eva, they would not only be discreet but also take extra care of her.

Gordon took her hand again. "I'll pray. Father, thank You for the gift of meeting—Rosy." Gordon stumbled on Eva's pseudonym. Had she noticed? "For this food. For our time together. In Jesus's name, amen."

Eva picked up her spoon and dug in with gusto. "This soup is amazing. You should try it."

She held her spoon up to him.

This...this was not princess manners, and he stilled. Could this really be the woman he'd given his heart to as a shy, bumbling, and brokenhearted boy? But as she held the spoon, her hand under it to catch any drips, her expression open, he knew. He recognized that look. It had been the same one she'd had when she approached the ten-year-old version of himself in the kitchen with dessert and milk. She'd plopped down next to him and offered him a slice of cake that his uncle had baked and just rambled on and on until he opened up and spoke to her. They both knew grief and the loss of a parent. It seemed to pull them together. It had been that moment he knew he would love her forever.

And now, she sat next to him, offering soup. He leaned closer as she slowly slid the spoon into his mouth.

His heart skipped a beat as her attention locked on his mouth, and he didn't release the spoon until she glanced back up. He let go of the spoon and winked. He froze. Had he really winked? Did people even do that? When a flush covered her cheeks, he relaxed. "Delicious. Now, try mine."

Gordon dipped his own spoon into his chicken tortilla soup and held it out to her, his hand under the bite, same as she'd done.

Definitely not princess etiquette. However, he'd rise to the challenge. Eva didn't hesitate to lean closer.

He'd planned on maintaining eye contact as he offered her this bite. But as she opened her mouth, his focus changed. Mesmerized by the way her lips parted and then closed around his spoon, he slowly removed the utensil. A tiny spot was stuck to the center of her bottom lip. Reaching his free hand up, he cupped her cheek, gently dusting the spot off with his thumb. Her mouth parted at his touch, and warm breath heated his skin.

Someone cleared their throat. Gordon dropped his arm and scooted back. The waiter stood there with the water pitcher. "Would you like more water?"

"Please." Eva picked up her napkin and dabbed at her mouth, her princess manners peeking out.

The waiter filled both their glasses and left. Gordon took a bite of his sandwich, hoping to clear the now awkward silence between them. "The concert doesn't start for a few hours. Would you like to check out the art galleries along the harbor before we return to the bazaar?"

Perhaps suggesting activities Gordon knew Eva would love gave him an unfair advantage, but he didn't care. He only had one day to give Eva what she'd always wanted to do. He'd make the most out of it.

"Is there time?" She practically bounced out of her seat.

Gordon couldn't help but chuckle. "If it interests you that much, I think we can make time."

"I don't want to miss anything at the bazaar, but I've always wanted to see those galleries. I mean..." She stilled momentarily and used her napkin to dab at her mouth again.

Gordon wanted to call her out on that information she'd just leaked. Most people knew the princess hadn't visited the galleries, and that she loved local art. It had been scheduled several times, but every time something had come up. One time the artist had become terribly sick, and they'd postponed the show a week, which had conflicted with the princess's schedule. There had been a lot of news surrounding the rescheduling. He knew she'd said it without thinking, and he should probably let it go, but he wanted to see what she would say. "You've never gone before?"

"Oh." Her face flamed red. "I keep very busy. I don't have a lot of free time. I actually haven't been out much because of it. I guess I could be called a workaholic. When I do have some free time, I tend to leave town. We have a cabin in the mountains."

A cabin. Ha. More like a lodge. Gordon had gone up every summer with her after he moved in with Orlin because his uncle traveled with the royal family. It had always been Gordon's favorite part of the summer. Eva could run free, and he had joined her. Without the pressure of the palace, everyone had been more relaxed there. "If you haven't spent much time exploring the city, we could do anything you'd like to. I'd be happy to be your unofficial tour guide."

Eva took another bite and swallowed. "Actually, even more than the harbor, I'd love to see your favorite place."

"Mine?" Of all the things she'd ask, this one caught him by surprise and warmed him from the inside.

The front door chimed when it was pushed open. Maria Kopal, the royal news reporter, and her cameraman, Danny, walked in. They worked for KAT-TV, and Maria was known for her bulldog tenacity. If anyone would recognize Eva, it would be Maria. They sat at a table not too far away. Maria sat facing Gordon. She nodded a greeting and continued to talk with Danny.

Eva's voice pulled his attention back to the table. "Yes. There must be one place in this city that you love more than the others. As a reporter, I imagine you've seen more than most."

He'd never taken anyone to his favorite spot, but if it meant getting her out of here before Maria and Danny noticed them, he'd do it. He took out his wallet, threw down some cash, and shrugged on his coat. "Let's go."

"Now?" Eva looked at her soup, then glanced around the

room. Setting her napkin on the table, she nodded. Gordon stood, grabbed her coat off the back of her chair, and held it while she put it on. Then he offered his hand, and she willingly accepted it as they quickly left the restaurant.

He hurried her up the small hill, away from the prying eyes of Maria.

"Where are we going?"

"To that scooter rental up there." Heat climbed up Gordon's neck as Eva hugged his arm, excitement radiating off her.

"A motorbike? For real? I've always wanted to ride one." He knew. She'd mentioned it a time or two. Or more.

Gordon chuckled and couldn't help but tease her. "Let me guess, you never have."

She shook her head. "Never before."

"Then today is your lucky day."

Really though, he was the lucky one.

Seven

Of all the people to see today it had to be Maria Kopal that walked into the café. She lived for reporting royal gossip, and while most stories were outlandish with only a snippet of truth, people ate them up. If Maria recognized Eva, her day of freedom would be recorded and used for entertainment purposes.

Thankfully, no one followed them, and there were no photographers hidden in the trees that lined the street. The sidewalks had been cleared of snow, and no one lurked between buildings. There had been no flint of sunlight reflecting off camera lenses, no phones recording them, no one seemingly peeping at them behind trees or ducking into cars.

Eva sat behind Gordon on a motorbike, her arms coiled around his lithe frame. His familiar outdoorsy scent brought back memories of campfires and fleeing from Beverly together. Once they'd found themselves in a tiny closet to hide from her. He'd been pressed up against her, and she'd hoped he would kiss her then. He hadn't. He'd always been a perfect gentleman.

When Gordon had offered to rent a motorbike for her, the

prospect of actually driving one had thrilled her, but the opportunity to snuggle up to Gordon had been an easy choice.

The wind nipped at her nose and ears whenever she peeked around him as he drove along the calm residential streets of the capital. How had Gordon known she'd want to leave when Maria walked in? Did he suspect her real identity? She should tell him the truth, but there'd be no whispering secrets on the motorbike.

Children played on the sidewalks, people walked their dogs, and the occasional person carried a cup of a steaming hot beverage. The sun, now high overhead, did little to fight the cold temperatures, but it didn't seem to bother anyone, especially not her.

With her arms wrapped around Gordon and cuddled up against his firm back, Eva was kept plenty warm with the thrill of the moment. She had one day—one amazing, fantastic day—to enjoy her dearest friend. To experience the things she'd never dreamed could happen.

Gordon maneuvered the bike into a parking spot and set the kickstand. He jumped off, took off his helmet, tucked it under his arm, and extended a hand to her. "My favorite spot awaits."

Heat flushed her neck. She'd done nothing but sit there and watch him. She put her hand into his and dismounted the bike, trying to maintain some sense of modesty. Princesses should always keep their knees together, so riding on a motorbike would never be acceptable. Beverly would pitch a fit.

Eva unclipped her helmet and handed it to Gordon to store. At least her wig hadn't moved—whatever Kendra had done to make it stay in place worked wonders. The quiet neighborhood offered an unusual hush after the bustle of the bazaar, the chatter of the café, and the wind in their faces as they'd driven across town.

"It's beautiful." Eva whispered the words, hesitant to speak out loud and break the almost holy silence of the park. Tall pine trees lifted into the air, casting long shadows, but even so, the beauty, the quiet, the stillness...drew her in. Welcomed her to be herself in the center of her city.

Gordon took her hand and led her into the park. She had often noticed the large green space from her window, but seeing it in person, it felt bigger. It stretched several blocks, so it had walking trails paved throughout, tennis courts, a large pond, and so many trees.

In the distance, a group of young children threw snowballs and played in the area dedicated for the children's park that included swings and slides. An older gentleman walked his goldendoodle, and a young mom pushed a jogging pram.

Thick layers of snow coated the grassy areas, some with footprints and animal tracks, other areas pristine. The sun reflected on the snow like someone had thrown handfuls of golden glitter across the surface.

"Do you think we could build a snowman? Just a small one?" Eva pointed to an area not too far off the path that might have enough snow to create a small sculpture.

Gordon shrugged and stepped into the snow, pulling her behind him. He dropped her hand and took out the gloves from his pockets and put them on. "When was the last time you built a snowman?"

Eva let out a deep breath. "Probably a dozen years ago or more. We had gone to the cabin, and I built one with y—" She glanced around. No cameras. No reporters. But after seeing Maria, it might be better to keep her secrets to herself. "We used to build them often, but then my governess informed me proper ladies don't romp in the snow."

Gordon tossed a snowball at her, hitting her in the shoulder. It fell apart, sending little bits of snow upward toward her face, down the front of her coat, and some landing on the bare skin of her wrists between her gloves and her sleeves.

Gordon's soft chuckle surprised her. "I don't think you're ever too old to 'romp in the snow.'"

Eva quickly packed her own snowball and fired it back at Gordon, completely missing her mark.

"Looks like your maturity has affected your throwing abilities." Gordon threw another snowball, and it splattered across her thigh.

Laughing at the absurdity of it all, Eva quickly packed a few more snowballs and lobbed them Gordon's way. The second one hit its mark. But he'd already thrown three, all of them leaving snow on her coat. He had no problem with his aim.

Gordon walked backward, his hands up, Eva packed a few more snowballs and stood with her arms full. "You wouldn't hit an unarmed man, would you?"

"If that man was you? I would." Eva lobbed another ball Gordon's direction, and he ducked, letting the ball sail over his head. He turned to watch it land a few feet behind him. With his back to her, she fired off her last ball, and it hit him, sprinkling snow all down his coat.

She bent to make another snowball. "A little rusty, but it's coming back."

Gordon walked closer, his expression changing from teasing to serious. He pointed behind Eva. "That's what I wanted to show you."

Behind her a small stone chapel stood in the sunlight. In the distance, she could see the palace on the hill. The scene in front of her could be something out of a princess fairy tale, and yet here this beauty sat right in the center of Lesa, the capital of her beautiful Nevive.

"Wow." Eva breathed the word out and stood, her half-made snowball in her hand. The stones were lined like bricks, the multi-colored finish adding to the charm. With the bell tower out front and the chapel behind, the building appeared to have been around a long time. "How have I never seen this chapel before?"

Eva dropped the snowball she'd been making and walked toward the building. The small cross on top of the bell tower reflected the sun, and this far into the park the noises of the street and the children's park had fallen away. Birds chirped merrily overhead.

Gordon fell into step beside her as they approached the chapel, and when they made it to the sidewalk, they stomped off the snow from their boots.

"I stumbled across it on a morning run. In the summer, you can't see the palace through the leaves, but right now, the view is clear." Gordon walked up to the door and pushed it open. Inside, five rows of wooden pews lined up around a center aisle. Stained glass windows filtered in light, casting rainbows on the concrete floor. At the front, a short step elevated the platform.

Gordon led her down the aisle, and for a moment, Eva could see the rows filled, a pastor at the front, and Gordon waiting for her as soft string music filled the warm room.

She blinked and the vision faded, but the dream lingered.

Gordon paused and studied the room. "I've never shared this with anyone. Never seen anyone else here."

"You said you found it running?" Eva thought she knew every inch of her country, especially the capital, the history, and the people, but this small building—it had history, a past that she had never learned. With the beauty of the carved wood pews, the simplicity of the stone walls, the color from the windows, she could almost imagine the heavenly hosts singing around her.

Gordon selected the third row and patted the seat next to him. His arm on the back of the pew, he crossed his ankle over his knee. His winter coat was open, revealing his sweater underneath. Positively cuddly. "I run through this park most days. Several years ago, a man stood in the doorway and invited me inside. Said I looked like I could use a place to pray. I've come almost every day since. I've seen him in passing, but only to wave. He works in the garden and keeps the place clean, but besides him, I've never seen anyone else here."

She settled next to him, careful to leave space between them. The chill of the wooden boards kept her planted in this reality—a runaway princess exploring the city with the man she'd always secretly loved.

The colors of the stained glass filtered across the pews. "I almost feel seen. Heard."

Gordon lifted his face toward the ceiling. Peace rolled off of him. "You feel like He doesn't hear your requests?"

Immediately, Eva wanted to grab the words back. Too personal. Too much. Princesses should never share such personal thoughts. Not even rogue, runaway princesses.

Eva knew—of course, she knew—that God saw her. The heart of the king was in His hand and all. But she wasn't king, or queen in her case, yet. There were times when she wondered why she was easy to overlook. Was she so easily exchangeable that someone else could step into her roll, her life and He, too, wouldn't even notice?

"I know He can hear me anywhere, that all I need to do is reach out, but there is something about this place, this quiet, that makes me feel a little more connected. A little closer."

Gordon didn't look at her, though, and she had no idea if he knew her true identity. "I think we all feel like that from time to time. I wonder if He hears me. But the reality is you are heard. You're a princess."

Oh. He knew. Would he chastise her for being out today? Why was he still with her or had even allowed her on the bike to cozy up next to him if he knew who she was? She intertwined her fingers and squeezed them tight. "A princess?"

"Yes. You are a child of the King, the Creator of the world. The Giver of Life. The Master of it all. That makes you a princess."

Oh. That.

She knew that.

As she sat there, looking up at the stained glass window, a thought wiggled in. She wasn't just Her Royal Highness, Princess Evalina of Nevive, she had an even more prominent title— Daughter of *the* King.

Gordon's voice broke through her thoughts, but she studied the colors dancing across the floor as a cloud passed over the sun. "You know, being a princess makes you anything but ordinary. It means you have your Father's ear whenever you need it. You have a calling. A purpose. It means you are extraordinary."

Gordon shifted in his seat to face her. Eventually, she met his eyes, but she couldn't hold his insistent gaze, the intensity of his expression. The dark spot on the floor under the pew in front of her looked a little like an elephant. If she tilted her head just so and looked through one squinty eye...yes, definitely an elephant.

It didn't seem to faze him, because he hammered home his point. "In truth, though, it's not always about feeling. It's a simple reality, the promise that He hears. That's what we can hang on to."

She knew, of course. Simple words. Almost a typical, standard pat answer but still truth.

Gordon's faith seemed so unshakeable. So easily held onto.

"He gives peace when our mind is stayed on Him. That's my paraphrase, but a promise to cling to."

A beautiful promise, but it didn't stop the doubt.

"Sometimes, I wonder if He really sees me. Or if like everyone else, He could exchange me for a different model." After all, Eva had only ever prayed for a love match, and here she stood on the precipice of a marriage she didn't want to a man she barely knew and didn't love. One who might not even be able to tell the difference between her and Kendra.

Everyone else might see a happy love story, but she knew better.

Gordon's hand found hers, and she released her hand to flip it over under his. His palm moved across hers, his fingers going between hers. "I may not have a job for much longer. I understand questioning God's plan, but I also know that with every terrible thing that has happened in my life, something good has come from it. My parents passed away, but I moved here. I met my best friend. Found a job I love in a country I adore."

Eva's hand tightened in Gordon's. "Don't you wish your parents would have lived?"

"Of course. But I also know that I'm right where I'm supposed to be. Unless I'm sent back to the US." He blew out a breath. Eva's thumb moved up and down over his hand to offer comfort.

"Why would you be sent back?" They'd never discussed this. He'd never said anything about going back to the US. He'd not enjoyed being so far away for university and had finished his degree in three years to come back.

"Technically, I'm not a citizen."

"I thought you applied years ago." Oops. She knew better than to speak without thinking. "I mean, you've been working at the station for so long. I assumed you were a citizen."

"Work visa. Even that may not be renewed."

"That's preposterous." It shouldn't be so difficult to obtain citizenship through the proper channels. "Why hasn't it been renewed?"

Gordon puffed out his cheeks. "The immigration office either loses my paperwork or says I haven't supplied all the information. I keep trying, but I wonder if it's God keeping me from becoming a citizen. I want to stay here. Nevive is my home. But maybe God's trying to push me in another direction and I'm just not listening."

Eva let go of Gordon's hand and scooted closer to rest her head on his shoulder. "I can't imagine you not here."

Gordon wrapped his arm around her and rubbed his hand up and down her arm. "I don't want to go. But God can use difficult situations for good. He never lets anything go to waste."

Was God going to use this marriage? She didn't want it. Didn't feel any peace about it. She had a solid resolution to follow through for the sake of her country, but that didn't mean it felt right. Did she trust God enough to work out the details, to make this situation the best for her?

Changing the subject seemed so much easier than answering any of those questions. "Do you know the history of this church?"

Muscles tightened under her cheek, and she sat up. Gordon gestured toward a plaque she hadn't noticed. "Apparently, it housed royal weddings. Years ago. I think it's been four or five generations since it was used. The bell stopped working, and no one knows why. The weddings moved to the abbey closer to the castle."

Eva had never heard that bit of history. How had she missed that? "I thought the royal weddings had always taken place in the abbey. What a shame they were moved."

His nonchalant shrug reminded her that he may not know her true identity. He nodded and looked around the sanctuary. "This is a beautiful place."

The small chapel would be so much more personal and sacred than the large abbey. The intimate and small group that would gather here would make a wedding more...desirable. Less showy and more real.

She closed her eyes and tried to picture it. And again, the image came to her quickly. The swell of music almost real, but when she looked into the face of her groom, it wasn't Alexander.

It was Gordon.

And that could never be.

GORDON COULDN'T DENY THE PRICK OF PAIN IN HIS heart as they left the quiet of the chapel behind them. No matter how fast he drove the motorbike, the longings he'd experienced in the chapel clung to him like a second skin, almost as tightly as Eva hugged him as he took a turn.

In the chapel, he'd had an impossible image when Eva had asked about the history. Eva walking down the aisle to him. It'd left his knees weak—and his heart hurting.

They had today.

Nothing more.

He rounded a corner a little faster and tighter than he normally would. But when Eva's arms tightened even more around him and she rested her head against his back, well, he had his reasons. Also, he had taken the scenic route down to the harbor, ensuring he could make the most of this ride, because never again would he feel Eva's arms around him.

For a while, a car had followed them. If it'd been a tail, he'd lost it, but paranoia had set in. He checked his mirrors again, and thankfully nothing seemed out of the ordinary.

The wind bit at his nose, stinging his cheeks, as the road curved. When he slowed down, looking for a place to park the bike, a puffy purple coat caught his eye. He pulled to the side of the road, watching a lithe teen girl weave through the crowd.

Eva's body shifted back, and he missed her tight hold. "Do you want to get off here?"

He shook his head, but he couldn't stop looking at the girl. Was she really the one from the bazaar earlier this morning? She would've had time to walk down here, but why? That was several miles.

"Is there something wrong?" The hesitation in Eva's voice pulled him back to the moment.

"No. I just...I think...it's nothing. Just a story I've been working on, but this doesn't make sense."

Eva relaxed behind him, and he realized that his strange behavior had made her think perhaps they had been followed, or that her cover had been blown. He turned on the bike to face her. "But there's nothing to be concerned about."

Was this the time to tell her he knew who she was under that disguise? Or did he just enjoy today for what it was?

"We could look into it. Follow the lead. I can be the Jimmy Olsen to your Clark Kent." Eva studied the area like she knew what he had been looking at.

"Well, look at you knowing your comic book characters. I don't know how long this will take." Gordon scanned the area.

The teen seemed to be moving slowly, watching the people around her.

"Let's do this. I've always wanted to see how you find your stories." Eva dismounted from the bike with more ease and grace than he could fathom.

He wanted to make today special for her, and if following a story lead made her happy...well, he could call it multitasking.

Popping the kickstand, he turned off the bike. He stored the helmets as Eva bounced on her toes. "You may be disappointed with how unglamorous the news is behind the scenes."

"I doubt it. If you're involved, I won't be disappointed." Eva's cheeks turned a stunning pink, and he couldn't help but reach for her. "Follow your lead, Mr. Tarpen. Don't lose sight of it. I'm right behind you."

Gordon linked their fingers and scanned the area. The purple puffer coat disappeared around a corner. "If you're sure. We'll have to hurry to catch up."

"Let's go." Eva fell into step beside Gordon, and they caught up just in time to see Purple Puffer Coat Girl weave into an oncoming crowd of businessmen exiting a brownstone building, all wearing winter coats and carrying an attaché case or backpack.

"What are we looking for?" Eva squeezed his hand. Her breathless voice and pink cheeks belied her excitement. "Is it the answer to why these men are all leaving work midday?"

"No. They were probably attending a meeting or something. Watch the girl in the purple coat." Gordon slowed their steps to almost a crawl, and Eva wrapped her free hand around his arm, giving the impression they were on a romantic stroll. But as they followed the girl, Eva paused. Her mouth dropped open, so perfectly round and tempting.

Nope. Bad thoughts. Eva's perfectly kissable lips would not help him win the anchor chair. Gordon forced his attention away from Eva and found the teen girl. Her hands held the arms of a man as she apologized to him. While they spoke, she let go of him, and so very easily her hand tucked into her own pocket. But it looked like... "Did she just pick his pocket?"

Eva tugged on his arm to move faster. "It was smooth. He has no idea. Do we stop her? We should stop her."

"Let's follow. I want to see what happens. We can get the wallet back to him once we confirm that's what she's doing." Gordon and Eva followed the girl, hand in hand. She managed to swipe two more wallets in quick succession. None of the victims suspected anything. The girl had skills.

As Eva and Gordon walked between buildings to follow the girl down an alley, the scent of day-old garbage met them, and the icy layer on the sidewalk caused Eva to slip. Gordon steadied her in time to see the girl open a wallet. She snapped it closed.

"Hey!" Gordon called, pulling Eva along as he jogged toward the girl who glanced up. Her large, brown doe eyes taking him in. Her eyebrows drew together, and a deep frown etched her face. She dropped all three wallets she'd taken and took off running. After launching herself on top of a dumpster, she caught a long bar that was the banister on the fire escape and swung over a fence into someone's backyard.

"Go! Follow her!" Eva pushed Gordon after the girl, but he couldn't leave the princess. Not alone in an alley next to a dumpster. Not even for his story.

"No. My days of rail swinging and fence jumping are over. This isn't the movies." After all, there might not even be a story. It had definitely been the same girl, so he'd know where to find her later. But why would she befriend Marge if she wanted to steal from her? Why was she stealing? And why wasn't the girl in school?

Eva picked up the wallets and handed them to Gordon. "You're right. It's not nearly as exciting as I thought it would be. A chase would have really been something else, though. We can turn these in, get them back to their owners. Didn't the police chief break up a large group of pickpockets last year?"

"Yes. But it's an easy and petty crime. Happens everywhere."

Gordon quickly stuffed the wallets in his pocket. Why would the girl drop them and run? Where were her parents?

Eva linked her arm in Gordon's. "We can drop these off at the local police station, but let's not tell them there's a pickpocket on the loose just yet. I can only imagine what the news stations…"

Eva's voice trailed off, and as they merged back onto the busy sidewalk out of the alley, she froze. "This would make for a good story. Are you going to…?"

At her struggle for words, Gordon could put her mind at ease. He had no desire to cause hysteria or put that girl in danger for ratings. "There's no proof yet. We don't know if she took any money, and we have the wallets to return. I don't have any video, and there's no story to tell. Yet."

Eva hesitated for only a second before her shoulders relaxed and she turned back toward the alley. "Perhaps we can find that young girl and discover what is really going on. I suppose I wasn't a very good Jimmy Olsen for you. I didn't even think to video for you. If I had thought to pull out my phone…"

"Nonsense." Gordon tugged her back toward the motorbike. He hadn't thought to pull out his camera either, and he was the professional. That's probably why, even though he had the longest résumé, he still hadn't landed a seat at the anchor desk. "I didn't even think to grab my camera. Now, let's swing these by the police station, and then we have options. I believe my day's not over. So, do you want to try and hit the harbor shops before they close, or return to the bazaar and listen to Johnny Rocco perform?"

"Johnny's such a great person. I've always wanted to hear him perform in front of a live audience." Eva bit her lip while she mulled over the answer. "They have the dance floor set up?"

"At the concert? Yes."

"Then the bazaar it is. I've watched many concerts off my balcony, but it's so far away, the people are tiny. I've always wanted to dance among the crowd."

"Then dance you will. Your carriage awaits." Gordon gave a mock bow and stretched his arm out toward the motorbike.

Eva flushed and curtsied in return. "You're most kind, good sir."

As Eva placed her hand into his and then mounted on the back of the bike, heat rushed up his arm. He sat on the bike in front of her and pulled her hands around his waist. As the sun set, the air rushing around them was almost too cold. With Eva snuggled into his back, Gordon could have driven on forever if he hadn't felt her shiver.

At a stop light, he rubbed her hands and arms. "We can return the bike and hail a cab. It would be warmer."

She shook her head. "No, I like the bike. You keep me plenty warm."

And just like that, the light turned green, and Gordon sped up.

It didn't seem so cold after all.

Eight

The cold air immediately greeted Eva as Gordon parked the motorbike at the police station and dismounted. And the shiver that ran down her spine almost hurt. Renting a cab would be far more intelligent, but riding through town pressed up against Gordon? Well, not all choices were made with intelligence in mind.

"It really is too cold to be on this thing." Gordon wrapped his arm around her and hurried her toward the door of the police station. Three concrete steps led up to the door of the three-story red brick building, and she stilled at the bottom of the steps.

This couldn't be a good idea. The last thing she should do was walk into a police station. If her father knew she'd gone missing, they'd be looking for her. Or what if Maria had recognized Eva and followed? She'd tried looking for a tail but hadn't spotted one. Hadn't seen anyone lurking to photograph her. However, if she walked into the police station, would it be like turning herself over? She wasn't ready to be whisked back to the palace faster than...well, fast.

She still had a concert and an evening of dancing with Gordon while Johnny sang in the background ahead of her. That sounded much better than an evening of lectures and scoldings if she'd been discovered.

"Would it be better if I didn't go in with you? I could stay with the bike and make sure no one takes it."

Gordon chuckled. "Nonsense. The bike is fine there. You haven't worried about the bike before. Remember, there's a low crime rate in Nevive."

"Low crime except for a teenage pickpocket." Father would want to know about that. Had another group moved in? How many instances of pickpockets had been reported recently?

Gordon lifted her hands placing them on his chest. She stepped closer, enjoying his warmth and strength. He might not know it was her, he might think this was just a day to enjoy, but she would remember that look in his eye as he rubbed his warm hands on her arms, up and down. The way his chest vibrated as he spoke. "Going in will be fine. They won't think *we* took the wallets. They know me."

Well, they knew her too. And he'd successfully unlocked a new fear. *Would* they think they had taken the wallets? Hopefully not. Everything seemed to be there still. But worse yet, would they see through her disguise? Would they ask for IDs? She hadn't even considered a fake last name, and she had no desire to continue to lie. At some point, it had to stop, and she'd need to come clean. Everything would be fine, unless they blew her cover and dragged her away before she'd been able to dance under the stars listening to Johnny Rocco while wrapped in Gordon's arms.

The street seemed awfully normal. No guards, no security, no one appeared to be following her. There didn't seem to be any big search for her. If they were looking for her, there'd be more activity. Right?

Even still, walking into the police station seemed unwise at best.

But those men needed their wallets, and Gordon didn't seem

like he'd leave her alone. Rather like in the alley. Did he know? Were they dancing around the truth? Was he too much a gentleman to call her out on her lie? Or did he want to spend time with her? Her heart leapt at the thought, but she couldn't read into this. It was just one day.

Gordon had held her hand and kept her close. Even now, he stood closer than he ever had, his chest solid under her gloved hands. His hands continued to move up and down her arms, warming her. His brown eyes roamed her face, landing lazily on her lips, before slowly making their way back to her own eyes. Something flashed in the depths, and he hugged her. Slowly moving closer.

Would he kiss her? Now? On the steps of the police station? It didn't matter—anywhere he wanted to offer her that tender touch, she'd be willing.

The distance between them narrowed, and she lifted her chin, closed her eyes.

Waited for the distance to close between them.

For the moment his lips would connect with hers.

But instead of his warmth, cold air rushed at her when he let go of her and moved back. She swallowed and turned away. Hopefully, the cold would hide her burning cheeks. Talk about reading the moment the wrong way. As he walked toward the door, his hand gripped hers. "In we go."

Without a choice, Eva followed Gordon up the steps into the police station. A blast of warm air met them as they entered the building.

Gordon walked up to the front desk, like he knew exactly where to go and what to do. He probably did. How many times had he been in the police station for work?

"Nancy, good to see you." Gordon walked with Eva toward the desk where an older woman sat, her white hair styled neatly in a longer pixie cut that framed her face. "You look as stunning as ever."

The woman smiled, and her entire being lit up at Gordon's words. She stood—her head not even reaching Gordon's shoulders—and moved around the desk, her arms open to hug him, until she noticed Eva. Nancy froze.

Oh no. Would Nancy recognize Eva? But it wasn't recognition that filled her eyes, rather it was curiosity as her gaze landed on their clasped hands. She tried to let go, but Gordon held tighter. She didn't want to make a scene, so she made sure there was a little extra space between them. Hopefully without making it awkward.

"Always a flirt, Gordon. But it's good to see you. And you brought a lady friend today?" Nancy dropped her arms and stepped closer to them.

Had she imagined that Gordon's hand tightened on hers? That he still held on a little more firmly? Or was it something she wanted and only thought she felt? His face didn't give anything away, although his ears were a little red. Did he bring *lady friends* to the police station often? Perhaps he had no idea of her identity, and "Rosy" was just a fling for the day. An uncomfortable sensation coiled in her stomach.

Nancy extended her hands to Eva, which forced Gordon to let go, so she could allow Nancy to take her hands and squeeze them. "Let me get a good look at you."

Nancy spread their joined hands and gave Eva a full perusal. Eva would turn in a circle if Nancy didn't have such a firm grip on her. "Gordon's never brought a girl with him. And you are a pretty little thing."

Eva couldn't hold back the chuckle that this tiny woman, who didn't come up to Eva's chin, called *her* little. And thankfully, this woman had answered that nagging question—Gordon didn't parade *friends* into the police station. Could today be more than a fling for him? The relief that bubbled through her could be blamed on the fact that she still had on all her outside gear in the warm office.

Before Eva could say anything, Nancy turned her attention

back to Gordon. "Where'd you find her? She's beautiful. Don't mess this up."

Gordon's neck, cheeks, and ears all turned a flaming shade of red. Eva wasn't sure she'd ever seen him blush.

Nancy dropped Eva's hands and immediately hugged Gordon. While she held him tight, she fussed and cooed and finally demanded, "Tell me her name."

Once Nancy let go, Gordon stepped closer to Eva, placing his hand on her low back. "Nancy, meet Rosy."

"Rosy. A lovely name for a pretty girl. Now, did you only come by to introduce me to your beautiful lady, or are you working today?" Nancy returned to her desk and moved her computer mouse, put on a pair of reading glasses, and looked up at Gordon over her glasses.

They hadn't discussed what they would say to the police. If they reported a pickpocket, then the police might try and hunt Eva down for future clarification if she gave a statement. And when they couldn't find her—well, it wouldn't be good if they started looking. Gordon pulled the three wallets out of his pocket. "We saw a—"

"We found these wallets on the sidewalk. Thought you could hunt down the owners and return them." The last thing they needed was a scandal or a rumor of a group of pickpockets when the chief had worked so hard to disband the huge circle last year. And she sure didn't want them to try and hunt her down. Anything she could do to keep from having to produce an ID or a last name. She wanted to enjoy her day with Gordon, not get lured into a criminal investigation. She would make sure her father knew the full details.

Gordon's hand pressed against her back, but he recovered quickly. "Yes, we saw them on the ground and picked them up."

Truth. They had picked them up. Nancy frowned and took the wallets. Opening each one, she noted their credit cards and IDs seemed to be in order. Inside, bills still sat nestled in their proper pockets. "It's unusual so many people would drop their wallets at once." Nancy leaned back in her chair and raised her voice. "Hey, Randy!"

Oh dear. Eva quickly studied her shoes as the police chief walked toward the lobby, his footsteps sounding on the hard floor as he got closer. The man had been in office since Eva had been young. He'd been to the palace several times and had known her since she was "knee-high to a cricket." His funny twist on an old adage. Would he recognize her and reveal her identity? There was no way the chief would let her leave the station without security if he discovered her.

What were the chances that she'd run into all the people that might easily see through her disguise in one day? Gordon, Maria, Chief Rodgers? Yikes.

Randy walked toward them, his large girth preceding him. His unruly white hair curled around his face. "You bellowed, Nancy?"

"Gordon's here with his girlfriend, Rosy." Nancy gestured toward them, and Eva inched a little closer to Gordon, staring at the scuff marks and scratches on the cement floor. They showed age and character. If she studied the scratches on the floor, she might find a picture or a face.

"Gordon has a girlfriend?" Chief Rodgers stepped forward, and there was little choice but to look up. Why hadn't Gordon denied that yet? They'd only just met that day, unless Gordon knew her real identity? But that didn't change the fact that they weren't together *together*.

"I didn't stop by to introduce Rosy." Gordon moved forward, and Rosy stayed behind him. "We found some wallets, and we wanted to return them."

"Found them? Where?" Chief Rodgers immediately switched from a teasing grandfather figure to police chief.

"On the ground on Central, outside the trade building." Gordon spoke his words carefully. Not lying but not giving away any extra. He'd quickly adopted her story without question.

"Well, thank you for turning these in. It's so weird. It appears everything is still there. We'll contact these men and return them. Is there anything else?"

"No, sir. That's all. Rosy and I are off to the concert at the bazaar tonight." Gordon linked their fingers and led her toward the exit.

"Rosy?" Chief Rodgers said her name, and she worked to smile, an easy natural expression, not the one of stress fighting to take over her stomach. Gordon stopped as the chief spoke. "Have we met before? You look familiar."

"I hear that often, sir. I think I have one of those faces."

The chief studied her, and Eva's smile wobbled, an uncomfortable thing, as Gordon nodded toward the door. "We better get going. We want to make it back to the bazaar to hear Johnny Rocco sing."

"Oh, to be young again. You two have fun!" Nancy hollered before the door closed behind them.

As Eva took a deep breath, the cold air filled her lungs. That had been a close call. Too close.

A quick survey revealed nothing out of the ordinary. No bodyguards, no one looking for her, no media. A white crossover slowed down in front of the station and drove by, but the driver didn't turn or seem to notice Eva and Gordon, as the driver looked the other way.

The sun sank low behind the buildings, the day short. Soon she'd be dancing under the stars, listening to Johnny croon one of his romantic songs.

With Gordon.

It kept getting better.

A dream come true.

Eva and Gordon walked back toward the bike. The seat was now cold underneath her. A cab would be warmer. But as soon as she wrapped her arms around Gordon, she knew...she'd suffer any amount of discomfort for this experience.

And she'd spend the rest of the night dancing in his embrace.

Tonight would be the perfect ending to the most incredible day.

THE RICH BARITONE OF JOHNNY ROCCO FILLED THE area, and couples swayed to the rhythm of his song. Gordon gathered Eva—Rosy—a little closer. Saying her fake name at the police station had reminded him this wasn't real. Whatever happened between them today wouldn't last.

They had a timestamp on the end of their relationship.

He held her close anyway, their bodies moving in perfect rhythm to the music. He'd never danced with her like this at a royal ball or even in their practice sessions, but tonight felt intimate. Informal.

And he was here for it.

For every moment of it.

The string of lights reflected on her wig, and he could imagine how breathtaking her real hair would be. Johnny started singing "I'll Be Home for Christmas," and he drew Eva closer yet. She came willingly, all but eliminating any space between them, and fell into step with him like they'd been dancing together for years. Which they had. But wow, did it feel like home with her in his arms. If only it could be.

"What are your goals for the future?" His voice held a husky note, like he needed to clear his throat.

She missed a step but recovered quickly. "That encroaches on real life and the future."

"It does." He'd agreed to one day. To live in this moment. But he'd been lying. He wanted all of her moments. All of her dreams.

Eva tilted her head and studied him until his ears burned. Large outdoor heaters lined the edges of the dance floor, making the area warm. With Eva in his arms, he might not need those heaters. She nodded and rested her head on his shoulder. He let the music settle between them, but he wanted to hear her voice again. "Tell me your dream vacation."

"That's easy. Today has been the perfect vacation." Her breath puffed on his neck before she lifted her head. "If I could do this again, go someplace and just be among the people. Walk, order whatever food I wanted, dance, build a snowman. Whatever I wanted, whenever I wanted, with whomever I wanted—that would be the perfect vacation."

He spun Eva out, and while she twirled away, Gordon could be ten feet tall. He couldn't stop the smile that spread across his face. The feelings bubbling up inside of him could stick around. Her perfect vacation pretty much summed up their day today. He'd been able to give her that, and he'd like to do it again.

As he caught her back into an easy embrace, she asked, "What about you? What's your ideal vacation?"

Part of him wanted to tell her wherever she was, but he stopped the words before they came out. That would imply more than one day, and he needed to keep it light. "A beach. The sun and sand between my toes."

"Any specific beach?"

"I love the Florida Panhandle beaches and have family there. I'm never opposed to a visit to see them. But I don't want to live there. If I could go anywhere, I'd love to see the Philippines, or Bora-Bora, or the Galápagos Islands. I haven't traveled as much as I'd like."

"You've traveled growing up though. With your uncle?" Eva frowned, as she realized that crossed way over the light and fluffy line. He wasn't even sure he'd mentioned his uncle during their time today. "I'm sorry, that's very personal."

He nodded. It was. He could share more along that line, but as she kept herself rigid in his arms, he opted to give her an out. Keep her relaxed, even if the topics of the questions were obscure. "Do you want a pet?"

"I've always wanted a cat."

"Not a dog person?"

"I'd love a dog, but it wouldn't work with my schedule. Other people would end up taking care of it. I wouldn't even be able to walk one, train one. That's not the job of a p—" Her voice cut off and she shrugged. A princess. He knew what she didn't say. "A cat could live in my apartment, and I could care for it myself."

He sidestepped leading her in a slow turn in time to the song. "Your independent streak is showing."

"So much of my life is planned for me. Taken care of by others. The few things I can control myself are important to me."

"Getting personal there, Princess."

Eva stilled in his arms and stepped back slightly. "Princess?"

Oops. Talk about a way to kill the moment. "Seems fitting if you have so little control over your life." He shrugged. Hopefully his casual tone didn't indicate that he could see beyond her disguise. Had seen past it since the moment he saw her. He should tell her that he knew—it wouldn't be hard. Just whisper in her ear. He glanced around the crowd, and something caught his eye. Could that be a camera lens?

No. No, just his paranoia coming through.

The music changed to something quick and peppy, and he changed up their moves, swinging her out and back in. She followed his lead perfectly, laughing at the change of pace.

By the time the song ended, they were both winded, and Eva's cheeks were flushed red. He drew her close again, and they swayed in a circle, when movement on the edge of the crowd again caught his attention.

This time he knew it wasn't paranoia but reality creeping back in.

Marco. Head of Eva's personal security. Staring right at them. Gordon led them deeper into the crowd of people dancing so there were several couples between them and Marco, but at one point Eva stumbled in his arms, and he knew. She'd seen Marco too.

"Gordon?" The quiet plea of her voice had him ready to slay dragons. Marco wouldn't stand a chance.

"Yes?"

Eva's expression held a note of determination as she glanced over Gordon's shoulder. "We agreed to one day, right?"

"That's all. Just one." The words stung, and his voice scratched.

"If I said I didn't want the day to be over yet, do you think we could leave?"

Why had there been no security all day? He'd never seen her without it, but it started to fall into place. "You're on the run?"

She shook her head. "I haven't been, but I might be soon. If you're willing."

Gordon stepped in a half circle, keeping his eyes on Marco as the head of Eva's security casually walked along the edge of the crowd, not moving closer to them, but not letting Gordon guide Eva farther away. "Let's do it."

Mindful of the couples around them, Gordon wove through the crowd, working to keep his eye on Marco. Then she nodded toward another guy in the crowd. "Do you see the guys in suits?"

"Yes." There were two besides Marco on the edge of the dance floor now.

She pointed toward an opening in the crowd. They stopped dancing, and Gordon grabbed hold of her hand as she started in that direction. Gordon followed behind to keep her sheltered from their view. "Let's stay away from them."

"Princess Evalina!" a voice yelled over the crowd, and Eva picked up the pace.

A young man Gordon didn't know but wearing the classic black suit stepped in front of Eva, and she gasped. He held out his hands as if Eva was a startled kitten. "Your Royal Highness, please don't make a scene. Come with us."

She shook her head, drawing up to her full height. Gordon had seen her relaxed today, but watching her transform back into Her Royal Highness, Princess Evalina startled him. She filled the role so well. "Thank you, but I'm not ready to return. Now, kindly step aside, so *you* don't make a scene."

"My orders are to bring you back to the palace." The man did not budge. Instead, he reached out to her, like he wanted to take her hand.

Unbelievable. No wonder Eva had enjoyed her freedom so much today. If Gordon needed a dragon to slay, nothing said it couldn't be the man standing in front of him in a black suit. Gordon dropped Eva's hand and stepped in front of her. "I believe the lady asked you to let her pass."

"That is none of your business." The man didn't even spare him a glance, instead reaching around Gordon to what? Grab Eva?

Eva's hand rested on Gordon's arm. The tremble made Gordon raise his arm to deflect the guard's reach. "Actually, she's my date. And as your princess, you need to do as she asks."

The man lifted his brows, but he turned his attention back to Eva, trying to step around Gordon, and grabbed her elbow. "Please, Your Royal Highness. Per your father's request, I need you to come back with me."

Eva tried to pull her arm free, but the guy seemed to tighten his grip.

Not cool. No one should be allowed to manhandle Eva in such a manner. Gordon seethed. "I suggest you let go, sir."

The man in the suit completely ignored Gordon and tugged on Eva's arm again, causing her to stumble forward. Eva's quiet voice held an edge Gordon had never heard. "My father would never ask you to use force. I suggest you unhand me at once. I will be speaking to Marco about this behavior."

Gordon quickly glanced around the group watching them. Where was Marco? He'd seen him earlier. Why wasn't he getting involved in this?

The security guard hesitated but didn't release his hold on Eva. It didn't matter who the woman was, no one should treat a lady this way. Even if this guy thought he was protecting the princess, he shouldn't grab a woman and yank her around.

"The lady said to let go." Without another thought, Gordon punched the guy.

The guard stumbled into a couple dancing behind him. The guy grabbed the guard's arms, keeping him from retaliating. Thank goodness.

Gordon had too much pride to shake his hand out, but that hurt worse than he thought it would. Though he probably should have considered the ramifications of assaulting palace security, he would never regret protecting Eva.

Now Marco stepped into things. He and another guard rushed toward them, so Gordon held out his hand to Eva. "If you still want to, let's go."

Eva didn't look around, didn't hesitate. She simply took Gordon's hand and followed him through the crowd. He would relive this moment the rest of his life, when Eva—not Rosy, because that cover had been blown to smithereens—had chosen him. Him.

Gordon wove through the crowd as couples gasped and broke apart in the mayhem, but many who had witnessed what happened happily helped their beloved princess get away. And somewhere in the distance Johnny Rocco continued to sing, something upbeat and trendy. The bass a constant beat that matched the speed of his heart.

Thankfully there were only three guards, and they couldn't be everywhere. Some blocked the guards while others had their phones out and cameras pointed at them.

So much for not being a headline tomorrow.

With the third guard behind them—another man Gordon didn't know—Gordon saw the guy he'd just punched rushing toward them. A kid really, who seemed very young to be on the princess's protection detail. He wasn't slowing, and Gordon knew the man would try to take him down.

"This way!" An older woman waved for Gordon to follow her. Without a second thought, he turned and guided Eva into an opening in the crowd which seemed to swallow them up.

Eva followed closely behind him. The crowd seemed to clear a path for them off the dance floor and into the bazaar. Gordon slowed their steps, trying not to draw attention to themselves as they wove through the crowd browsing the booths. They slowed as they walked past the carousel and skating rinks, working to blend into the crowd.

Finally, it quieted as Gordon left the bazaar and moved into the shadows between two buildings. The uproar of the dance, the fight that broke out, the music, and the people faded into the distance.

Slowing down even more, Gordon needed a moment to regroup. Now that people knew the princess was wandering around, she would need security. Her disguise no longer offered her protection. People had probably already shared videos on social media, if they hadn't been sharing them live.

Eva fell into step beside him, and they walked farther into the shadows. "I'm sorry, Gordon."

This was it. The moment they had to talk, probably say their goodbyes.

But before he could speak, his feet wobbled on a patch of ice. While Gordon tried to find his footing, his feet skated back and forth. His free hand started to windmill, and in order to regain his balance, he tried to let go of Eva's hand. But she latched onto him tighter as she, too, lost her balance on the ice.

The ground rose up to meet him, and he put his arm out to break the fall, but it gave way under the momentum, and he went all the way down. He rolled, trying to ensure Eva had righted herself.

But just as he rolled over, Eva landed on him. He caught her, and a hiss escaped as his wrist throbbed. He held her though, just breathing. Twice in one day they'd ended up on the ice. Twice he'd held her in his arms.

This time though, her weight was completely on him, his hands on her back. Her breath puffed out, as he just savored the feel of her. The ice crept through his coat, but he didn't move. Didn't want to break the spell.

Eva, his Eva, ran her fingers over his face, down his arms. Concern etched her eyes as she checked his head. Her fingers wove into his hair, massaging his scalp. He lifted his head slightly as her hands moved to the back of his head. She took special care as her fingers ran over his skin.

He'd been a fool to agree to one day. He knew it wouldn't be enough. But this moment, right here, Eva in his arms, touching his arms, his skin, his face—it just felt right. He never wanted to let go. Instead, he wanted to close the distance, brush his lips against hers.

But before he could move, she scrambled off him, and he hissed in pain again.

"Oh, Gordon! I'm so sorry." She extended a hand to him. "I didn't mean to hurt you."

He took her hand with his good wrist and stood, his back damp after lying on the ice. She quickly caught his sore wrist, pulling his jacket sleeve up.

"That doesn't look so good." She wasn't wrong. But her hand skimming over his skin didn't feel so bad. In fact, he rather liked her gentle touch. "We need to get that checked."

He withdrew his wrist out of her grasp. It did hurt, but he'd never admit it. "I'm fine."

"You're not fine." Fire flashed in her eyes and her voice brooked no nonsense. The princess had returned.

He needed that reminder. The beautiful woman in front of him wasn't a fling for the day. No, she would one day rule the country. "Eva, you've been identified. We can't risk it."

She dropped his gaze, her cheeks turning a brilliant pink. "You knew. When did you figure it out?"

"Since I saw you in the market."

That got her attention. She glanced up at him and took a step back. There could be none of that. He might not be able to have a lifetime, but he wasn't ready for their day to end. He reached out and took her hand, keeping her in place.

Watching their linked fingers, she whispered, "I can't believe you didn't say anything."

With his sore hand, he lifted her chin with the crook of one finger. "I can't believe you thought I wouldn't know immediately."

Eva held up a thumb and forefinger, separating them an inch or so. "To be honest, I may have been a little hurt when you didn't immediately call me out."

Gordon shook his head as he used his sore arm to cup her cheek. "And blow your cover? I would never."

"I wanted to see the bazaar. Experience some freedom. I'd been cooped up with a cold, and well, I just wanted some fresh air. I never dreamed I'd see anyone who would recognize me. And instead, I ran into you, saw that snake of a reporter at lunch, and walked right into the police station." She shrugged. "I'm sorry I lied to you."

"I'm not upset. I pushed you this morning, wanting to see what you'd say. I could tell you were alone, without security."

She seemed to hesitate, a battle raging in her mind. Gordon let his hand drop from her face, mindful of his sore wrist. Eva tried to free her hand from his, but he held tight. He wasn't ready to lose that connection to her.

She stilled. Her voice quiet. "I'm sorry. You didn't have to stay with me. As you saw, I've been perfectly safe today."

"Eva, I pushed and then stayed because I *wanted* to be with you."

"Really?" The uncertainty in her voice had him letting go of her hand as he wrapped his arms around her. Only he'd forgotten about his wrist, and as Eva leaned back against his hands, he inhaled sharply.

She reached behind her and brought his sore wrist in front of her, gliding her fingers over his blotchy skin. "We have to get that checked."

Gordon made a fist then stretched his fingers. "It's fine."

"Gordon." Eva ran her fingers over his wrist and gently pressed a red area.

Gordon couldn't stop himself and jerked away from her touch.

"You need to get that checked."

"Your security is more important. You'll be recognized if we go to the hospital. We've been standing here too long as it is. We need to get on the move. As much as I don't want today to end, we should get you home. And I need to face the music, or uh, repercussions of punching your security officer."

Eva lifted one eyebrow and held up her finger. "First of all, he deserved that. And I will see to it you do not face any charges. Second, we just ran from security. If I wanted to go back, I would have gone then. I'll go back in my own time. Third, I know just where to go to get this checked. Come on. Follow me."

The problem? He would follow her anywhere. Except once she returned to the palace, he wouldn't be able to stay with her. Regardless of what she said, he'd be arrested for assaulting palace security. He hadn't thought that through at all. Violence was never the answer, and he'd just turned his brain off. Sure, he'd been trying to protect Eva, but that was the guard's job. Just because Gordon didn't agree with his methods didn't make physical violence acceptable. His uncle would be ticked.

All too soon, today would be over, and he'd face the consequences of his actions. He'd never regret the day with Eva, though, and he'd accept whatever came his way for doing what he thought was best.

After spending the day with Eva, holding her hand, being close, one thing was certain—he would never be the same.

Nine

Chemical smells filled the exam room, and the overhead lights buzzed, but the clinic was quiet. Eva had called Dr. Renolds on the way over. Although the man had a private family practice, he also volunteered at the children's hospital once a month and on the weekends. Eva had met him years ago and now requested him when she needed a doctor. He'd always been good to work her into his schedule, and tonight was no different.

"The good news is it's not broken. The bad news? You've sprained your wrist." His deep gravelly voice belied his age as he gestured to the muscle that had swollen on Gordon's wrist.

A shiver ran down Eva's spine, and Mrs. Renolds wrapped an arm around her shoulder, tugging her from the room. "We'll let you two finish in here. I'm going to take Eva to get cleaned up."

The older woman guided Eva into another exam room. Eva washed her hands and splashed some water on her face. Mrs. Renolds handed her a towel and settled on the exam table. She gestured to the seat next to her and Eva hesitated. Mrs. Renolds moved with a tenacity that came naturally. She seemed so comfortable and confident in her own skin, while Eva wanted to curl into a ball, hide from reality.

Eva glanced in the mirror. Her wig had slanted across her forehead—probably from when she fell on top of Gordon. But she'd been so concerned with him, she hadn't noticed.

Mrs. Renolds patted the table insistently. "I can help you take that off. With your cover blown and news circulating, there's no need to keep wearing it."

"News reports?" Eva hopped up on the exam table, nowhere near as easily or gracefully as Mrs. Renolds, who went to work removing the wig. So much for staying under the radar. Of course, the news would be circulating after what happened at the dance. Which, before the punching had started, had been glorious. For a few moments, she had snuggled into Gordon, listened to his steady heartbeat, while her head rested against his chest. His strong arms had pulled her closer. It had been a dream until she'd seen Marco. And the new intern.

Eva closed her eyes, as her hands shook. She felt bad that Gordon had punched Smithy, but he'd basically asked for it, demanding she come with him. Never before had security been forceful with her, but as an intern, he was still learning the ropes, and she didn't often have a reason to interact with him. Father must be pretty angry to demand she return at all costs, but since he'd been the one to suggest the trip, something else must have come up to play a part in that request.

"That was one impressive punch that young man threw. It's not an easy feat to take out one of your security guards." Mrs. Renolds removed a few more pins and lifted the wig off.

The weight of the wig gone, Eva ran her hands over her hair, quickly undoing the braid used to hide her red locks. She had to admit it felt good to take the wig off. "I had hoped no one caught that on camera."

"Several people did. The news station even picked it up." Mrs. Renolds dropped her voice an octave and mimicked a news announcer. "'Our very own Gordon Tarpen is in on the action. We have reached out to him and are waiting to hear back from him.'"

Eva flicked some dirt off her leggings, letting her own hair fall around her face. "I should have gone back with Marco, not caused a scene. I just wasn't ready for the day to be over. All I wanted was to have one day—a moment in the scheme of things—to just experience life. To be simple and ordinary. To be seen by someone."

To be with Gordon. Not that she wanted to say that out loud. Besides, she was supposed to be getting married soon, and unfortunately, Gordon wouldn't be her groom. That thought chilled her more than any spill on the ice could.

"You are anything but ordinary."

Mrs. Renolds's calm, serene voice soothed some of the ache Eva had been feeling since she'd run from the guards. Why would her father send them after her? Hadn't he been the one to encourage her independence?

"You are an extraordinary woman, Eva."

Gordon had said the same thing earlier. When he'd known her true identity. He'd seen past her facade, seen past her walls, seen past her disguise. He'd known who he'd spoken to. Calling her a princess but insisting her title held a double meaning. "I've been told that before. Today even. I'm beyond thankful for my life and responsibilities, but before things are taken completely out of my control, I wanted to visit the Christmas Bazaar. Drink cocoa, walk the streets, dance with a stranger." She gulped. Gordon had been no stranger, and she'd not even tried the cocoa.

What she had done, though, was danced with Gordon. Held Gordon's hand. Hugged him tightly as they rode a motorbike through town.

Gordon had taken center stage of her adventure.

Even though he'd seen through her disguise, he'd still offered her his hand. Still wrapped his arms around her. Allowed her to snuggle against him on the motorbike. Encouraged it even. When she thought he might kiss her, he'd known it was her and not some random girl he'd picked up at the bazaar.

Today had been so much more than ticking things off her bucket list. It had been a hidden dream becoming reality. It was like God had heard her deepest, most secret desires and brought them to life.

Like He'd seen her, heard her prayers, and responded.

Giving her everything she wanted. But only for a day.

Mrs. Renolds ran her fingers through the wig, brushing out the tangles that had accumulated. Then she wiggled her eyebrows and grinned. "I daresay, Gordon is no stranger."

Anything but. How could she describe their relationship? The man she wished would love her? "He's a lifelong friend."

"Oh, honey. That man wants more than friendship. He wouldn't be throwing punches, protecting you in a fall, worrying about your wants if he didn't care for you."

Hope flared. Could Mrs. Renolds be right? But there was no room for hope, not with a pending engagement hanging over her. Besides, Gordon had never shown interest before. One day in town wouldn't change that. Even if she wanted it to be true, she had to look at the big picture, not just a few stolen moments. That punch wasn't because he secretly held feelings for her—he'd been trying to protect her because Smithy had crossed a line. Gordon was a gentleman and would protect any woman. "Sure, he cares. We've been friends forever."

Eva jumped off the exam table, rubbing her hands on her arms. Would she ever warm up?

"I daresay, it's more than that." Mrs. Renolds bent down and opened a cupboard underneath the exam table and removed a thin blanket. She shook it out and wrapped it around Eva's shoulders.

Grateful for the small amount of warmth, Eva pulled the blanket tight. Funny how she hadn't noticed the cold today when she'd been with Gordon, but now she had to actively keep her teeth from chattering.

Mrs. Renolds ran her hands up and down Eva's arms. The friction helped to warm her. "I believe that young man might have a thing for you. Will you pursue it?"

"I'm not sure your observation is correct. If it was, I'm not sure there is time to find out. Parliament says I have to be married by my birthday in a few weeks. If I am not, I forfeit the throne. Gordon's not a citizen, and even if he was, I couldn't force him to marry me just to let me keep my throne."

Mrs. Renolds tsked, and Eva could picture her making that sound when she tried to correct unruly children who came into the clinic.

"So, you planned this day to what? Have a day with him? Live out your fantasies?"

"No. I didn't plan on seeing him today. I just wanted to experience the bazaar. Running into Gordon had never been part of the plan. It was a gift. A dream. But only for a day, and now the day is done, and I have to go back."

"That's easy enough. Just call your security. Or I bet we could easily flag one down without a scene. Especially if we drove toward the bazaar."

Eva's stomach tightened, and a shiver ran down her back. She hadn't been lying to Gordon when she said she wasn't ready to go back. She should go, though, since the day was ruined anyway. Gordon's sweet patience and protection had landed him with a sore wrist. She shouldn't ask him for more.

Eva turned away from Mrs. Renolds. She should just text Marco. He'd pick her up and she could return to the palace discreetly. Since there'd been enough of a scene as it was, she really shouldn't try to cause more. She had no idea how the PR department would spin this.

"Of course, if you're not ready to go back, you could come home with us. We have two guest rooms. It will be perfectly on the up-and-up if anyone questions it. It will give you some more time to talk. We'll make sure you're safe and unfound."

Eva spun around and hugged Mrs. Renolds. "Thank you. I'm just not ready for the magic of today to end. It's not even seven yet."

The older woman's arms came around Eva and hugged her tightly. Her hands patted Eva's back. "Of course, dear. Now, let's go tell the men. You need a warm shower and a change of clothes. We can do both at home. Then you can talk with your young man and figure out the future. This romantic wants you to find a way to be together."

An hour later, Eva sat in the kitchen in clean jammies she'd borrowed from Mrs. Renolds and a warm cup of apple cider. Beverly would pitch a fit not only at her behavior today but if she could see this outfit. Flannel, both the bottoms and the top. A cute set she would pick for herself. Not to mention she smelled like a tropical fruit basket, because everything in the bathroom had a fruit fragrance—so different than the products she regularly used. But she loved the newness of it. The simple, sweet fragrances might be something she bought for herself moving forward.

Dr. and Mrs. Renolds said good night and took their own cider to their room, leaving Gordon and Eva alone.

"Want to sit on the couch?" Gordon stood from the kitchen table, extending his hand to her. Even now that the ruse was up, he continued to offer his hand.

She picked up her mug and took his hand. Sparks climbed up her arm and zoomed down to her toes. Nothing seemed to warm her like his touch. If she kept hold of him, would it cut the chill still clinging to her? She didn't get the chance to find out, because he let go so he could hold his own mug. The doctor had wrapped his other wrist, although he said he wouldn't need the wrapping for long.

Gordon led her into the living room to the couch near the Christmas tree in front of a large picture window. Outside, the Christmas lights that decorated people's homes lit the view against the inky sky. Inside, the lights were off, but the glow of the tree illuminated the room in a festive manner. A gas fireplace across from the tree heated the room and added to the merry ambiance. A romantic atmosphere for a conversation that made her palms sweat and her toes numb.

They sat on the couch, their mugs on the coffee table in front of them.

"Blanket?" Gordon didn't seem to mind close proximity, as he scooted a little closer.

"Please." Eva spread the soft throw across their laps, then handed Gordon his mug and reached for hers. As she settled in, he put his arm on the back of the couch, his hand resting on her shoulder. He stayed close, like he enjoyed the nearness as much as she did.

"I'm sorry for the ruse today." Eva sipped her cider, relishing Gordon's warmth and strength. She could get used to relying on him.

"I don't think you could fool me. I'd recognize you anywhere."

He'd recognized her.

He saw her.

There were not many people she could say that about. Not many people truly knew her. "People see what they want. I didn't really think anyone would see me."

"I do. Like I knew it was Kendra out with Alexander this week."

Eva wiggled her toes. Gordon knew when it wasn't her? He saw her that clearly? She pursed her lips to keep from smiling like an idiot.

Gordon's good hand drew a circle on her shoulder. "I don't understand why you need a body double."

Eva shrugged. No one knew really. "In a lot of ways, I'm not sure. Father wanted extra security after Mom's accident."

Gordon scrunched his eyebrows together. "The rock climbing accident with Aunt Erica? That was an accident, nothing nefarious happened."

Eva nodded. The accident that had claimed her mother's and Gordon's aunt's lives. "Yes. Father had concerns I might be reckless. So, Kendra was found. She moved to the palace and after a while became one of my closest friends. I always thought it was more to keep me sheltered than a security issue."

"But why Kendra? She looks nothing like you."

"Exactly. We have similar facial features, but no one would really notice that. When we travel, people assume she's a companion. Father utilized her more when we were younger. He said he wanted to keep me safe. I've always felt a little like Rapunzel locked in her tower. The sad reality is that most people don't know the difference and never look beyond the red hair and green eyes."

"But people close to you know the difference." Gordon seemed indignant on her behalf.

Eva swirled her cider in her mug, and Gordon set it on the coffee table for her. Then he draped his arm around her again. "Not always. One time when we were younger, I was in the other room, and Kendra was dressed like me. Father said something to her, not knowing she wasn't me. I guess...I've always wondered if I mattered. If my own father couldn't tell the difference, how would anyone else?"

Gordon's hand tightened on her shoulder, and he used the fingers on his bandaged hand to lift her chin. "You matter, Eva. I see you. But more than that, God knows each of His children, and He sees us all as individuals. The Good Shepherd calls us by name."

A single tear escaped and rolled down Eva's cheek. Gordon caught it with his thumb.

Eva savored his tender caress. She knew people respected her position, but to see her personally the way Gordon did? It was a rare treasure.

Her throat tightened. "Thank you for today. For seeing me. For showing me the park. The church. For letting me follow a story lead with you."

Gordon's thumb ran down her now dry cheek and left a fire in its wake. Every part of her tingled as he examined her, noticing her cheeks, her nose, her lips. He stalled there, before he rubbed his thumb over her cheek again.

The air between them changed. It electrified. The space between them seemed to close.

"Eva." Gordon's husky voice sent another shiver that had nothing to do with the cold racing down her spine. In fact, she'd finally warmed up. Might even be hot.

He tucked her hair behind her ear. His hand lingered, then ran down her neck. Her breath became shallow, and her heart pounded against her chest.

"I…" He pulled his hand back, creating space she didn't want. The sparking and sizzling faded.

He glanced away, and a wall went up between them. She recognized that wall. It had always been there. Today had been different because she'd peeked behind it, but with a single breath he'd built it back up.

But if there was any way she could knock down that wall, she should try and find it. Today would be over before she knew it, and she'd like to move forward without questions. If she didn't find out what he was hiding, she might always wonder.

"Tell me what's going on with Alexander." If he could, Gordon would kick himself. He didn't really want to know, but he'd almost kissed Eva. Almost given in to every fantasy he'd ever had and closed the distance between them, almost pressing his lips against hers, right here in the doctor's house.

Did their one day include kissing? Boy, did he want it to. However, he shouldn't even consider it, knowing Alexander would soon be her fiancé.

So he'd pulled back, creating space he didn't want. He'd held her hand all day, pushed every boundary they had, and maybe he needed to put some boundaries back in place. If only to help ease the heartbreak that was sure to come.

"He's a gentleman. He's kind, compassionate. Nothing like Lord and Lady Veelsh. They aren't wrong. He would make an excellent king. Kendra says he's always been very kind, and she has always been a good judge of character." Eva straightened her back, her princess persona falling perfectly into place.

He hated that he'd done that to her, brought that back out. "I sense a but."

Eva blew out a breath. "There can be no but."

"There is one, though." Gordon pushed because he wanted to hear her truth. If she voiced her concerns, there might be a way he could figure out how to help her. He might have stopped himself from kissing her, but he didn't want the emotional walls up yet.

Eva pursed her lips. He absolutely should not be so focused on her mouth. He had to find a way to break this pull.

"Gordon..."

Just call him a glutton for punishment. His name on her lips drew him closer. "Tell me."

More of a demand than a plea. He expected her to put him in his place. Tell him to mind his own business, because he should. He deserved it for pulling back and the mixed signals he was obviously sending.

Instead of anger, Eva seemed to withdraw. Her quiet voice trembled as she spoke. "I don't love him. I hardly know him, as Kendra has been attending all the dates we had planned because of some silly cold. They seem to have a great connection that I just can't find with him. But for my country, he would make a good king."

"But not a good husband." Gordon supplied the words that were a knife to his heart, because he, *Gordon Tarpen*, would make a good husband. He would love her, care for her, see to her needs.

But he couldn't be her husband.

Eva let her head fall forward, her hair covering her face. "He will make a good match. We can learn to love each other. Arranged marriages are not uncommon in royal lines. My great-grandparents had an arranged marriage, and they managed to fall in love and live a long and happy life together."

She sounded so firm. So resigned. "If you don't want to get married, why are you pursuing a match?"

"It's because of an archaic law that's been dug up. All female heirs must be married by their twenty-sixth birthday to take the throne." She straightened her posture and lifted her chin. Her face completely devoid of any emotion.

Irrational anger flamed inside Gordon. "So, you just throw your freedom away? Because of some archaic law someone has dug up?"

"I've hardly thrown it away. I've done everything I can to fight against it. I've met with the historians, studied each time the law has been brought up. Father has met with countless lawyers. I will fight it until the last minute, but it does not appear there is a way to win. With this particular regulation, I believe compliance may be the only outcome."

"So today was what? The chance to escape and do what? Stick it to Parliament?"

"Nothing so rebellious. Just a chance to relax. To be myself. No one ever sees me, and now they want to dictate my future with a marriage I don't want." Eva's voice sounded calm enough, almost practiced. But the disappointment, anger, frustration, resignation warring in her eyes were enough to make Gordon catch his breath. "At least I thought no one saw me. Until you."

"At lunch you said all we had was today." The words hurt just as much now as they had earlier. He wanted so much more than what he'd agreed to, but no amount of work, no amount of effort could make him what she needed, no matter how much he tried. So, he'd agreed to this one day. One day to live the life he wished he could have. A life with Eva at his side. Or maybe rather, a life at her side.

Eva broke eye contact and reached for her mug. She picked it up and took a sip then cradled it in her hands as she studied the Christmas tree. A smile crossed her lips as she seemed to weigh his words. Just as a princess should. She seemed to collect her thoughts before she finally spoke. "One day. To be myself. To experience my country. To be among my people. To be free. And then you saw me, stuck with me, and made today more than I could have hoped."

When she looked back at him, his insides heated as Eva studied his face. After setting her mug back on the table, she closed the space between them. Space he'd created. She lifted her hand, warm from holding the cider mug, and cupped his face. Her fingers moved slowly, her thumb skimming along his bottom lip. "You've made today more than I could have hoped. Ordering off a menu at lunch. Seeing the chapel. Searching for that girl. Riding the motorbike. Dancing at the bazaar. You have no idea what you've given me."

He'd known exactly what he could give her the moment he had seen her. He'd known he could give her the things she'd always wanted. After years of conversations, passing texts, stolen moments together, he'd remembered what she'd longed to do and had tried to make her dreams a reality. "I remember what you've said. I didn't get you to the hair salon today, though. No haircut for you."

Eva chuckled, her hand still warm on his face. "I'm not sure I'd want to cut my hair anymore. I've grown to like the length. Pun intended. Not to mention it would cause problems with Kendra's wig. Every haircut has to be approved. I'm surprised you remember my desire to cut it at all. That was years ago."

"I remember everything, Eva." And he did. Every moment with her was a treasure. A gift he tucked away and savored.

Gordon placed his hand over hers, intertwining their fingers and drawing them over his cheek to his mouth. He kissed her fingers, her skin soft and warm. Her breath hitched slightly, and he lingered, allowing his lips to savor the sweetness of her skin, the delicious and unusually fruity fragrance.

He kept hold of her hand and lowered it to the space between them. "If you could have another day like today, what would you do?"

"Spend it with you. Just like today." So honest and open. Her response had been quick, like she didn't have to think it over. Her cheeks flushed, and a smile teased her lips.

"A repeat? Everything the same?"

"Not the same, but with you. I'd like to walk a dog. Go rock climbing like Mom did. I've always wanted to learn. Slide down a fire pole. I'd want to go to a park and swing. Or go to a water park and go down a waterslide. Oh! Or jump off the high dive into a pool."

He could see it, the perfect picture she painted. He'd do all those things and more.

But today would end. Tomorrow would bring heartbreak. She'd been so quick with her response, he wanted to return the openness. Let her know what today had meant to him.

He loved her. Today had been a dream for him as well, but he couldn't say the words, not when she would marry someone else. His stomach tightened and his throat burned as he held the words in.

She wanted a love match. He could be that for her, but not when he didn't qualify. He'd worked so hard to become a citizen, only to fail over and over. He couldn't offer what he couldn't give. "You have to know, Eva, I'd give you the world. I have connections at the fire department. We could run over now."

She chuckled. He'd chickened out and thrown in some humor. They could no more make it to the fire station than they could have a future together. Too many obstacles in the way. Too much security on the lookout. Not to mention, she wore flannel pj's, and he wore pants that were a little short and a T-shirt he'd borrowed from the doctor.

But if she said the word, he'd figure it out. Find a way to make it to the fire department. He'd always wanted to make her happy.

He traced the lines on the back of her hand, then flipped it over and did the same on her palm. Memorizing this moment. The feel of her hand cradled in his larger one. Her perfectly manicured nails, the two freckles below her ring finger.

He knew this woman. Had loved her for as long as he could remember.

A new heat burned under his skin—not of awareness and awe, but anger. He would love her all the days of his life. He would make her the center of his world. But some stupid law stood in their way.

Not just one law. A few laws. And he couldn't change them. Couldn't even fight them.

He swallowed. He would not allow this time to be tainted by negative thoughts. Only one day. The thought repeated in his head like a drum beat.

Glancing back up, he caught his breath at Eva's expression. He continued to gently trace lines on her hand. She leaned closer, her pupils dilated, and her mouth parted slightly. He'd love nothing more than for Eva to close the space between them, lean into him again, to enjoy these last moments together.

But he couldn't ask. Not when he knew this day was ending.

Almost like she had been thinking the same thing, she scooted closer and rested her head on his shoulder, pressing herself into his side.

Excitement rushed through his veins. He knew every spot where they touched. He wrapped his arm around her shoulders, as she tucked in next to him, their breathing synced.

They sat in silence. Gordon watched the flames lap at the logs, never burning but dancing and leaping. The beauty of a gas fireplace. He missed the scent, the sound of the real thing. Almost like today. Today had been the real thing, burning into him, searing his mind and heart. But he had to accept that this fire between them would burn out, and he'd be left scarred and hurt.

"Gordon?" Eva's quiet voice drew him out of his musing.

She turned and looked up at him. Her hand gently caressed his cheek, then moved to the back of his neck, her fingers finding their way into his hair. Who knew that simple touch, the repetitive motion of her fingers moving in and out, back and forth could be so mesmerizing?

Her pupils were so big he could hardly see the green of her eyes, and she tugged him closer, guiding his mouth down toward hers. He came willingly.

When her breath washed over his face, he hesitated. The drum beat in his mind sounded at a deafening level.

One day.

One day.

What if he accepted this kiss, that shouldn't be his?

He should stop this.

Push her away.

But his body refused to acknowledge reason. Refused to stop this moment that he had dreamed off.

He searched her face, waiting for reason to step in. To realize this kiss should be forbidden.

But oh, he wanted it. Wanted her to close the gap between them. He wouldn't do it. Couldn't. But if she...

"Eva." He whispered her name. A plea? A warning?

As their breaths mingled together, Gordon also knew that he wouldn't deny her. If she wanted this, if she desired this moment, he would accept the heartbreak that would come.

Kissing Eva would be a memory he would hang onto forever. But it would come with pain, knowing he'd never again be able to claim her mouth again.

Right now, he wanted to show her how much he loved her. Wanted to make promises for a future he'd only dared to dream of.

He wanted to pull her tight. To allow their mouths to dance together.

Sure, the heartbreak would be worse, but he wanted to taste her. To breathe her in.

Gordon held still, allowing Eva to take the lead. She looked up at him, questioning. His heart slammed against his chest.

Once. *One day. Please, Eva.*

Twice. *Do it.*

Three times.

She pressed her soft, warm lips to his.

Everything clicked into place. His purpose. His calling. Her hand in his hair tugged him closer, her other hand fisting his shirt. He wrapped his arms around her, and she sank into his embrace.

His mouth moved with hers in a dance he'd love to repeat the rest of his life.

The freedom, the familiarity, the newness, it all just resonated belonging. Like he'd found his place in the world.

Like this was his moment. She was his person.

This kiss, this life-changing feeling. He'd carry the memory with him for years to come.

And as she married—

His mind rebelled. Coiled away from that thought. But still, the realization dawned on him. He held another man's future wife in his arms.

He couldn't allow himself this moment. He should not allow himself to enjoy a kiss that never should have been meant for him.

He broke apart, ripping his mouth from hers.

She pressed back, her hands bracing the couch, hurt flashing in her eyes. He'd done that, caused that pain, and it slayed him.

But he couldn't disrespect her. She deserved the world, not a stolen kiss in the shadows.

She stood up quickly, crossed the room, arms wrapped around herself, her back to him.

Everything inside of him longed to stand, to follow her, to hug her close, to comfort her. To finish that moment in a gentle manner. But he couldn't move.

She could never be his. His to protect. His to love. His wife.

Somewhere in the house a clock chimed. He counted the beats—twelve.

The day had officially ended.

They'd agreed to one day.

And it was over.

Ten

The clock finished it's twelfth chime.

The day had ended.

What a terrible way to end the most glorious of days.

A lump formed in her throat, and Eva worked to swallow it down. What on earth had she done? He'd never ignited anything between them until today. Even then, all he'd done was hold her hands, put his arms around her, dance with her. There had never been a kiss until now.

Not with Gordon, not with anyone.

She'd always wanted her best friend to have her first kiss, and she'd jumped in headfirst, desire clouding her judgment. She'd wanted to peek behind his walls, not lay one on him.

She'd given Gordon her first kiss, and for a short time, he'd kissed her back.

Until he'd ripped away, almost pushing her off the couch.

She breathed in, counting to six, holding the breath for four, and releasing it slowly. She had to get her heart rate under control, but that wouldn't happen if she couldn't slow her breathing. It wasn't like she'd run a marathon. Nope, just kissed her best friend.

Who knew she'd use her training for the crown for this? She didn't run her hands through her hair or rub her temple. No, she squared her shoulders and took another shaky breath, her arms at her sides.

"I'm sorry." She owed him an apology. While she should make eye contact when she said the words, she kept her back to him.

"Don't do that."

She heard Gordon cross the room behind her, but she couldn't turn to look at him.

He gripped her hand, the heat of his body close. "Please. This isn't what I want."

Her ears burning and it felt like her skin was on fire. She'd finally warmed up, and now she might melt. Of course he didn't want this—her kiss. Her. He'd made that perfectly clear when he rejected her.

She might be sick.

Space. She needed space. But the heat emanating off him made her want to curl into him. Bury her face in his strength. Even after she'd completely acted out of line, he stood behind her. He'd always been there, and she craved his presence. Even now. Especially now, because kissing Gordon had been the most amazing thing—at least before it ended.

But she'd had enough embarrassment for one day. No way would she turn around and cause more. After he'd ended their kiss like it had been the most terrible experience, she had to put boundaries back in place. Make sure things went back to normal. She would let him put his walls back up and not peek behind them. Resurrect her own barriers that she'd let down since the dance.

Oh, she needed to go home. The clock had struck midnight. Talk about turning into a big fat pumpkin. Why hadn't she gone with Marco at the dance and saved herself this mistake? Too bad she couldn't have a do-over.

She glanced around the dark, quiet room. If only she could disappear into the shadows.

She needed her purse.

She could escape if she got her phone. Ugh. She should have called her father earlier, instead she'd been so wrapped up in her freedom with Gordon.

A quick glance revealed she hadn't left it in here. Had she put it on the kitchen counter?

"Eva, please, let's talk." Gordon squeezed her hand. She pulled away, upset she'd allowed him to offer that small comfort. She didn't deserve it.

"I'm sorry." She'd said it once, but it seemed a good thing to say again. She walked into the kitchen, and the small light over the stove illuminated the room enough for Eva to see her small handbag on the counter by the back door.

Quickly crossing the room, she picked up her purse and took out her phone. She turned it on and as soon as it booted up, the messages started rolling in. She had at least two dozen from Marco. She fired off a text with her location, telling him to come to the back door. The time had come to accept her fate.

Yesterday had been a dream. Or a nightmare. One where she threw herself at her best friend and ruined their friendship. How could she have misread the situation so grossly?

Marco responded with his ETA. She shoved her phone back into her purse and took a deep breath. Gordon's hand landed on her shoulder, and she shrugged him off. She couldn't do this. Couldn't allow him to comfort her stupidity.

"Eva, I think you misinterpreted what I meant." His voice held a quiet plea she didn't understand. One she couldn't dissect.

"Oh, no. You were very clear. I understood. And I am sorry I put you in an uncomfortable situation." She wrapped her arms around her waist. They weren't nearly as comforting or warm as Gordon's, but if she didn't hold herself together, she might crumble.

Just five minutes. Then Marco would be here, and she would walk away from this. Forget this moment had ever happened.

Who was she kidding? She'd replay that kiss over and over.

Relive the shame of Gordon pushing her away for a long time to come.

Gordon let out a sigh. She could almost see him running a hand through his hair, his other on his hip. It would be so easy to turn and wrap her arms around him. But she couldn't. She'd already embarrassed herself enough for one day. Maybe a lifetime.

He placed his hand on her arm, causing a chill to run down her spine. "It's not that. I mean, this is what I want. More than anything in the world. But I'm not...I can't..."

She nodded, her back still to him. She couldn't turn around to face him. She knew this couldn't work. He had no interest in her. All day they'd been together, and every time they got close, he pulled away. He might as well have spelled it out in neon lettering.

Not. Interested.

Had she picked up on that? No. She'd only seen what she wanted to see. Normally, she picked up on social cues. She'd been trained to do so. But today had been about letting go of reality and dreaming—a magical, romantic day with the man she'd always loved.

Gordon tried to pull her around, but when she didn't move, he stepped in front of her. His hands gripped both her arms, the bandage of his wrap thick and heavy even through the flannel of the pajamas she had on.

She took a deep breath and forced the smile she'd practiced her entire life, then looked up at Gordon. A lifetime of training allowed her to plaster on her best I-am-a-princess-and-I-am-calm face. She might never have thought she'd pull it out in an I-just-kissed-my-best-friend-and-got-rejected situation, but it certainly applied. *Thank you, Beverly.*

His hands squeezed her arms. "Don't do this. Don't push me out. Don't put on your mask. Not with me. Eva—"

She shook her head, working to keep her face neutral. "I'm not sure what you mean."

Liar. Liar. She could practically taste the lie as it rolled out, but if she wanted to cling to any dignity, she needed to keep it together.

"Don't put thoughts into your head that I didn't say. I wanted nothing more than to kiss you. All day. There were so many times." Gordon bent down, his breath washing over her as his attention dropped to her lips. "Then to take all your kisses. But you're promised to someone else. Even if I wanted to steal you away, I'm not qualified."

Eva rolled her lips in. That didn't make it any better. He wasn't willing to fight for her, wasn't willing to try. "That's not a reason. It's an excuse."

"It's the truth, Eva. I'm not a citizen—"

"Because you're so stubborn. You have to do everything on your own. Work all the details out all by yourself. Don't you think one phone call to my father, even mentioning the situation to me at any point, would have solved your citizenship problem? If we knew your paperwork was getting lost, we would have stepped in. But you won't ask for help. You won't fight for us." Eva jutted her chin out and gestured between them. "If you wanted this, you'd make it happen. You never have."

Gordon stepped back. His eyebrows pulled down and he let go of Eva, his hands falling to his own sides. "All I've ever wanted to prove was I'd be a good match."

"There's nothing to prove. You would have been a good match. A perfect match, even. But you wouldn't let go of your pride long enough to make that a reality."

"That's rich coming from you. You who are willing to throw away what we have because of some stupid law." Gordon stepped forward again, his hand outstretched.

"What's there to throw away? Tell me."

Gordon opened his mouth, but nothing came out. He couldn't tell her anything, because she'd imagined it all. Just like people saw her when Kendra stepped in, she'd only seen what she wanted to see. A figment of her imagination.

Not reality.

Eva dug in her purse and removed her phone out again. Marco had sent a message saying he'd arrived. "The day's over. It's after midnight and Marco's already here."

Tucking the phone back into her purse, she wiped at her cheeks even though she hadn't let a single tear fall.

Yet.

They'd come, but she couldn't start now.

A knock sounded on the back door, and Eva stepped around Gordon. Her hand rested on the doorknob, and she closed her eyes. When she stepped out of this room, there would be no going back. She'd really be walking away from Gordon. From her dreams of a happily ever after. From any hope she had of there being a someday with him.

The cool metal of the doorknob brought her back to this moment. "Thank you for spending your day off with me. Please tell the Dr. and Mrs. Renalds I said thank you for their hospitality."

She stared at the round brushed nickel knob. Half hoping Gordon would stop her. Half hoping a magic Christmas elf would appear and turn back the clock sixty minutes so she could keep herself from making such a colossal mistake.

When she opened this door, she had to step out and fully embrace her role as princess. As a woman ready to sacrifice her wants, her desires for the betterment of her people. For the growth of her country.

When she walked out this door, she would no longer be able to hold onto her fairy-tale dreams revolving around Gordon. She would go straight to her father and apologize for running away. Hopefully, Alexander would forgive her escapade. She would learn to love him. Eventually. For the sake of her kingdom.

She would throw herself into loving Alexander with wild abandon. After all, love, well, it was a choice.

"Eva—" Gordon's voice ground out low and scratchy, almost

like it caused him pain to speak. It hurt to hear her name on his lips. It might be the last time.

She hung her head. She had to open the door.

"Gordon." She remembered his arms around her as he took her around the dance floor. The way he'd held her close while Johnny sang, or while protecting her during the fall on the ice, the way his solid back had felt as she'd hugged him when they rode the motorbike across town. "Thank you for a truly unforgettable day."

Even if she needed to forget it, today would hold a special place in her memories. It would always be the dream of what could never be.

She squared her shoulders, straightened her back, let out a deep breath, and forced her smile back into place. She could put off the inevitable no longer.

She opened the door.

Marco stepped aside to make room for her next to him as he scanned the room.

Thankfully, he didn't say anything, and Eva walked away without looking back. She kept moving forward.

Toward her future.

Toward her decision.

Toward her people.

Because if she looked back, she'd see her heart with a man who didn't want to fight for it.

GORDON SLUMPED INTO A KITCHEN CHAIR, HIS ELBOWS on the table, his head in his hands.

Eva had walked out, and deep in his bones, he knew things would never be the same. Gone were the days of carefree fun. Gone were the text messages filled with gifs. Gone was the laughter.

Hope had died tonight when he pulled back, effectively reminding her of her role and her duty to the kingdom. Practically pushing her into the arms of someone else.

Running his fingers through his hair, he tugged on it. He'd told her he could never be the one.

It had been the truth, as much as he hated it.

And she'd called him prideful. Told him he didn't fight for her.

His scalp burned, but he deserved the pain. Wanted the pain. It hurt less than the knowledge of what he'd done to Eva. It hurt less than the sting of her words.

His phone vibrated in his pocket, and he pulled it out. Kevin had sent several messages and had called four times. Gordon had ignored them, but this most recent message had a picture.

Gordon opened it and froze. He pushed back from the table and walked into the living room. They'd left the window uncovered. Why hadn't he closed the curtains? Even with the lights off, between the glow of the tree and the fireplace, Maria Kopal had found them. Snapped a picture and blown their story up.

The picture showed a couple in a cozy embrace. He'd held Eva, pressed her closer, and she'd practically melted against him. Their lips connected.

The moment had been perfect.

The way she had relaxed into his embrace. How they had explored tentatively, and how ultimately it had been like finding home. A moment Gordon would never forget, and now apparently the world would remember it too.

The one kiss they'd shared had been caught on camera.

The headline changed the moment the picture had captured from something intimate to scandalous. *Perfect Princess's Fall from Grace.*

Gordon quickly scanned through the news story. In typical Maria style, the story contained very little fact and a whole lot of speculation.

Her Royal Highness, Princess Evalina found kissing KEVE-TV news reporter Gordon Tarpen. At the time of publication, it's unknown how long the pair have been together or why the princess left the palace, but the couple looks quite cozy in a private residence just ten miles from the palace. How the local reporter thawed the Ice Princess is still to be discovered.

We have reached out to the palace and Alexander Moriffiti and are waiting to hear their response.

What will this mean for the Not-So-Perfect Princess? Only time will tell.

Gordon's phone buzzed again, and he changed screens to read the text message.

KEVIN

Better get in here fast.

GORDON

On my way.

Gordon hung his head. The pain meds for his wrist were not helping the headache that had started to throb, and there wasn't enough coffee in the world to solve this problem.

Quickly changing out of the borrowed clothes from the doctor and back into his not-quite-fully dry clothes, Gordon ordered an Uber. He had ten minutes to brush his teeth and leave a note for the Ronaldses, thanking them for their hospitality.

Twenty minutes later, Gordon sat inside Kevin's office. Silence filled the room, suffocating and thick. It would be easier if his boss would scream at him. Instead, Kevin sat behind his desk, clicking through his computer. He must have found what he wanted, because he pinned Gordon with a look.

"What's the number one rule for reporters?" Kevin sounded like a college professor, if college professors had greasy hair and wore frayed jeans and old rock band T-shirts.

Every eager journalist learned the rule early on. "Don't be the story. Report the story."

"Exactly. You broke that rule in so many ways." Kevin turned the screen around to a video of Gordon and Eva, still in her wig, sitting at the café at lunch. Gordon held his phone up as they took a selfie, and she laughed, and then bumped against him. Flirty, cute, fun. They appeared to be a happy couple. Gordon's stomach tightened, and the cider from earlier threatened to make a reappearance.

"A picture's worth a thousand words. And Maria has two videos and a photograph of you and the princess. I don't need to tell you how much that's worth." Kevin clicked the mouse, and a video of Gordon and Eva dancing at the Johnny Rocco concert appeared on the screen. The video cut to Gordon throwing a punch and pulling Eva away from the crowd. It was almost a package, not just a simple video.

Gordon wiped his damp hands on his jeans. Pain shot up his injured wrist, but he ignored it. These videos showed a different story than the actual events of his day with Eva. "These clips are taken out of context."

"KAT-TV is crowing over this breaking news." Kevin clicked the mouse again, and the photo Gordon had previously seen filled the page. Gordon couldn't deny that the picture caught a moment that gave the appearance of a happy couple very much in love. "Tell me, did you know it was her?"

Gordon sat up straight. He would not break, no matter what happened. "Yes."

Kevin shook his head. "When did you know?"

"The moment I saw her." He wouldn't lie. And he didn't really know what Kevin would say even if he did.

"So, it was a clandestine meeting between two lovers?" Kevin stared him down, like a father who'd found his son causing trouble.

Gordon refused to shift in his seat. He hadn't been caught with his hand in the proverbial cookie jar. Okay, maybe he had. Even so, they'd done nothing wrong—except run from her security. But she'd not been ready to go back, and Gordon had only wanted to give her everything she desired. "No. I saw her this morning quite by accident."

"Tell me you were taking photos and videos for a story you were going to bring to us." Kevin pinched the bridge of his nose like the words pained him.

Ah, the reason for this middle of the night meeting. It had more to do with a story than a scolding. "I knew it would be the story of a lifetime. I also knew that if Eva wanted today to be a news story, it would have been clear from the get-go. Since she was out without security, a press release, or even a friend, I had no intention of breaking her confidence to build my career."

"Eva, is it? Liam hasn't been wrong. You do have a strong connection to the palace."

Gordon rubbed his temples. Talk about a tell-all. He'd said her nickname without thinking. He needed sleep or a redo of the day. Too bad no one had created pain medication for heartbreak.

"To me, she has always been Eva." But no more. She could no longer be just "Eva." He'd seen to that and would need to remember they could no longer be that close. Not even in his mind. Especially in his mind.

Kevin leaned back and crossing his arms over his chest. "It's why you refuse to do any reporting on the royals."

Gordon nodded.

"Okay, so here's the deal. I don't like it, but this is coming down from my boss. Either you turn over your photos from today and report on the Not-So-Perfect Princess's day of freedom and ensure your spot as anchor, or you take a break."

He would never hurt Eva—Evalina. Never make her out to be a fallen princess. Today had started out innocent enough and developed into a day he'd like to relive. The ending? Not so much. "If I share my story, she will still be the princess the people love. I would show her day out on the town wasn't a fall from grace but instead a day she interacted with the people and explored the capital of her country." He could do that.

"That's not the story, and we both know it. The people want to see all the gritty details."

Gordon shook his head. "If there aren't any?"

"There are." Kevin gestured at his computer screen, the picture of Gordon and Eva kissing still on full display. "Obviously, there are. Tell this story and you'll have the desk. Don't and..."

"I don't have a job." Gordon might be sick.

Kevin clasped his hands on his desk. "I'm not going to lie. That's a possibility. This is a huge story, and we could have had quite a lead on our competitors. Instead, Maria has turned this story into the biggest dirty entertainment news this country has ever seen. You had the chance to tell a story, and you lost it. Now, the tone has been set. I'm not sure you could change the narrative even if you tried. People won't care about the Perfect Princess anymore, they'll want to know how you thawed the ice princess."

"Even if I came to you with this story, Maria jumped on the release prior to what we would have, taking control of the narrative." There had to be a way to fight against this. There had to be another way. Gordon stood to pace Kevin's office.

"Perhaps." Kevin sighed. "But the station would have had a previous narrative to go on. Now whatever we do is reactionary."

He couldn't sell Eva out. He *wouldn't* sell her out. He paused behind the chair he'd been sitting in, gripping the back with both hands.

Kevin's face softened. "If you take a break, I may be able to save your job. The anchor position would be out of the question, but perhaps in time, you could return as a reporter."

Give up the dream of being an anchor? He studied his hands, hands that not too long ago had held the woman he loved. He might not be able to be her love match, but he could keep the promises he would never be able to vow. He would stand by her, protect her, love her.

Never before had he used his connection to the palace for his career. He wouldn't start now. She might have called his independent streak pride, but he'd cling to it. He sat back down as he squared his jaw. "How long of a break are we talking?"

Kevin steepled his fingers in front of his face. "I wish I could say. But honestly, until things calm down. Two weeks? A month? Until the next big scandal hits? I filled out the paperwork for you. I just need you to sign it."

Kevin opened a drawer in his desk and pulled out a stack of papers. He handed it to Gordon.

Gordon took them and scanned over the documents. His body ached from the day, and the hammer that someone seemed to be using to pick away at his brain wouldn't stop. Not to mention his wrist still throbbed. The words at the top of the paper caused him to pause. "A leave? Those are unpaid."

He sagged back into the chair, his determination to be strong, to protect Eva shaken. She would never ask him to give up his job. The check his uncle had given him helped, but without a job it wouldn't last long.

Kevin nodded. "Yes. But it also means we can't give your job away."

"There's no other option? You're certain?"

"You could report on how you thawed the ice princess. We can get you on-air with the morning news. I have no doubt you took plenty of photographs today."

The mental picture of how many times he'd snuck a picture of Eva filtered through his mind. He could tell quite the story, but not the one Kevin claimed everyone wanted to hear.

Lose his job or betray Eva, ugh, the princess? Why was it so hard to think of her this way? Talk about a rock and a hard spot.

Without his job there was no way he could get citizenship unless he called the king. But without a job, could the king help? He bowed his head and closed his eyes, trying to block out the tide of emotions. He'd already lost Eva, seen to that when she walked out of the doctor's kitchen and he didn't go after her.

Would it hurt to report on today? If he put out the real story, it might help save her reputation. Even if Kevin said the management wanted the gritty details, Gordon could still tell the story of what happened. Of a leader who wanted to be with her people, of a woman poised with class interacting with local businesses, of a carefree girl experiencing life's simple joys. Would the station put a scandalous spin on his words? Not if he was live. Then the audience could draw their own conclusions.

But could he sacrifice Eva's privacy for his job and the attempt to clear her name? Could he tell the story without ripping open his heart and letting the entire country, probably the world, see how much he loved her?

Kevin had been thorough and knowledgeable with the paperwork, filled out every detail.

"I'll give you a few minutes. The morning producer will be in shortly, and we have a quick meeting before I'm finally done for the night. If you're going to report, come knock on Cindy's door. If you're out, leave the paperwork on my desk."

Kevin pushed back from his desk and closed his door on the way out.

Gordon rubbed the back of his neck, trying to work out the knots that had formed during this conversation. If only he could call the king, find out what would be best.

The king! Gordon dug out his phone and found the king's personal cell. The number had been programmed into his phone years ago and never used. The king had insisted on giving it to Gordon in case he ever needed it.

The call went directly to voicemail. The wall clock read two in the morning. The king likely slept without the knowledge of what Maria had reported. Or could the king be so angry that Gordon had assaulted one of the guards that he ignored the call on purpose?

Gordon tapped his fingers on the desk. If he had a chance to help Eva, he'd take it. If opening up about the day would protect her, he'd do it.

Kevin burst into the office and closed the door. "Sign the papers."

"What? No, I ca—"

"If you want to keep your job, sign the papers. Trust me." Kevin took a pen out of his jar and handed it to Gordon.

Without much more thought, Gordon scribbled his signature across the paper.

Kevin grabbed the papers. "Now, get out. Don't let anyone see you. I'll call you when you can come back."

Flipping his lights off and leaving the door cracked, Kevin hurried out of the office. Unsure what had changed Kevin's mind so quickly and completely, Gordon took the cue to leave. The cold air stung his cheeks, a welcome reprieve from the pain that threatened to consume him from within.

He walked out of the parking lot, careful to stick to the long shadows of the early morning darkness.

Turning the corner away from the news station, Gordon headed toward his apartment. He kicked a pebble, the soft plink-plink as it skirted down the street a companion in the midst of the suffocating quiet.

Most people slept, while Gordon's entire world had imploded. Uncle Orlin always said nothing good happened after ten at night. Perhaps he'd been right all along. If Gordon would have gone home, the kiss wouldn't have happened. Eva wouldn't have walked out of his life. He might still have a job.

At least his uncle had given him enough money to catch up on his apartment and make sure he could keep it for a while. But how long could he stay before immigration kicked him out? Without a job they had no reason to let him stay. Would they send him back to the States?

He walked up the steps to his apartment, his footsteps heavy on the stairs. When he opened the door, he found a single envelope lying on the floor. He picked it up and recognized the handwriting of Mallory, his landlord.

His finger slid under the envelope flap, and he pulled out the single piece of paper. A sticky note fluttered from it to the ground, and he picked it up.

G-

Sorry I couldn't give you a heads-up. The building sold, and since you don't have a long-term contract, the new owners want you out by the end of the month.

M

Great. Just great. He should call his cousins in Florida. Where else could he go while he looked for a job? At least he would have a place to stay there.

Yesterday had been one of the most memorable days, but since the clock struck twelve, he'd lost everything.

Eva.

His job.

His home.

And the sun hadn't even come up yet.

Eleven

Upon Eva's return home, her father and Maurice, the head of the palace's public relations met her. After her father hugged her and told her to meet him in the morning at his office, he left her with Maurice, whose shoes made an angry tapping sound as they walked her back to her apartment. Eva had always heard that a picture was worth a thousand words, but she'd never understood what that meant until she'd seen the picture of her and Gordon kissing.

And what a story that picture told.

Also, who knew a story could be so wildly distorted based on one picture?

One picture would be bad enough, but the overachieving reporter had managed to capture videos too. Plural.

Hopefully, no photos had yet been released of Eva walking into the palace in flannel pajamas. That would only give people even more to speculate on.

"I need the details of the day." Maurice's irritation at being woken up in the middle of the night carried through his words.

Eva stopped walking and waited. Maurice walked at least a

dozen steps before he stopped and spun around on one heel to face her.

"I will give you the overall view of the day. But I have no desire to share any personal details with you." Eva raised her hand to keep Maurice from interrupting. "I understand your job, and I am sorry that my choices today have caused you a mountain of work. But this is my life, my emotions, my heartbreak, and I'd like to keep as much as possible out of the headlines."

Maurice's facial features softened, and he stepped forward. "I'm sorry, Your Royal Highness. I was harsh. There is no way to keep this story from spiraling, but I will do my best to keep it to a minimum. We had gotten wind that the story was breaking. It would be a minimal story, if only you'd have come home with your guards..."

Now it made sense—why her father would send security. It had been reported that she was out and about.

After discussing the highlights of the day, Maurice developed a response plan, but he warned Eva that it would most likely not take. The story Maria had told and the narrative she created would be hard to change. With the story breaking overnight, the morning news stations would have already placed it as their lead, and the palace's response would be just that—a response. Hopefully, it would tamper down the salacious spin, but the picture of Eva kissing Gordon couldn't be changed.

She had, after all, kissed him. In front of an open window with enough light to allow a camera to take a clear and detailed picture.

"Rookie mistake," Maurice said. "Next time consider your surroundings."

Well, there wouldn't be a next time. There *couldn't* be a next time.

"Don't forget the king wants to see you first thing in the morning." Maurice checked his watch as he ended their discussion. "Or in a few hours now."

Maurice finally left and Eva caught an hour of sleep, if she could call it that. Now she stood outside her father's office. Double-checking her outfit, she straightened her black suit coat, the color seeming appropriate this morning. Never mind her melodramatic flair. Eva ran her hand down her skirt to dry her damp hands before she patted her hair, pulled back in a soft French twist. Now or never, she had to face her father.

With her eyes closed, she took one deep breath. Normally, Renee would open the door for her, but Eva had managed to either beat Renee to the office, or her father's assistant had already arrived and sat within the closed office.

Eva had skipped breakfast, not that she wanted anything to eat before she met with her father. Now that she'd experienced freedom, the sweetness of Gordon's full attention, the heartbreak of his rejection, and the betrayal of a single photograph taken out of context—the day might not have been worth it. Especially since she'd have to face her father's anger at refusing security. At least she knew why he'd sent them.

If she'd known one day of freedom would cause such an uproar, she would never have gone into town. Never wished to attend the bazaar. She would have stayed within the palace walls and saved herself the humiliation, not only of an unwanted kiss but of an unflattering worldwide headline.

Not only did this single act of rebellion cost her the friendship of the one man she'd never wanted to hurt, it could cost her everything. Her future. Her throne. Her dreams.

A deep breath.

What was done was done.

She had to accept her foolish mistakes and work to correct them. She would accept all of her father's anger and promise to never do anything so reckless again.

Raising her hand, she knocked on the door and waited for her father's call to enter. It came, and Eva walked into the office. The king sat behind his large cherry desk in a navy suit, his hair styled perfectly. He closed his laptop on the center of the desk when she entered. His coffee mug sat next to the computer, steam still rising and curling into the air. At least one of them looked like they hadn't needed copious amounts of under eye concealer to appear rested.

Eva dropped into a quick curtsy. "Morning, Father."

"Have a seat, Evalina." He emphasized the *L* in such a way that Eva knew this conversation would be with her king, not her father.

Settling into a large brown leather chair across from the king's desk, she noted that while he spoke like the king, the worry lines in his forehead indicated her father had a lot to say too.

"I saw the picture and the videos."

Of course he had. The entire kingdom—probably the world—had seen them by now. Last she'd checked, she'd been trending. #iceprincessthaws #perfectprincessfallfromgrace #royalrunaway

"I realize the implications of the story. I am sorry for the drama I am causing, and I am ready to take full responsibility for my actions."

The king lifted one eyebrow and pressed his lips into a grim line. "Are you? Do you realize what this story could mean to you? To our kingdom?"

Eva placed her right hand over her left. Did she know that she could lose the throne? Yes, of course she knew. If Alexander wished to discontinue the relationship they had started, she would be hard-pressed to find a suitable match before her birthday in less than two weeks.

Although she regretted the trouble she now faced, she would cherish the good memories of the day. The conversations she'd had with Gordon. The exhilaration of riding a motorbike through town. The music pulsing around her as she danced while Johnny Rocco sang. Their mad dash through the busy crowds to follow the teenage girl. She'd still need to discuss that with her father, but not right now. She might not wish all of yesterday away, but she did understand the problems she now faced. "I regret my actions have caused pain."

The king, his silver hair styled perfectly, let out a breath and rolled his shoulders. Gone was the king, as her father propped both hands on the desk as he tilted his head to the side, concern etched across his face. He studied her without judgment. "Do you love him?"

She gave a small shake of her head. "He is unqualified to be my husband, and my feelings—"

"Matter. I realize he doesn't meet royal protocols as your partner. And I never forget my kingdom, but my question right now is simply for you as your father, not your king. Do you, Eva—not princess, not Rosy, not whatever other alias you want to give yourself. Do you, Evalina, love Gordon, the man who has always made you smile?"

Tears stung the back of her eyes, but she blinked hard. No more. There had been enough after Maurice left. What did it matter if she answered truthfully? It didn't change anything. The answer leapt to her mouth without thought. "Yes, but—"

"There are no buts. I had wondered but had no proof."

Eva squeezed her hands together. "This does not change what Parliament has ordered. I have only a short time left to get married. I need to speak with Alexander to find out if he's still interested in a future together or if he'd rather not progress our relationship."

Father knocked on the desk and reclined back in his chair, crossing his right leg over his knee. "I'm not sure Alexander is the man for you."

"Just a couple of weeks ago, you thought he might be a good match." Eva gripped her hand harder to keep from fidgeting.

"Before I knew you loved another man."

"I am a princess. I can turn off those feelings. My duty comes first."

Her father shook his head. "It's not that easy."

"My country should be first." Eva stood and moved behind the large leather chair she'd sat in. She rested her hands on the back and adjusted her stance to a practiced poised one Beverly always hyped, and her relaxed smile fell into place. Beverly would be proud. "My duties as princess are far more important than matters of the heart."

Her father sighed. "That's not true, and I'm sorry my actions have allowed that belief to manifest in you. You are so much more than a princess. There is more to life than these four walls."

"Not that I'd ever had the freedom to explore those things until yesterday. Since Mom's accident I've been cooped up behind palace walls. But if yesterday's adventure taught me anything, it's that we have wonderful people. They are kind, generous, fun. I want to fulfill my calling to do what's best for them."

"That's a lot to unpack." Her father took in her words. He seemed to mull over his answer before he spoke. "I am sorry. I did take your safety too far after your mother died. You carried so much of her spunk, her adventurous spirit, and I couldn't imagine losing you too."

Eva shrugged. "So, you locked me up like a princess in a tower."

"That's part of why I encouraged you to go out. Embrace a little freedom. It had been brought to my attention that you might be a tad too restricted." Her father stood and came around his desk and rested his hand on her shoulder.

"Why would you do that? Look at the mess it caused. If I'd stayed inside..."

"But you had the time of your life. Besides, I sneak out, and I've never had a problem. I wanted you to experience some freedom."

No wonder the idea to go out incognito had been so quick from her father. Of course, he did it too.

But if he didn't want her so restricted— "Why bring Kendra in at all?"

It had always upset Eva that Kendra had been allowed to go to all the "fun" things. Eva had even seen Kendra with her father in the ballroom. They'd been dancing and having what looked like a grand time. He'd never danced with Eva like that before. "You created a second daughter to have all the fun with."

"Oh, Eva." The king rubbed his forehead. "Kendra has never taken your place. We used to practice, and it took a lot of work to make our interactions natural. But she has never, *never*, taken your place."

"Practice?"

"Often. We would be in the ballroom, and she'd hug me. I'd have to call her your name and work to act natural. We even danced together for a few father-daughter moments that I wish I would have shared with you. If I could do it all over again, I would."

"I saw that once. I assumed you didn't know the difference between us."

Her father reached for her hands and squeezed them both. "I've always known the difference. Just like I knew Kendra had taken your place around the palace yesterday."

"Did you really tell the security team they needed to bring me back at all costs?"

Her father let go of her hands and motioned for the seats. He took one and she sat in the other. "No. We had caught wind that a story would break, and I wanted to make sure you were here. I sent your team to quietly bring you back. Lessen the story. Smithy, the over-eager intern, has been talked to. And he's quite upset that a civilian clobbered him. I told Marco that Smithy is lucky we don't press charges for how he handled you. Marco assures me it won't happen again. Gordon impressed me, though. He had every right to take that swing."

It helped to know her father hadn't really sent the team to pull her back at all costs. Even though it was pretty much what Maurice had said, it eased her mind to hear it from her father. Here she'd escaped into town thinking no one would notice the switch, and it hadn't gone unnoticed at all. While she'd thought she'd been invisible, multiple people had seen her. Her father clearly saw the difference between her and Kendra.

Gordon and Maria saw through her disguise. How many other people had and just didn't report it?

Her father reached across his desk, picked up his coffee, and took a sip, allowing a moment of quiet to settle between them. "The second part of what you said, we do have really great people in Nevive. They are kind, loyal, and amazing. But often what's best for the people is what's best for the ruler. Have you prayed about any of this, Eva?"

Eva froze. Her father so seldom talked about his faith, even though she knew he spent time reading the Bible daily. They'd stopped talking about their personal beliefs years ago.

Her silence must have prompted him to continue. "I have not remarried or dated since your mother. Mainly because I haven't felt the time is right. Not because of laws or rules."

He'd considered a relationship after Mom passed? Call her surprised.

"Don't look so shocked. There is..." He cleared his throat and looked away briefly. "Someone I have considered. But the timing is wrong. I haven't felt at peace to move on my feelings. But I also have not considered anyone else, because of..."

Eva couldn't help a smile. Her father had a crush. The news lifted the weight of her current predicament. "Do I know this woman?"

Her father set his coffee cup down and crossed one leg over his knee, playing with the hem of his pants.

"I do! Oh, please tell me it's Renee."

Shaking his head, the king stood up and walked back around the desk to his chair. "It is not the right time. It may never be. Don't go sticking your nose in this. I'm telling you because if Alexander is not the man you have feelings for, you do not have to follow the expectations you've placed on yourself. There is a way around this law."

"You've found a way around the marriage law?" *Oh please, say something came up yesterday.*

"It was more hopeful speech, but I do have another meeting with a lawyer today."

Eva sank back in the chair, the heaviness of her situation settling back on her. Nothing worked. They couldn't win. She didn't have a choice. "If there's no way around it and I still have to marry, Alexander is the best option. We've chased down every possible way to fight this. Historically, legally, traditionally—I would like to fight. I would like to marry for love. But I also want to be queen someday."

"All hope is not lost." Father opened his laptop and started typing. "Several years ago, I added a line into a bill. It turns—"

"Father, I'm not giving up. But we've tried all those avenues. I don't believe any line in a bill will change things. I must be married by my birthday. We have two weeks."

Her father's fingers stilled over the keyboard. "Eva—"

She held up a hand. "I know, Father. You want my happiness. But I will prepare for the inevitable. I don't want to marry but I will. I can't keep hoping something might work out in my favor. I am prepared to do what is needed. I've been trained my whole life to do this. If Alexander is willing, he is the best option I have. Please, you agreed not too long ago. Do you happen to know where he is?"

Her father shook his head. "Eva, please. Your happiness—"

"Is not on the line. I want to serve my people. I do not want to give up my role as princess. That will make me happy. This is my choice, and I will find happiness in it." She would. It would hurt to let Gordon go, to let the dream of a love match go, but she had to prepare for the future. She had to accept what needed to happen. She couldn't hold out hope for a future that would never be.

Her father pressed a button on his phone. A knock sounded on the office door, and Renee walked in, dropping to a quick curtsy. Her father gave her a small smile, an ever so small movement that most probably wouldn't even notice, but after their conversation this morning, Eva picked up on it. "Renee, do you know where Alexander is?"

"Breakfast in the dining room."

Eva stood. "Then I guess I will go find out if there is still a chance for us."

"Eva, please. We can have hope. Trust me to find a way for you to be happy."

Eva bowed her head slightly. "As long as you let me continue to do what I must, I'll let you look for a way out."

"Very well. Renee, we have much work to do today. Did you arrange a call with the American lawyer?"

Renee nodded toward Eva and sat down in the second chair. "I did. He said he'd never seen a law like this one and he'd be happy to do some more research. We have a phone call with him this evening around four."

Father would scheme. He'd plot and plan, but they both knew they might not find a loophole in this particular law. She'd let him continue to search, but she'd work on finding contentment in this.

"Thank you. Truly. I'm grateful you're willing to continue to fight this. I'll go find Alexander." After exiting the office, Eva made her way to the dining room. Her stomach grumbled, but food would not help her nerves. Neither would caffeine, although it might take the edge off the pounding in her head.

She entered the dining room quickly and found Alexander and Kendra together. She approached the table, and they both stood to greet her.

Two empty coffee cups sat on the table. At least someone had been able to relax this morning.

Kendra hugged her, forgoing the normal curtsy. Eva had never been more thankful for a friendly hug. "It's going to be okay. I'll let you two talk."

Eva caught her friend's hand before she could walk away and squeezed it. "I'll come find you in a bit."

Kendra walked away, her posture stiff and her facial expression tight. Something wasn't quite right, but Eva couldn't pinpoint what was wrong. Perhaps Alexander had already told Kendra how upset he was and her friend was worried for them.

She turned back toward Alexander, his face relaxed. He didn't appear upset or angry. "Could we go for a walk?"

Alexander gestured toward the door. "To the garden?"

Eva nodded and they stopped at the coat closet to bundle up. She'd long ago started leaving a coat by the garden door so she could walk whenever she liked without having to hunt down one of her own. She slipped into a black trench coat that tied at her waist, adding her scarf and gloves. Thoughts of Gordon skimmed her mind, but she pushed them away. She'd need new gloves, ones that didn't remind her of the way Gordon's hand had wrapped around hers. Tucking her gloved hands into her coat pockets, she headed toward the door where Alexander stood, his navy peacoat on, waiting for her.

Stepping outside, Eva was hit in the face with the cold air, and a chill raced down her spine. Just yesterday she'd welcomed the bite of the air, enjoyed the snow, and even ran through it. Of course, she'd kept warm pressed close to Gordon.

Today, the cold cut through to her bones, chilling her blood, and making her teeth chatter. She clenched her jaw tight. Princesses did not chatter their teeth. She took her hands out of her pockets, forcing herself to relax and be as natural as possible. Besides, Beverly would not be pleased if she knew Eva walked with her hands in her pockets.

Beside her, Alexander strolled quietly, his steps even, his movements fluid. When his hand brushed against hers, he held it, guided it into the crook of his elbow, and stepped closer. The warmth, while nothing like Gordon's, did help to take the edge off the cold and ease her nerves.

"We could talk inside. It is a bit chilly today. A storm is moving in." His breath puffed out as he spoke.

He wanted to talk about the weather? Her entire life seemed to be coming apart at the seams, and he wanted to talk about the forecasted snow?

Had he not seen the picture? Perhaps he didn't pay attention to local news. Highly likely. She'd never had a lesson on how to apologize in this situation. There had been no rule book or princess class on how to say *I'm sorry I ran away and kissed another man.*

No sugarcoating would make this easier. Might as well jump into it. "Alexander, I owe you an apology."

He nodded. A flash of something crossed his eyes, but he masked it quickly. He did know. At least she didn't have to tell him. Small mercies.

He studied her but continued to lead her deeper into the garden. Did he want to lead her in so deep no one would see his reaction? Where were her bodyguards now? Did she need them? After yesterday it's likely they were even closer than normal. Kendra wouldn't have left her alone if Alexander had a temper.

"I am sorry for the picture and for the videos. I can say that the story they paint isn't exactly true, but I did sneak out, spent the day with another man, and..." *Gave him my first kiss.* "If you'd like an explanation, I'll oblige."

Alexander's brows furrowed, and he stepped away. Eva was forced to let go of his arm, bringing hers back to rest at her side. As the cold wind blew through her, she missed the warmth he offered.

"I understand how the camera can catch things. But, Evalina, I don't think you realize I'm a catch too. I could date. I could find a wife in the traditional way. I could wait for love."

Eva couldn't maintain his piercing gaze. He had every right to be upset, and she'd not begrudge him those feelings. "I'm sorry to take those things from you. I know that this hasn't been the easiest way to make a connection. I'm not sure why you're willing to give up all that. We haven't had a chance to really get to know each other."

"But we have. I've enjoyed our time together. We have chemistry. I thought we were starting something that could last."

Alexander stopped, his hand gripping her elbow and turning her to him. He studied her face. "I thought you felt it too, but then I realized it wasn't you on the helicopter if you were also in town."

Eva turned her head away, blinking rapidly. He honestly hadn't known. Couldn't see the difference. If he had a connection with Kendra, did she feel it too? Alexander's gloved hand guided her face back and he studied her. His thumb moved across her cheek. "It wasn't you, was it? On any of those dates after our first lunch. How could I have not seen that?"

Alexander dropped his hand and turned away. Eva had never wanted to play with his emotions. "I'm sorry. It's a well-kept palace secret, and we weren't sure we could trust you with it yet."

"It was Kendra." Not a question, a realization.

Eva stepped forward, her hand on his arm. "I am sorry, Alexander. You would have been read in before the wedding. I understand if this changes how you feel about our arrangement."

Alexander took a few deep breaths, his shoulders rising and falling slowly. Eva closed her eyes while he took another. As he turned back toward her, her hand fell away, and she opened her eyes again to find him resolute. "While I hate that my cousins are forcing your hand, I do think we could be a good team. I think we could be good for Nevive. But I won't enter a relationship with a woman who plans on having a side piece. If we move forward, it's with the understanding that when we say 'I do' it will be us against the world. There will be no one else. Not for you. Not for me. You will be my one and only. If you can promise that you will be faithful, I still think we can make this work. Forget my cousins, forget the pressure of Parliament. I said I would do this, and I meant it. I'm a man of my word. We may not love each other now, but we could possibly grow into that. I won't go anywhere, unless you want me to."

Alexander appeared earnest, and he certainly sounded it. But did he not want to talk about Gordon? About Kendra? Would he really accept the switch that easily? Without more information, more conversation? "You don't want to talk about Gordon or Kendra?"

Alexander closed his eyes and rubbed them before he reached for her hand and looked directly at her. "We have a past. But we both have a reason for doing this. You for your country. Me? Well, to not have to rule. You—well, ah, Kendra, I guess—said I would likely still be able to practice medicine some, but not to the full extent I wanted. I assume since she spoke for you, that is still the case."

"Why try for the throne if you wanted to continue to practice?"

Alexander scoffed. "You've met my cousins. I tried to tell them I didn't want to rule some country I'd never been to, but they wouldn't listen. I've never wanted to disappoint my parents, and my cousins said this is what my parents wanted for me."

Lord and Lady Veelsh were pushy people. From the beginning Alexander had been willing to give up ruling. He'd never said he wanted to. Perhaps he'd been as manipulated as she had when it came to this marriage. "I'm not sure what it would look like, but we would work to make practicing medicine happen."

Alexander nodded, and they stood there together. It seemed they both needed a moment to let this new reality set in.

"Evalina?"

"Yes?"

"If we do this, promise me no more lies?" His voice held pain.

Alexander might not have shared all his reasons, but whatever they were had caused him a lot of pain. Did he feel Kendra had lied to him? Was that why he would let whatever they had go so quickly? "Kendra—"

"It's okay. She had a job. Just please, no more lies? I'm happy to sign an NDA if needed." Alexander closed his eyes, and when he opened them, the emotions that had been churning in them were gone. In their place stood a steely resolve.

Truth. A good foundation for any relationship. "I promise. From this point on, no more lies."

Alexander relaxed. "Thank you. That makes us a team."

A team. She let that settle in. They could be one. He'd be her partner. Someone to go through life with her.

Together they could face whatever life threw at them.

He opened his arms, and Eva hesitated only momentarily before she hugged him, resting her head on his wool jacket. No sparks, no bubbles, no tempting heat, but Alexander's warmth, his strength were comforting. He seemed willing to fight for what they had, as simple and new as it was.

She would make this work.

She could forget Gordon.

She had to.

Her country needed her.

Alexander's hands moved up and down her back, and she nodded against his jacket before pulling back just enough to look up at him. "Okay. Just to alleviate your worries and to tell the truth. My actions yesterday were not normal. I promise I would never cheat on my husband."

As she tucked her head back against his chest, right under his chin, the wind calmed around them. The sun peeked through the trees, chasing the shadows and chill away. They stood there for several heartbeats. Eva let his arms comfort her, the promises they'd made settling in her mind.

After a while, Eva stepped back, and Alexander ran his hands down her arms, and he dropped to one knee. He pulled a small red velvet box out of his pocket.

Her eyes stung. Eva closed them, hoping the tears would stay put. Her heart didn't pound against her chest, and her knees didn't shake in excitement. When she knew tears wouldn't fall, she found Alexander waiting with a smile. Even though his eyes lacked deep emotion, they did hold a promise. He opened the box and held it up to her. Inside was an antique-style round diamond ring. Eva brought one hand to her chest, more to rub the ache, and forced her princess smile.

Alexander took her left hand, his thumb moving over the top of her gloved hand. "This was my mother's ring. My parents had a healthy and loving marriage, and I thought it might bring us luck. Will you marry me, Evalina?"

Nothing in this moment screamed happily ever after, but an earnest man offered her his future even after she'd been caught kissing another man. He promised to do right by her and her country. He'd promised friendship and faithfulness. With the hope of love to come, she couldn't and wouldn't find a better match before her birthday.

Her heart split in two as she let out a single word.

"Yes."

"You need a shower." Uncle Orlin tossed a towel in Gordon's face. "Get up."

It had been eight days since Eva—the princess—had kissed him and walked away. He still hadn't convinced his brain not to think of her so informally. It had been the best day of his life. Followed by the worst.

No job. No home. No visa.

Merry Christmas to him.

Gordon grabbed the towel and sat up. He sniffed his arm. Phew. He hadn't showered after the gym last night. He'd barely been able to drag his sorry behind back to his uncle's and collapse on the couch, not even bothering trying to make it to the guest room. He'd moved out of his apartment and taken up residence six days ago.

Living in the palace inside his uncle's suite hadn't been terrible.

He'd managed to hide away without seeing anyone but the occasional security on the way to the palace's private employee gym.

Uncle Orlin opened the blinds and let the sun in. "If you get your rear in gear, I'll have coffee and breakfast in ten."

"What time is it?" Gordon stood, stretching. He'd been merciless to his body last night, and the muscles still screamed this morning. He rubbed his wrist, still sore, but he'd taken off the wrapping. He couldn't handle the reminder of the gentle way Eva—the princess—had held it. The weightlifting had probably not been the best thing to do, but he needed to push himself. Needed to blow off some steam or he might combust. Physical activity had been the only way to keep his mind off the princess and the announcement of her engagement.

Her engagement.

To another man.

A man she didn't want to marry.

He'd known it would happen, but that didn't make it hurt any less. Didn't mean he wanted it to happen.

The palace had released pictures. This time it had actually been Eva in the photos. While the couple resembled happy—big smiles, cozy poses—the joy didn't reach the princess's eyes. Instead, she appeared resigned.

He'd done that. He'd pushed her away and into the arms of that...jerk.

Except Alexander appeared to be anything but a jerk. No, he'd stood up for the princess. Had her back. Defended her.

Meanwhile, Gordon had been silent. Hidden away from the public's view.

He'd pushed Eva—no, the princess—away because it couldn't be him. He'd pushed her right into the arms of the man who could be by her side.

"Ten minutes, Gordon. Get up." Oh man, his uncle still stood there watching him wallow as the heartbreak had returned. At least when he was asleep, he could pretend there was still hope. "Time for you to check your phone. It's been pinging for over an hour. Kevin wants something."

Uncle Orlin left the room and turned on some Christmas music in the kitchen. The scent of bacon quickly came from that direction.

Gordon grabbed his phone. Sure enough, he'd missed six messages from Kevin.

KEVIN

Are you ready to come back to work?

Have a chance to save your job.

You won't like it. But you need to do this.

The rest of the messages read about the same. Gordon's stomach dropped. If he wasn't going to like it, it was a story on the royals. He hated how news stories on them never showed who they really were. And now, if he wanted his job back, he'd have to fall into line and report on them. It likely wouldn't stop at royal news —he'd be groveling and reporting on the worst stories just to get back to work.

At least if he had to report on the royals, he'd have a chance to see Eva—the princess. Talk to her. Apologize. He'd opened their message thread at least twenty times a day, typing out messages. Except he'd deleted them all. If they talked, it needed to be face-to-face.

Uncle Orlin had stopped giving him any kind of updates on her. Told him it wasn't his business how the princess was doing. He wasn't wrong, but Gordon wanted it to be his business.

Wanted to know every detail. Every thought. Was she eating? Did she feel okay? Why wouldn't she? She couldn't be as broken-hearted as him. She had to forget, move on. Had already accepted Alexander.

After the photo of their kiss, Gordon had had phone calls from all over the world requesting interviews. He'd refused them all and changed his number. It had hurt to know Eva no longer had his number, but she wouldn't contact him anyway. Not after what had happened between them.

GORDON

I'll do it. Whatever it is.

KEVIN

I'm going to keep you to that.

Be in my office in 30.

Gordon showered and stepped into the kitchen.

Orlin handed him a sandwich wrapped in brown paper. "Figured you needed to get on the road. Take this to go. Bacon, egg, and gouda."

Gordon accepted the sandwich, noting the way his uncle moved a little slower. His hair had thinned slightly, and he had a few extra wrinkles. Had Gordon caused those this week? It certainly wouldn't have been easy to have a mopey and moody nephew around. Yet his uncle never complained. Never gave any indication that Gordon made things difficult or unpleasant. Gordon hugged him. "Thank you."

"It's just a sandwich." Uncle Orlin turned to wipe the counter but not before Gordon could see the grin his uncle worked to hide.

"It's so much more, and you know it," Gordon called as he put on his winter coat, but his uncle walked into the front room, holding a cup of coffee and a plate with his own breakfast sandwich.

"I suspect that Kevin is going to ask you to do something you don't want to. You need to do it. Be the reporter you are. See the princess. Try and speak to her. If you have to get in under the guise of the media, then do it." Orlin's face brooked no argument.

"What aren't you telling me?" Anything could have happened while Gordon had wallowed the last several days away. Several long hard days to be exact since he'd frozen like an idiot and let her walk away.

Orlin set his plate and mug on the coffee table and crossed his arms over his chest. "It's not my place to speak on this. But you need to find her. Talk to her. You love her and you need to tell her."

"I'm not a citizen."

Orlin muttered under his breath. Just before Gordon opened the door Orlin spoke. "Talk to the king."

With one hand on the doorknob, Gordon allowed the reality of his situation to press down on him. He had nothing. No job. No citizenship. No title. What could he offer a princess? "I can't."

"Excuses. You're so bent on doing everything on your own. You're not an island, Gordon. You don't have to do everything alone. You don't even have to prove yourself to anyone. You are worthy. You are enough. God made you to be the man you are and brought you here. It's been a wild ride, but your selfishness will ruin your life if you don't set it aside. Talk to the king."

Ouch. Gordon let go of the doorknob and turned back toward his uncle. Gordon mirrored his uncle's stance and crossed his arms over his chest. *His* selfishness? Wasn't he putting Eva first by letting her go? That was an act of selflessness. "I can't just call the king."

Still muttering Orlin sat down on the couch. "You have his number."

Okay, so Gordon did. And he'd called it a total of one time. That single time it had gone directly to voicemail, probably because it had been the middle of the night. Maybe because the king had already seen the photos and had ignored him purposefully. There were a lot of reasons someone might try to call the king, but whining about his lack of citizenship? Not a good enough reason.

"I have to go." Gordon turned and yanked the door open, effectively ending the conversation. Before his uncle could say anything else, Gordon jogged to the car he'd been borrowing from his uncle.

A few minutes later he walked into the newsroom. The buzz of the reporters hushed as he walked toward his desk. He heard a few whispers but couldn't make out what people said. For the better. He didn't have any desire to hear more gossip.

Liam stood up and gave three lazy claps. "Look what finally crawled back in. The man who denied our station the greatest news story of the year."

Gordon flexed his hand. He'd love to bury his fist in Liam's nose.

Oh. No.

Gordon unclenched his fist. Never before had he wanted to do that. Sure, he'd fought for Princess Evalina at the dance, but before that? Never had he wanted to let anything come to blows.

Tonight, he'd take this desire and try out the punching bag in the corner of the gym. That would blow off some steam and keep his temper in check.

Gordon shook his hand, trying to come up with a witty comeback, but before he could respond, Kevin yelled from his office. "Gordon. You have fifteen seconds to get in here."

Saved by the bellowing boss. Probably for the better to ignore Liam. He was moving on. Thankfully, Gordon wouldn't have to deal with him in the future, so he clamped his mouth closed and headed into Kevin's office.

His boss worked on his computer and didn't bother to look up when Gordon walked in. "Close the door and take a seat."

This couldn't be good. If Kevin wanted the door closed, Gordon was either getting ready to be fired or yelled at. Again. He shouldn't have eaten that sandwich.

With the door closed, the silence in the office seemed suffocating. Gordon sat, ran his damp hands down his jeans, then shrugged out of his coat.

Kevin typed on his computer, frantically chewing a piece of gum. His glasses sat lower on his nose than normal. He'd added a security string to them, so when he took them off as he turned toward Gordon, they dangled around his neck.

"I have a story. It won't take long for the rest of the newsroom to hear it and clamor for this. Princess Evalina is holding a press conference this afternoon. I want you to cover it."

"Me?" Gordon's chest tightened. He knew he'd be asked to report on the royals, but this? Finally, hearing the request... Kevin might as well have kicked him in the gut.

"Yes. If you want to come back, the boss wants to see that you're a team player. He says that if you're willing to use your connections to report on the princess, that will go a long way into rebuilding trust. Try and grab a one-on-one...something. Anything. I want you back and it needs to start here. Start pulling your connections."

Nope. No. Gordon couldn't stop his palms from sweating and his heart rate from kicking up to speeds he didn't think he could hit on the treadmill. "I—"

Kevin raised his hand, cutting Gordon off. "I know you've always refused royal stories. I didn't realize it was because of a personal connection. I may have pushed for more from you. But you don't have a choice anymore. Fill these requests or you're out of a job. Not even the leave can protect you."

That hardly seemed fair or legal. But pushing the leave through at the last minute the way they had probably wouldn't hold up. "I may not be here much longer. My visa hasn't been approved."

"If you prove yourself, I'll ask the boss to make some calls. I don't want to lose you." Kevin picked up his coffee and took a sip then made a face. "Cold. I suggest you grab what you need and head to the palace. I'll cover for you here."

Gordon stood and stopped at the door. "Thanks, Kevin."

"Don't thank me yet. Just go get this story."

Gordon opened the door and walked out. It was a good thing he'd showered and dressed like Orlin had ordered this morning. Because ready or not, he was about to see Eva—the princess.

Twelve

A low murmur buzzed through the open door into the long, bland palace hallway outside the media room. Inside the room, local and international press members waited for whatever Eva would say.

She'd always thought this day, this announcement would be filled with eager energy, excited nerves.

Love.

She'd pictured sweet looks and flirtation like Prince William and Catherine had exchanged. Even now the couple oozed affection.

That could be her goal. Someday she and...sigh...Alexander could share that.

Yet she wouldn't have sweet flirtation, hidden touches, or even the anticipation of a stolen moment after the press conference today.

Someday.

Hopefully.

Since Alexander had proposed seven days ago, they'd spent a good bit of time together, getting to know one another. But even after seven days, no spark had developed. Sure, Alexander happened to be a standup gentleman, but he wasn't Gor— Nope. Not that again. Alexander was a standup gentleman, end of story. Yay.

Only, her mental flag waving and cheering didn't sound as peppy as she needed it to. She'd give anything to have Kendra here. They'd talked about what happened between her and Alexander. Kendra had admitted that she'd grown fond of him, but that the country would always come first. However, her friend had asked for some personal time, promising to be back before the wedding.

Would Kendra come back though? Eva still didn't know what had happened between the pair. Would this marriage cost her that friendship too?

Taking a deep breath, Eva closed her eyes and blocked out the noise echoing from the reporters just beyond the open door.

They'd be thrilled to run back to their stations with the news that Her Royal Highness, Princess Evalina of Nevive would be married after a surprisingly short engagement on Christmas Eve. In five short days.

She could already imagine the rumors...which had run rampant after the picture of her and Gordon.

A warm hand settled on her low back. Steady, calming.

Alexander had arrived.

He leaned down, his voice low. "Are you having second thoughts?"

His face oozed compassion, understanding, as his hand moved in a small circle on her back. Her body flushed. Could he not be so perfect? For just a few moments could he act like a jerk? Get angry? Yell? Be something other than an agreeable human being?

Other than his few statements that he was a catch the day she apologized about running off and kissing another man, Alexander had shown very little emotion. A stable rock in the midst of her tornado of emotions. The calm to her storm.

But not...

She couldn't finish that thought. The good news was he'd be super easy to be married to. She hoped.

Doubling down on her decision, she forced her best princess smile, then lifted on her toes to speak into his ear. "I can't have second thoughts, but you can. Are you sure this is what you want?"

Instead of nodding, he took her hand and led her away from the security. He turned his back on them and pressed Eva up against the wall, one hand by her head, blocking her from the view of prying eyes.

His voice was low, as his minty breath washed over her face. "I'm good for my word, Evalina. I made you promises, and I will keep them."

Something flashed in his expression. Disappointment? Dread? It disappeared fast, replaced with a certainty she wished she could latch onto.

If Alexander could continue to agree to this loveless marriage, then she could too. One thing bothered her though, even after their time together—why was he so willing to follow through with this farce? Not a farce...an arrangement.

She couldn't let those thoughts creep in now. Not when the entire world's press waited for them to announce their upcoming nuptials. "No doubts. Let's do this."

Alexander nodded. He studied her face. A question lingered between them, but he didn't ask. Instead, he pushed back from the wall and stepped aside. Eva nodded to Marco, who said something into the security microphone he always wore.

Smithy stood against the wall. His black eye from Gordon had faded, and the incident seemed to have calmed him down. He had apologized for the way he'd treated her, and although she thought about asking to have him removed from her detail, he was young. One foolish mistake shouldn't ruin his entire career.

Alexander gestured for Eva to lead the way to the stage, then he followed a bit behind and to her side. She motioned for him to stand next to her, and she took his hand as they stepped on stage.

Approximately one hundred press members were there, cameras flashed, and phones were pointed her way as she walked up to the center podium. It was a much smaller crowd than normal, as she'd not given much notice, sending the notification out mere hours ago.

The only saving grace of talking to these reporters was knowing that Gordon wouldn't be there. He never reported on the royal family, and after their day together, she was sure he never would.

She'd broken down last night and turned on the news to at least see him, but Gordon hadn't been on. Turned out he hadn't reported anything since their day together. He also hadn't shared the events of their day, opting to be silent.

She'd taken a trip to the kitchen to visit Orlin, but she hadn't asked any of the questions in her heart. How was Gordon? Was he okay? Where was he? Had he lost his job? Was he even still in the country? She couldn't. It honestly shouldn't matter. But Orlin knew what she needed and had made her favorite cookies before she'd even arrived. Instead of talking, they'd sat in silence drinking tea. He'd been the one to teach her that though cookies might not solve the problem, they always helped.

She'd promised Alexander she would be faithful, and she'd meant it. Mentally would be the hardest, but she would purge Gordon from her heart and her mind.

Alexander squeezed her hand. The room quieted down, and people waited for her to speak.

"Good afternoon. Thank you for coming on such short notice." Eva dropped Alexander's hand and placed both of hers on the podium. Alexander fell back a few steps to stand behind her as she spoke to the press.

The urge to grip the sides and hang on for dear life almost overwhelmed her, but she forced her hands to lie flat. This was it. The way it had to be. Once she announced this, there was no going back. She glanced at Alexander. He nodded to her.

There might not be love between them, but the friendship they had developed in the past few days would be enough. "I invited you here to share my good news."

The press applauded, and Eva turned back toward Alexander. She offered him one of her hands, and he took it, stepping up next to her behind the podium. He smiled, his blue eyes sparkling. Taking courage from his seemingly affectionate gaze, she continued to speak without looking at the reporters. "I have decided not to have a long engagement, and my wedding will be next week on Christmas Eve."

A rush of calls and yells came from the crowd. Eva lifted her eyebrows to question Alexander if he was ready for this, and he nodded. She turned toward the reporters and together they faced their audience. She held up her free hand, waiting until she could continue. One by one she made eye contact with the reporters on the front row, as the room slowly quieted down again.

Just before she reached the end of the row, her breath caught, and her entire body froze.

Gordon.

He stood at the end of the row, holding his phone, recording her speech. Their eyes locked, and heat climbed up her neck. Her ears burned. Her tongue stuck to the roof of her mouth.

Forcing her attention away from Gordon, she studied her notes. Where was she? What was she supposed to say next?

Why was she standing here?

Why was *he* here?

Alexander cleared his throat and spoke for her. "The wedding will be held at the Nevive Abbey. Local police have already been notified to help make the necessary arrangements for the service and events that take place that day."

Thankfully, Alexander could step in and finish, because Eva couldn't remember how to speak. Might not remember how to breathe.

Gordon.

Like a magnet, her eyes sought him out.

He stood there, his hair neatly styled, his long muscular body relaxed. But his face had gone pale. Surely, he'd heard about her engagement. The entire world had heard by now.

But that didn't answer her pressing questions. Why had he come today? Never before had Gordon covered one of her press conferences. What was he doing here?

Oh goodness. Would he bring up the photograph? The videos? The kiss?

Would he break his silence today of all days?

Alexander dropped her hand and pressed his on her low back. She'd been staring at Gordon. Again. This would not go unnoticed.

Alexander must have finished sharing the details she'd meticulously planned out, because he asked, "Are there any questions from the press?"

The entire crowd except Gordon raised a hand and started clamoring for attention. Marco stepped forward with a mic and handed it to a man in a gray suit.

"Matt from British Entertainment News. Alexander, this question is for you—how did you feel after the picture with Princess Evalina and Gordon Tarpen was released?"

Alexander stepped closer to her, his chest steady against her back. He smiled down at her before looking back at the crowd. Wow, he had better acting skills than she'd given him credit for. "I'm so glad we are getting this question out of the way. That picture was taken out of context. The princess and I have talked about it. I hold no hard feelings toward her or Mr. Tarpen. In fact, I'm grateful to him, because it brought Evalina and me together even quicker than I had hoped."

Alexander looked back down at her. For a second, even she believed that he had deep feelings for her. It sounded like a good speech, like a man in love. But it still bothered her that he would agree to this. Why give up on love? He said he had his reasons, and that he hoped for love between them. Even so, it seemed the air had been sucked from the room as all the reporters turned their attention to Gordon.

Matt held tight to the mic and looked down the row. "Gordon, you've been quiet on this story. Do you have anything to say?"

Eva glanced at Gordon, who stood frozen until his Adam's apple bobbed. He hadn't said a word about their day. He'd probably received as many calls and requests for interviews as she had, and yet he didn't have the luxury of palace security. He had shouldered that all on his own. And now he faced the same firing squad of reporters she did. Except she'd been trained for spotlight moments. She had a team standing behind her and Alexander beside her. Gordon took a small step back, then looked both ways like he wanted an exit. She had the power to save him from this. To put an end to this line of questioning.

With a quick breath, she spoke before Gordon could respond. "I don't believe Mr. Tarpen attended this conference to be questioned. I will say that Alexander is correct, the story was taken out of context. It captured a second of an entire day I planned to be among the people I love so much. The people of Nevive. The photo and videos twisted my outing into something that it was not. While Mr. Tarpen and I have known each other since childhood, there has never been a romantic connection. I believe that is enough for now. We will see you for my wedding. Thank you for coming."

As she stepped back from the podium, the press continued to yell questions. Security allowed her and Alexander to exit, but just before she stepped off stage, she turned to see Gordon.

Immediately their eyes met, and she stopped.

I'm sorry.

She had so much more she wanted to say. So much more she wanted to convey in that one quick look. But she hoped he understood. She never should have put him in this position, and if she could have a do-over, she would have held herself in check.

Regret was a terrible companion.

The door closed behind her with a thud as the last security member stepped through, blocking her view of Gordon.

Alexander rubbed her arm up and down. She nodded to him, and he dropped her arm before turning to speak to Marco. Something about security for Gordon. Eva couldn't listen, though. She needed to get away.

Away from the press.

Away from the questions.

Away from Gordon.

GORDON STOOD IN THE POOL OF REPORTERS. THE ROOM quieted down immediately after the door closed behind Eva.

How on earth would he get out of here without being mauled for a soundbite?

It was time to man up and answer the questions everyone had been asking. If he fessed up to the reporters that he loved Eva, had always loved Eva, they might get off his back.

What good would it do, though? She'd just announced she was marrying another man.

A security guard stepped forward and stood next to Gordon. The rest of the reporters slowly packed up and left the press room, not a single question hurled his way.

He'd thank Eva—ugh, still with the informal nickname. The princess. He'd thank the princess for the thoughtful act, but she'd left.

Gordon stood at the rope with a burly security guard next to him until the last reporter left. The large pressroom had simple white walls, with golden accents. The maroon carpeted floor allowed for some of the noise to be dampened. Simple yet elegant paintings lined the wall as well.

When the door closed behind the final reporter, Gordon let out a breath.

"Thank you." Gordon turned to the security guard, but he was gone. Vanished almost like a ghost. How did they manage to move so quickly and quietly? He could use some tips, because he seemed to be annoying his uncle with every movement. Gordon closed his eyes and rubbed at his forehead. That wasn't true either. His uncle had been nothing but kind and gave no indication that Gordon was a nuisance. Uncle Orlin just said things Gordon didn't want to hear. If Gordon had anyone to be angry with, it was himself and the decision he made to push Eva away.

The princess. Not Eva.

Seeing her had brought back all the anger. All the doubts. All the...well, he couldn't stand here with the proverbial black cloud hanging over his head all day.

He'd give the reporters a few more minutes to clear out of the parking lot. Gordon opened the notes app on his phone and wrote down a few thoughts. Eva had announced her wedding in five days.

Five days.

How could *he* report on this story?

Without addressing what happened, it would be impossible. He'd been made a part of the story. In some way, he'd have to acknowledge his day with the princess. Or would he? He could just simply state facts. Not give anything else.

Once upon a time, that's how news reports worked—just facts, no speculation.

Kevin had put him in a terrible position. Because even if he stuck to the facts of today, the interaction with the anchors would bring up questions he didn't want to answer. Live-on-air there wouldn't be anyone to step in and take the spotlight off him.

Basically, he'd been given an ultimatum: tell his story or lose his job.

Gordon tucked the phone in his pocket and headed for the exit. Only two security officers remained inside the doors, but neither looked at Gordon as he walked through the double doors and out of the palace.

Standing on the steps, he glanced up at the towering building behind him. If he stalled, Eva—the princess—might come out. Find him and say hello.

They could talk things through.

A pipe dream. He knew she wouldn't. The look she'd given him had said so much.

I'm sorry.

Goodbye.

He'd received the message loud and clear, like a fist to his chest. She wouldn't come out, and that short look had been the only goodbye he'd receive.

He'd wanted to catapult over the velvet rope and launch himself onto the stage and through the door like some ninja spy. But what good would it have done?

It would just prolong the inevitable.

Goodbye would still be the only outcome.

Gordon pulled his phone out and recorded some video, the shadows creating a beautiful image. It would be good B-roll for his story. If he could manage to put something together.

Just facts. Nothing more. A pre-recorded package with no live intro or handoff.

"I've always enjoyed this view of the palace." A deep regal voice spoke from behind him.

Gordon fumbled his phone.

He knew that voice.

It could only belong to one person. He turned to the king, who wore a black leather bomber jacket, jeans, and a black ball cap. His aviator sunglasses hid much of his face.

Gordon lowered his head to bow, but the king grabbed Gordon's elbow, stopping his movement. "Don't do that. You'll blow my cover. There are reporters just outside the gates there."

Gordon glanced around and realized that the king's usual

entourage was absent. A few extra guards stood along the wall. "Your Majesty?"

"That might give me away too. Please, call me Tom."

"Tom?" Did all of the royalty have a second name they used in public?

"It's a good name. Not mine and no one will suspect a thing. Eva is hardly the first royal to sneak outside the castle walls. Now walk with me and don't blow my cover. I rather like this jacket and hat. It's worked for a while now."

Gordon walked a step behind the man he'd looked up to as a father figure. Even so, he'd always be the king first and foremost.

"Relax, Gordon. You're drawing attention. Walk next to me." The king gestured and slowed his step, waiting.

Gordon hesitated but obeyed his king. They walked down the castle drive and out the gates. A few guards dressed in casual clothes were following behind, but they hardly looked like they were guarding the king.

"You love my daughter." The king spoke the words with a quiet confidence. No pity, no shame, just a simple fact.

Heat climbed up his neck. Of course he did. He always had. Did the king know? He shoved his phone and his hands into his coat pockets. "Yes, sir."

"Enough to let her go."

Anger flared in Gordon's bones. Of course he'd let her go, and it had been the hardest and most terrible thing he'd ever done.

"I've never had a claim to her." Gordon bit out the words, his throat tight.

The king nodded, his eyes hidden behind the dark glasses, but he turned to look the other way, his hands swinging casually by his side. He motioned toward a bench and sat down, indicating Gordon should as well.

"I disagree, son. Whether you want it or not, her heart belongs to you."

Gordon's heart rate picked up. Had it? Surely, not anymore. "I never asked for it."

"I know. I daresay, she has yours too."

Gordon nodded. No denying the truth. She'd taken his heart when she walked out of the Renoldses' house. Since then, the cavity in his chest seemed hollow. Empty.

He'd turned into a moping idiot. Gordon shifted on his seat.

The king's intense gaze like a laser honed in on any movement, any emotion. "The day you had together, you didn't disrespect my daughter."

Gordon turned to look at the man beside him not as his king but as Eva's father. The hat covered his hair and shadowed most of his face, his jaw cleanly shaven, and his posture relaxed. But even so, this man had power. Authority. It just naturally came to him. Even in his casual clothes, people walking by glanced his way.

Gordon knew he would use all of his power to protect his daughter. "Sir, I could never disrespect, Ev—uh, Princess Evalina."

"Please, she's never been Princess Evalina to you. Don't start now."

"I have to. I can't think of her as anything else. She needs to rule the kingdom, and I would prevent her from doing that."

"That's why you let her go? Told her not to come back?"

That's not really what he'd said. But he hadn't encouraged her. Hadn't asked her to fight for him. He'd basically pushed her away, and he'd regretted it ever since.

He couldn't and wouldn't ask her to give up her dream of being queen.

"In so many words." Gordon nodded. Again. How could the king know the intimate details of his day with Eva? Did he have superspy techniques Gordon didn't know about? That would make an amazing news story. Far better than the one he had to write today.

He drummed his fingers on his knee. Eva could have shared the details of the day.

Movement caught his attention. Three palace guards standing not too far away, all dressed to blend in. One casually propped against a light post, scrolling on his phone, the second jogged up and down the street, never far from view. The third sat on a bench across the street "reading" a book.

"Eva wasn't really alone that day, was she?" Gordon nodded to the men. He hadn't seen them. He'd searched—everywhere they'd gone he'd been watching for someone. Scouting for her security but he'd not noticed them at all. "They're good at what they do."

The king smiled. "They are. And they knew you were looking for them."

The king looked out over the street in front of them. Cars drove by, and an older couple walked their dog. He waved to them, and they nodded a greeting. "I'm glad she had the gumption to get out among the people. But as I'm sure you know, not much happens in my palace that I don't know. It's easy really. The maids know everything. I just need to listen to learn what they know."

"Sir?" At least that ruled out Eva telling her father.

"You could have had quite the news story."

The king turned to Gordon, and a white-hot heat rushed through Gordon's veins.

"Never. If you think I'm the kind of man, the kind of friend, that would use my connection to the crown to further my career—"

The king chuckled. "Hardly, Gordon. Please. You've never called for that exclusive I would have given you. So, I sought you out. I have some news I think you should know."

Gordon shook his head. "Sir, I won't use you—"

"This is information you want to hear. You can do with it as you please." The king looked across the street and nodded. The man on the bench closed the book he'd been "reading" and stood and walked into the café behind him.

Gordon hadn't taken the time to notice where they had sat down. Old brownstones lined the street. Half a dozen were businesses, but the rest were residential. Tall trees cast long shadows with the usual streetlights. Pockets of snow were piled against the trees and the buildings, but the sidewalk and roads were clear. The sun shone down, cutting the chill of the air.

The guard exited the café with two paper cups, and as he approached, the king stood, putting his hand on Gordon's shoulder briefly to keep him seated. The king accepted the cups and handed one to Gordon.

"Thanks, Jake." The king sat back down, and Jake returned to his post across the street on a bench with a book back in hand.

"Patty makes the best coffee. Whenever I need an escape, I come for a cup of hers. Sometimes I simply come out to get a to-go cup." The king took a long drink of his coffee, looking more like a regular guy than the man who ruled their small country.

Gordon took a sip of his coffee. Not surprisingly, it was fixed just the way he liked it.

The king held the cup in both hands and turned toward Gordon. "Anyway, I believe the news I have to share will be of great interest to you. About five years ago, I approached Parliament about a change in the law. Although I had no idea they would force her hand into marriage, I could see the writing on the wall, and I wanted Evalina to be happy."

"I want her happiness too." As good as the coffee tasted, Gordon couldn't take another sip. He turned it in his hand, but his stomach soured at the thought of Eva marrying Alexander.

"I couldn't flat out change it, but I did manage to add a nuance in a bill everyone wanted passed. No one minded that I had added a little extra. The law stating that royalty must marry either a citizen or a titled individual now has a nuance, a caveat, if you will. As long as the reigning monarch approves, there are no rules in place for whom the heir has to marry."

Gordon squeezed the coffee cup, and the lid popped up. Thankfully, he reacted quickly enough that he didn't spill the hot beverage all over his hand. Putting the lid back on, he looked at the king. "Sir? I believe the law states that the princess must marry before her twenty-sixth birthday. Hence the rushed wedding."

"It does. However, if I, as the current ruler, approve a spouse for my daughter, my choice trumps the law's requirements of her spouse. As the father—and king—while I may not be able to delay the wedding, I can have the final say in who my daughter marries."

The words sank in. And the coffee slid from Gordon's hand. This time he couldn't catch it, and the beverage spilled on the sidewalk. Hot coffee burned his hands and legs.

Jake stepped forward with napkins, and Gordon thanked him. Were the guards prepared for every situation?

Gordon cleaned up his hands, and Jake took the now empty cup and lid to a nearby trash can.

Gordon sat back and rubbed his hands on his jeans. "I'm sorry, but are you saying Eva doesn't have to marry a Nevive citizen or royalty?"

The king nodded. "That is what I am saying."

Thoughts swam through Gordon's head—a future he'd never dreamed possible. What did Eva think about this?

The king took a small black velvet box from inside his coat. "I happen to think you would be a good fit for my daughter."

"Sir, she just publicly announced her wedding in less than a week. You think I can change that?" Gordon wanted to pace, but he forced himself to stay seated.

"Like I said, I can't change the law stating she has to marry. She still has to fulfill that part of the law, but you could change who the groom will be." The king grinned. "I believe if you review her speech, she never once said she was marrying Alexander."

Gordon let the words sink in, trying to remember Eva's speech. He'd honestly been so taken aback by her appearance—she'd lost weight, she looked tired—that he hadn't focused on what she'd said.

The king continued speaking but Gordon didn't hear anything. He looked back at the king. "I'm sorry, sir?"

The king stood, and Gordon stood with him. "I have no doubt you love my daughter. You let her go when you thought it was best for her and my country. You have proven yourself to be a man of integrity, a man of faith. A humble man, willing to set aside your own wants for the needs of someone else. I can't think of a better man to stand by my daughter as she leads this country. While you still have room to grow, you will be a great asset to our people, if you can let go of your pride and win my daughter back."

Gordon still couldn't quite wrap his mind around what the king had said. The burns on his hands and legs meant this was real, not a dream. Still, the king had sought him out. Told him to go after Eva. Gave his blessing even.

The king held out the small black box to Gordon. "I picked this ring from our vault. Evalina has always admired it. And although it's a bit presumptuous on my part to pick the ring, I think you will be happy with this one."

Gordon hesitantly reached for the box. "Sir, when Eva left, it was not...good. What does she think about this nuance you added to the law?"

The king put his hands in his pockets and chuckled. "We have not spoken about it. She seems... stubborn on this issue. I suggest you learn how to grovel. Prayer would be a good place to start."

The king walked away. Two men joined him to walk on either side, and Jake followed behind, looking like a man on a casual walk. Gordon looked down at the box in his hand, his palms damp.

He had the king's blessing.

He had a ring.

He had a chance.

"And, Gordon?" The king's voice broke into his thoughts.

The leader of Nevive walked backward, a teasing grin on his face. "Don't lose that. It's a special one."

A dark chuckle escaped, and Gordon held the box up. "No, sir. I wouldn't dare."

The king turned back around and continued to walk to the

palace, his retreating form just like any regular guy taking a walk. Not the king of the country out for a chat with his hopefully soon-to-be-son-in-law.

Gordon tucked the box into his coat pocket. Never once had he dreamed he might be given a chance to win the heart of the woman he loved. God had given him more than he'd dare ask or think.

Please, Lord, help me win Eva's heart and hand.

He had five days to change the course of a royal wedding and fix things with the woman he loved.

Thirteen

With only four days to go, Eva sat in the small chapel she'd been to with Gordon, her hands empty. How did people survive before cellphones? She'd turned hers off and left it back in her apartment to try to take time to focus, and yet, all she wanted was to escape into a game, to scroll through her newsfeed, or to type up a message to Gordon she wouldn't send.

Anything to forget that she was about to be a married woman in just a few short days.

By now, when she should have her outrageous feelings for Gordon under control, still all she wanted was to hear his voice. See his name pop up on her phone. All the more reason she'd left it behind.

Forced self-control when she thought she might break down and call him.

It didn't help that Kendra still hadn't come back. She missed her friend. There had been no one to talk to about any and all of the emotions raging through her. Let alone to make sure her friend was okay after such an abrupt departure.

Light filtered through the stained glass windows and quickly darkened before brightening again. The partly cloudy sky outside even affected the mood inside the chapel. Generations of previous heirs had sequestered themselves within the walls of the chapel for a week ahead of their wedding or coronation before the construction of the abbey next to the palace. How had they made it all alone? Did they not think they would go crazy?

Maybe it was better the tradition had died out.

Lord, how can it be so quiet, and I still can't hear You? Do You even know I'm here? Do You see me at all?

No response. The quiet of the chapel almost engulfed her, pressed down on her.

"You're not an easy person to find." The deep voice of her father filled the chapel. The acoustics were amazing. A choir would sound celestial, and the end of the silence would be a blessing.

Someone to talk to. Eva scooted over to make room for her father on the pew next to her. "Did you know the heir apparent used to take time in this chapel to pray before big life events?"

At the front of the chapel, the stained glass picture drew her attention as the sun once more must have dipped behind a cloud. Jesus stood tall, talking to a woman in the garden, the empty tomb behind them. The light filtered through the room, casting colors and shadows in beautiful patterns. What would it feel like to have the Savior's full attention like that? To be fully seen?

Her father settled in the pew next to her, his arm coming around her. "And he would sit right where you are, studying that same picture. I wasn't able to sequester like our ancestors had, but I did take time here like you are."

"Why doesn't the bell work?" It would be a welcome pause of the overwhelming silence. Eva leaned into her father, soaking up the comfort of a companion.

"No one knows. Previous rules have requested that several workmen try to repair it, but none have been successful."

"I wish we could hear the bell toll. To have the majestic sound ring through the land after the wedding."

Her father relaxed next to her. "I've always loved the place. The windows, the quiet, the solitude. I haven't been back in years, but I'm glad to see Fredrick is still caring for the property."

"Fredrick is the manager?" He must be the man that Gordon had seen.

"You could call him that. But he's always loved this building. Maybe I'll talk to him about the bell tower. I've not tried to have it repaired. Maybe it's time. But even without the bell, this place...it's like a place to come when you need to quiet your soul. When you need to meet Him like Mary met Jesus in the garden." Her father nodded toward the window at the front. Mary's blue robe with a red sash bright as the sun peeked out from behind a cloud.

"I remember that story. Mary was the first one Jesus appeared to after He rose from the dead. I was always jealous that He saw her, called her by name. I wanted to be seen like that."

"More people see you than you realize, Evalina." Her father crossed his foot on his knee, his navy suit pant leg riding up, showing off his navy socks. The tiny pink flamingos on them were his subtle way to show some style, though completely wrong for the season. No one would see the small detail on his dress socks.

He checked his watch. It was a slow and casual move, but Eva knew he had a busy schedule.

"What brings you by?"

"I know you are pushing forward with this wedding. There's no way we can stop it from happening, but perhaps Alexander isn't the best option for you?"

Eva snorted. So unprincess-like. "I'm not sure there are any other options with a wedding in four days."

Her father shifted in the pew so he faced her fully. "You marry the man you love."

Her father's voice didn't hold a joke, his eyes didn't twinkle, and his jaw held a stubborn tic, but Eva had no idea how he could be serious. The man she loved?

"I spoke to Gordon." Her father couldn't have said anything more surprising.

Her hands grew damp, and her feet were like ice. How could she be both overheated and freezing at the same time?

A million questions fired in her brain. How was he holding up after the story broke? Why hadn't he been on TV since then? He reported a simple package of her announcement. But he hadn't been on camera, and she hadn't seen him since. What happened? Why was he at the press conference in the first place? He hadn't tried to talk to her, and he'd been pale. Well, not that he could talk to her. But still. Was he eating? Why had her father talked to him, and what had they spoken about? A million more questions fought for dominance.

She picked a safe question and worked to keep her voice even and not the high-pitched squeak that wanted to come out. "Did he tell you he's applied for citizenship several times, but his paperwork is continually missing? He's not yet been approved?"

Finally, she managed to offer her father a tidbit of new information. Not that it seemed worthwhile to gloat over something like this.

"He didn't mention that. His paperwork is *continually* lost?" Her father tugged on his pant leg. A sure sign he'd filed this revelation away for future dissection. If something underhanded was in play, he would hunt it out. "Lady Galveston's son is the head of immigration. I'll have a conversation with him."

Too little, too late. It would take longer than four days for Gordon's paperwork to go through. The fact that it was the week before Christmas? Government offices were closed, and Gordon's fate was sealed. "It doesn't change anything."

"It doesn't." Her father's nonchalant response had her wishing she could stomp her feet. Scream. Anything to let off some steam.

Why dangle the hope of love in front of her only to tell her nothing had changed?

She stood and walked out of the pew, up to the front of the chapel, where she stopped in the midst of the colors of the stained glass cascading across the floor.

"Why tell me to marry who I love if you know I can't?" It hurt too much to say his name.

"But you do love him."

Eva spun around, walked down the center aisle toward her father.

"Do you need me to say it again?" Her voice cracked. "Yes, I love Gordon. I always have. But I...I made a fool of myself. Not that it matters, because it's impossible to marry him."

Her father shook his head. "You took your future into your own hands. Latched onto what you wanted and jumped in. I have wondered for a while about your feelings, but years ago, I wanted to make sure there was a way for you to have the happiness I had with your mother. I couldn't have seen an ancient law forcing a timeline upon you, but I wondered if there might be a way someone would try and force your hand to manipulate you or the throne. I added a line into a bill that passed without question—the heir apparent can marry anyone the reigning monarch approves of."

Her father stood and rested his hand on her shoulder. She turned back toward the front of the chapel, her breaths short and shallow.

This new realization didn't offer her the comfort her father wanted it to. Gordon had pushed her away. He hadn't fought for her. Even if she could marry Gordon, he hadn't wanted the future she offered. Not everyone wanted a royal title.

Not that she'd asked him that specifically. But the embarrassment of him breaking the kiss—it still caused her hands to tremble and her ears to burn until she went numb all over.

"I don't..." Her words hitched, and she forced herself to take a deep breath. "I don't believe Gordon is interested."

"*Pffft*." Her father rolled his eyes. "Please, the entire world knows he's interested. You don't throw a punch for just anyone. Not to mention the way he held you as he kissed you. The care he took of you as you traveled all over Lesa."

Eva hugged herself. If only her father spoke the truth, but he hadn't been there to see how that kiss had ended. She certainly wasn't going to enlighten him.

"And Eva, sometimes a father knows. I have no doubt he loves you every bit as much as you love him."

Eva covered her mouth as she took a ragged breath. She couldn't hold out hope, not anymore. She had to let the past go. "I'm not sure how things could change in four days. He hasn't reached out to me. He hasn't tried to contact me."

Her father stood behind her now. He wrapped his arms around her, and she relaxed against him. The light brightened behind Mary, illuminating her next to Jesus, whose entire focus was on the woman in front of him. Forever etched into the glass. What would it be like to feel the intense gaze of her Savior on her like that? To know He saw her?

"You know, I've always loved that story." Her father studied the stained glass window in the front of the chapel. "Mary, like many of Christ's followers, was distraught by His death. Yet as she stood in the garden, devastated to find His tomb empty, He appeared. He called her by name. In His compassion, He sought her out."

It's all Eva had ever wanted—to be seen for herself, not for her title, not for her place in the kingdom, not for who she would be. Not Her Royal Highness, Princess of Nevive, Evalina Rosalind Marie Bexley. Just Eva.

However, now that she'd been the focus of the news, she realized it had been nice when no one saw her. No one but Gordon. He'd always seen her.

What was it that made Mary so special, though, that Christ had sought her out?

Her father tilted his head. "You know, it's always amazed me that Christ paused in the middle of whatever He was doing to talk to Mary. To comfort her."

"Pause what He was doing? Like rising from the dead?"

"Sure. He was going about His Father's business. He asked Mary not to touch Him, because I'm sure she wanted to hug Him. Her friend, her Savior, once dead now alive again. But it's more than that. Christ could have appeared to any of His disciples. But He chose Mary."

"Lucky girl to get the attention of the Creator of the universe."

Eva's father's chin grazed her hair as he shook his head. "I don't think she was special. I think that Christ, as our shepherd, knows each of us. He calls each of us by name. He sees us. He knows us. He died for us. And He rose for us. I think Him stopping to talk to Mary is an excellent reminder that He does know us individually. He knew that Mary, more than anyone else in that moment, needed Him, so He came."

Her father squeezed her a little tighter and then stepped back, dropping his arms. "You need someone who reminds you that you are seen. You often think that you're invisible, replaceable, which couldn't be further from the truth. Your Savior knows this, and Gordon reminds you of it. If you want a union with Gordon, I would bless it, and you could marry him. Forget all previous rules —he is an eligible match. I need to get back to the palace. But don't give up on Gordon just yet. I think he could still be an option."

The front door of the chapel echoed as it closed. Eva didn't need to turn around to know that Marco had re-entered to stand at the exit. Never really alone, always watched.

Always seen.

The light through the front window darkened and then brightened again, like the sun had moved behind a cloud and come back out, only this time, the light shone brighter through the area around Christ.

The Good Shepherd who knew His sheep.

He called them by name.

Eva lifted her face, and a bronze plaque glinted in the light. Eva crossed the room and read the inscription. *I am the good shepherd. I know my own and my own know me.* All this time she'd been questioning whether God knew her, but did she know Him? Had she taken the time to learn about Him? Of course He knew her. She'd followed Him as a young child but had never taken the time to get to know Him better. If she had, she would have known He saw her. Knew her. Loved *her.*

Lord, I haven't been listening, but I want to. Help me to follow Your call on my life. I want to be loved and seen. Maybe I haven't been because I don't see myself the way You see me. Help me to know You.

In the still of the chapel, with time flying by at breakneck speed before her wedding, Eva heard the whisper of her name across the depth of her heart.

She may not want this marriage, may not know what the future held, but whatever God brought her way, He would help her to face it. Because the Good Shepherd not only knew His sheep, He didn't leave any behind.

Four days. He had four days to stop Eva from marrying Alexander. Gordon sat at the picnic table in the middle of the bazaar next to Marge's coffee truck and tapped his phone on the table.

"You survived." Marge sat down across from him, her gentle presence a balm to his wandering mind.

Yes. He had. Reporting on Eva's wedding announcement had been painful. But he'd cut a package, left it with Kevin, and quit.

"I never want to face that again. That's why I quit."

Marge's jaw dropped and she thumped her own coffee down on the table. "You quit? Why would you do that? I thought you were up for anchor."

"I was, but now…" Now he hoped for more. He had his sights set on marriage, and if that worked out, there wouldn't be space for his job. If he had to choose between his job and Eva, well, there was no choice. Eva would win every time.

Marge leaned forward and dropped her voice. "Tell me you're going after the girl."

Gordon grinned and dropped his head closer to Marge, as though he was sharing a great secret. "If by *girl* you mean Eva, then yes. I want the girl."

First, he had to get ahold of her, though. He'd been calling and calling, but each call went directly to voicemail.

"It's about time." Marge sat back and tapped the table.

Out of the corner of his eye, a purple puffer coat wove into the crowd. He zoned in on the crowd, but he didn't see anything out of the ordinary.

He'd wondered if the teen would come back. There had been only a handful of thefts at the bazaar, but now a couple hundred dollars were unaccounted for.

He had no proof Purple Puffer Girl was also the bazaar thief but call it reporter's intuition.

"Oh, Gordon." Marge's tone called his attention back to the conversation at hand as she too stared off into the crowd where the Purple Puffer Girl had gone. "Let that go. Don't chase it."

"Why not?" Gordon searched the crowd again but didn't see the girl. "Think of the story."

"You just said you're not a reporter anymore."

"True. But…"

Marge smacked her hand on the table. "No buts. Why do you always try to prove you're the best?"

Her words chaffed. He wanted to be the best. That wasn't a bad thing. Wasn't he supposed to always be doing his best? "I'm not sure I follow."

"There's no need to harass that girl. You don't know her or her story."

"And you do?"

Marge searched the crowd too, a sad frown crossing her face. "I don't. But you don't need to go after this. Why are you trying so hard to find a story when you've already quit? I don't think you need to try so hard. The way you work, you won't ever get to wherever you're going. You keep moving the finish line. You'll continue to push the bar higher, the standard farther. In your mind, you will never be enough. But you're missing something important—you won't ever achieve anything that will make you good enough. The truth is you are already enough. You want to know why? Because God already loves you. The princess already loves you. Your viewers adore you. You don't have to work for any of that. Let it go and move forward."

Marge grabbed his coffee cup, nodded a goodbye, and left before Gordon could say anything else. His phone vibrated in his hand, but it was just a message from Uncle Orlin about dinner. He ignored it and opened his phonebook to call Eva.

Got voicemail.

Again.

If he had Kendra's number, he'd try calling her. Uncle Orlin had been no help, even with the ring in hand. He'd simply said Eva had taken some time to reflect before her big day.

Reflect? On what? Where?

There it was again. The purple puffer coat. The girl stood in line at Marge's truck. The older woman talked to her and rang her up. They chatted casually as Marge loaded three hot drinks into a carrier and her daughter, Jamie, handed her a bag with a pastry.

Gordon stood and followed the girl as she wove through the crowd, Marge's words tickling the back of his mind. Maybe he had to prove to himself that he was good enough. That his intuition was correct. He could still find out about the stolen bazaar funds without turning it into a big story.

He tried to give her enough distance that she didn't see him when she scanned her surroundings. At the edge of the bazaar, she turned down the same alley he and Eva had escaped.

He followed her in, and behind the dumpster were two small children waiting for her, their conversation quiet but clear.

"You took so long. I was afraid you weren't coming back." The voice of a young girl, maybe three or four, trembled as she grabbed for the cup the older girl passed her.

The teen then passed a cup to a boy a few years older than the young girl. The children were clean, but their clothes were old and worn out. While the two younger children appeared well rested, the teen girl had bags under her eyes.

"You didn't get one for Mama, Lizzy." The little girl pointed at the tray with only one remaining cup.

The boy scoffed. "She's not coming back, Sarah."

"Demitri, try to be nice." Lizzy, the purple puffer girl, rebuked the boy with a tired sigh, like they'd had this conversation more than once.

This wasn't some huge pickpocketing ring moving back in. It wasn't even a group of thieves. These were children trying to make the best of a terrible situation. It didn't make it right, but Gordon recognized the desperation radiating off the children. Especially the teen girl.

"Hey." Gordon stepped out of the shadows. The children startled and the teen moved in front of her siblings, spreading her arms and purple coat, hiding the children behind her.

When she recognized Gordon, she tried to herd her siblings away from him. "We don't want any trouble, Mister."

"I'm not here for trouble. But I may be able to help." This

wasn't a story he'd report on the news, but it was one he could report—to the right people.

"Help." The teen snorted and turned, still trying to usher the younger kids away. "Thanks, but we're fine."

"I'm sure you are. But I bet you could use a good hot meal. Come with me, and I'll make sure you don't have to worry about food today."

"Please, Lizzy. I'm hungry," the younger girl, Sarah, said.

"I'm tired of pastries." Demitri rubbed his stomach and smacked his lips.

Lizzy bent down to talk to her siblings.

In order to give them some semblance of privacy, he opened a message to Chief Rodgers, sending him his current location.

GORDON

Hey. I have three kids that may need a home. Or at least some care. I'm hoping to take them to Ria's Café for a meal.

Gordon tucked his phone away, knowing the police chief would send someone, and waited for the children to finish their discussion. Lizzy did not look pleased, but the two younger children pleaded with her.

Lizzy turned back to him and crossed her arms over her chest. "Fine. The kids are hungry."

Once they walked to the restaurant and the kids were eating, Chief Rodgers arrived, thankfully in jeans and a ratty sweatshirt so he looked more like a friendly Santa rather than the police chief. The kids took to him like a long-lost grandpa. Even Lizzy seemed to relax in his presence.

Through the chatter of the younger children, Gordon learned that their mom had brought them to Nevive from the US after their dad was deployed. She'd grown up here and although the kids had never visited, she'd come hoping family would help while their dad was deployed. One day she'd gone out and never came back.

Lizzy had done what she thought she had to in order to protect her siblings, but she had never met her mother's family and had no idea how to find them.

The police chief had called social services, but finding a place for the children proved to be a challenge. Gordon had been on the receiving end of his uncle's love and care, so he knew how to help the children. When Uncle Orlin learned there had been no open home to place the children in temporarily, he'd immediately agreed to take them in.

Now at his apartment, they'd not wanted to sleep in separate rooms. So he'd arranged for all of them to sleep in a single room, moving beds around, so they had enough space.

After Gordon closed the door to the children's room for the night, he went into the kitchen and sank onto a stool, while Orlin wiped down the already clean counters, waiting for tea water to boil.

"I never would have guessed this is how my day would end." Gordon sighed and placed his head on his arms. "I never did get ahold of Eva."

The electric tea kettle finished heating the water and Orlin set about making tea. "You won't. She turned off her cell until after the wedding, and she's taking time to pray since she can't completely sequester before the wedding with the short notice and all."

Gordon's heart rate sped up. If she wasn't using her phone, how would he get in touch with her? He couldn't get close to her, not with security and her busy schedule. He could hide in the palace kitchen with Orlin. Maybe she'd come down. Or he could...

"You know, you remind me a lot of Lizzy." Orlin set a cup of tea in front of Gordon and sat on the stool next to him.

"I'm sorry? How?" Lizzy's purple puffer coat, along with her siblings' coats, had already been washed. Orlin had them all hung up in a row on pegs by the back door, their shoes tucked against the wall under the coats.

"She's stubborn. Independent. Doesn't want to accept help. The difference is, she knows she has to because of her siblings."

Gordon took a deep breath, his jaw tense. "You're not the first person to say that recently."

Orlin nodded. "You're such a smart guy, Gordon. I don't know why you can't see that it's okay to need help. Even Christ surrounded Himself with people while He was on earth. He had a crew that He loved. He let them in. Took them with Him to pray. To eat. To travel. He gave them things to do. He made friends, connections. Loved people. Let them in. You? You like to live on your own. Just like Lizzy. And her stubbornness would still have her sleeping on the go, wondering where their next meal was coming from."

Everything Orlin said was true. He'd been so stubborn, wanting to do everything on his own. Prove his worth at his job. Become a citizen. And none of it had worked in his favor. He still hadn't been able to meet the impossible standards to become Eva's husband. Now, he'd quit his job, he'd lost his apartment, and he still hadn't become a citizen. Worse yet, even though he had the king's blessing to pursue Eva, if he didn't figure things out in four days, well three now because today was over, she would marry someone else.

What had he done?

A strong hand landed on his shoulder. No words were spoken. Gordon didn't want to look up and see disapproval or anger. Although warranted, Gordon didn't want to know how deeply he'd failed his uncle. Eva. Himself. And worse yet...God. When his uncle had opened his home, continued to offer support and a landing pad again, now for an adult who couldn't make it on his own, Gordon had continually pushed him away. A lot like the moody child he'd been. When Orlin continued to stand there, his hand on Gordon's shoulder, there could be no more hiding. Finally, Gordon studied his uncle's face. There was no disappointment in his expression, only love.

"Now, you lean into God. Realize you cannot do it without Him. Ask Him how to move forward. From my standpoint, He's given you amazing connections. Pray about which ones to call on. Build your own team. But also realize that without God, you won't be able to. You need to depend on Him."

A team?

He did have an amazing network of people rooting for him. And he'd shut them all out.

Eva had been right. He'd been prideful. He thought he had to do everything on his own. But he couldn't. Just like he couldn't save himself, he couldn't do everything by himself.

He needed grace.

He needed people.

He needed to depend on God, who had already proved Himself by giving His Son to die on the cross. If ever someone had proved themselves dependable, it was his God.

Uncle Orlin picked up his tea. "I'm here. I'm on your team. But I think you need to figure out how you're going to move forward. If you want Eva, you're going to need to call in all your connections."

Orlin turned off the overhead light as he left, leaving only the glow from the Christmas tree in the family room. Gordon picked up his tea and walked to the tree. A golden ornament hung in the branches, two bells with bows encircled by a golden oval. The words *First Christmas* were etched in the ring. Orlin seldom spoke of his wife, but their love story had been one for the books. Fast and deep, and it had ended when Aunt Erica died in a rock climbing accident with the queen, Eva's mother.

Lord, I've made a mess of things. Help me to follow Your path and fix this.

Peace rolled through Gordon. God could help him walk through anything.

With today practically over, there were only three days left.

Three days to build a team and win the woman he loved.

Fourteen

One day—two nights—until she said "I do."

Eva paced the length of her room with her arms wrapped around her waist. She'd give just about anything to have Kendra here. Her friend still hadn't returned after Eva had told her about the engagement and her conversation with Alexander. She promised she'd be back before the wedding, but with time ticking away...hopefully, she'd be back tomorrow.

Stopping at the balcony door, she opened it, welcoming the chill of the evening. Snow fell softly over the city beyond the palace walls, but it didn't stop people from scurrying around the bazaar. Christmas lights twinkled through the town as last-minute shoppers hurried in and out of the stores she could see.

Someone knocked at the door, but before Eva could respond, the door opened. "Yoohoo! I'm back!"

Eva hurried out of her room toward the front of her apartment and threw her arms around Kendra. "I was just thinking about you. I've missed you. Are you okay?"

Kendra squeezed her back, and Eva had never been more thankful for her friend.

Eva broke the hug and grabbed Kendra's hands and led her to the couch. "I know you said that you're okay with what's happening, but you took leave, and I was worried you weren't coming back. Are you really okay?"

Kendra's laugh spilled into the room, warm and familiar. "First of all, it's freezing in here. Did you leave the door open again?"

Eva jumped up. "I'll go close it."

After returning from her room, with a couple of throws she kept in there, Eva tossed one to Kendra, who quickly wrapped it around herself. Eva mirrored her actions and sat next to her on the couch. "Tell me...how are you really?"

Kendra nodded. "Fine. Honest."

"But you liked Alexander, and I'm supposed to marry him. This is a mess."

"It's not. I did think he was a wonderful man. I still do. And if things were different, perhaps I could have allowed myself to develop feelings. He was never meant for me though, and I would never interfere in your relationship with him."

Posh. Kendra, her loyal friend, would never meddle like that. "I never considered you would. But I have been worried about you. Alexander seemed so firm, resolute in his choice. I'm sorry I didn't see your feelings before."

"You had a lot on your plate. You were focused on Gordon, and I knew nothing could ever happen with Alexander. He values honesty above everything else, and I was dishonest."

"Because of your job—"

"Regardless, I could have told him. Like I said though, I never meant for the flirtation between us to blow up the way it did. You need to be queen. I would never help the man who wanted to take it away from you. Although, I don't think that's Alexander. I think he's just as coerced as you are." Kendra stared off into the room, a far-off look on her face.

Eva knew that look all too well. It spoke of heartache, betrayal, disappointment. "If you have feelings for him..."

"Eva." Kendra immediately gave her a harsh look. "No. It is not in my future. You need to be queen. But I've heard that you could marry the man you loved. Why are you settling for Alexander?"

Eva's mouth might as well have been filled with cotton balls. She blinked quickly and took her own turn looking out over the room. "I'm not settling. I can't force Gordon…"

"Poppycock." A giggle spilled out of Kendra.

Eva found her friend wiping her eyes, a teasing grin on her face.

Kendra snorted. "I've always wanted to say that word. Who says that? But it's such a good word. Say it."

Eva raised an eyebrow. "Poppycock." And despite her best effort, she chuckled too.

"Ok, but seriously." Kendra reached for Eva's hand. "There is no forcing. Have you talked to Gordon?"

Eva shook her head. "What's there to say?"

Kendra tucked Eva's hair behind her ear. "How about start with 'I love you.'"

No.

Nope.

She'd started a kiss, he'd stopped it. She couldn't, she wouldn't, initiate the words she longed to hear from him. "I can't. I can't take any more rejection."

"Your phone's been off, so how do you know he hasn't been trying to reach you?"

Eva stood and walked away, pulling her throw tighter. "I don't. But if he wanted to stop this, why isn't he here? Knocking on my door? Fighting for me?"

"Okay. I see what you're saying. But seriously, knocking on your door? You do remember you're the princess and outside a select few, people can't just…" Kendra held up her hand and mimicked knocking on a door while making a clunking sound.

Eva turned back to her friend. "I know. Enough about Gordon. For you, I will stop this wedding in a heartbeat."

Kendra raised a hand. "No. Alexander is a good man. Did I

think he was handsome? Yes. You'd have to be blind not to. But I didn't fall in love with him."

"But you left—"

"I did. I didn't want to face Alexander after he found out I lied to him. But I also needed some time away for personal reasons, which we will have to discuss in the future. I promise as soon as I'm ready to share the details, you will be the first to know. So now I'm asking you to trust me." Kendra smiled. There was no hesitation, no lying, just her friend, open, honest, supportive.

"Thank you."

Kendra stood and crossed the room to stand in front of Eva, taking her hands. "No, thank you. It's not every day your friend volunteers to give up everything they've worked for to let you have a shot at a guy."

Eva chuckled again. "And it's not every day a girl has a friend she'd want to do that for. But I would for you."

Kendra hugged her. "I know. Now, this wedding is happening...what do I need to do?"

Eva led her back to the couch to share the to-do list. Kendra seemed so fine and when she was ready, Eva would support her through whatever had taken her away. And with only one day left, at least Kendra was back.

GORDON SAT IN HIS UNCLE'S APARTMENT WITH THE children piled on the couch together quietly watching a Christmas movie that Gordon couldn't name or follow. He should be out there banging on the palace doors or trying to sneak past security from the kitchen. Would it be hard to put on the palace uniform and just take something to her apartment?

But Orlin had needed someone to stay with the kids for a

while, and with absolutely no idea how to stop the wedding, he'd agreed. Call it a brain break. He tapped his phone on his knee.

Twenty-four hours. That's all he had left to stop this wedding, and he was no closer to figuring out what to do than he had been days ago.

Nothing he'd done had gotten him any closer to Eva. Nothing. He'd tried calling the king this morning, but he'd not heard back from him yet. He should be anywhere but here on the couch.

His phone vibrated in his hand, and he fumbled it. Maybe Eva had finally turned on her phone, or the king had called back.

No such luck. An unknown number had sent him a message. Had the media figured out his new number? He swiped to unlock his phone and opened the message.

UNKNOWN NUMBER

> Hey, Gordon. It's Kendra. Are you really going to let this wedding happen tomorrow?

Kendra? Gordon dropped his phone. Last he'd heard, she'd taken a few days off. Sarah got off the couch and picked the phone up then crawled into his lap. "You okay? I don't think you hurt your phone."

Gordon drew the little girl closer. "I'm ok. Just surprised by the text."

Sarah rested her head on his shoulder, relaxing in his arms. He opened his text message and responded.

GORDON

> Not if I can help it.

Immediately three little dots appeared, and Gordon held his breath, waiting for her words to appear. Sarah's warm breath puffed on his neck as she relaxed further, asleep in his arms. If only he could relax.

"Want me to take her?" Lizzy stood above him, her arms outstretched, ready to take Sarah.

"No. She's fine where she is."

Lizzy squinted at him but returned to the couch next to Demitri.

His phone buzzed in his hand.

KENDRA

Good. Get to the chapel in the park.
She'll be there for at least two hours.
Don't mess this up.

GORDON

Thank you.

Those two little words hardly seemed sufficient, but he hadn't even realized Kendra would be on his team. Sarah snuggled into him, taking a deep breath and letting it out.

As much as he wanted, he couldn't leave the children alone. He messaged his uncle.

GORDON

Need to go meet Eva. Can you come home?

UNCLE ORLIN

Be there soon.

Soon couldn't come soon enough, and thirty-five minutes later didn't feel like soon. By the time his uncle walked through the front door, Gordon thought he might burst. He quickly stood and handed Sarah to Orlin. Even in his impatience, he didn't have the heart to wake the little girl. They were finally safe, and they could sleep without worry.

Gordon grabbed the car keys as he rushed out the door, popping a breath mint in his mouth.

As soon as Gordon made it out of the palace, he ran into his first roadblock. Already police were blocking off roads for tomorrow's wedding and processional.

Chief Rodgers stood along the side of the road, and Gordon rolled down the window and waved at him. "Any way around this?"

Chief smirked. "If you're royal. Otherwise, you have to go clear around. There's a few streets open, but you'll be weaving. Where are you going?"

"The big park."

"You're better off to walk." The chief nodded and took a step backwards. "Oh, Gordon. One more thing."

Gordon paused. If Chief Rodgers needed something it would be important.

The chief bent down resting his arms on the open window frame. "I'm struggling to find a place for the three children to stay. Do you think you could get the paperwork filled out and have your uncle sign it? If you send it to me by tonight, they'd have a place for Christmas. We could find long term housing later. I'll keep working on it."

"I'll get it done." And he would. The children needed a safe space, and Gordon knew his uncle would provide that. Gordon waved goodbye as the chief reached for the tip of his hat.

Without much choice, Gordon found a parking spot and started the walk to the park. He'd be pushing it at this point, but nothing would keep him from Eva. After two blocks, he'd had enough of the wind. With his head down, he tried to keep the chill from tearing at his face. He grabbed his phone to check the time, but his pocket was empty. Back ones too. Must have left it in the car.

"Do you have the time?" Gordon asked a man dressed for work, with an overcoat and wool hat on.

The man responded. Gordon had some time, but he'd be cutting it close. He picked up the pace.

Seventy minutes later, he jogged up the steps to the church and burst in the front doors. The warmth of the building a welcome relief to the cold air outside.

Only the area was empty.

He'd missed her.

Gordon plopped down in the back pew. He still had to make it back to the car, but he'd warm up before he started the walk back.

The sun had set by the time he made it to his car. He'd missed seven calls from Kendra, one from the king, and more texts than he wanted.

Kendra's last text said it all.

KENDRA

> If you want this stopped, you're going to have to work harder.

If only she knew. But he'd do whatever he could.

GORDON

> Tell me what I need to do.

Maybe he still had hope.

Fifteen

Three hours.

That's all Gordon had left.

The countdown to the wedding had sped by entirely too fast. Even with a team of support behind him, Gordon didn't know if he could change the outcome set in motion. Especially after he'd missed her at the chapel yesterday. He'd been able to push through the paperwork for Orlin to keep the children. So, if push came to shove, they would have someplace to stay.

"What do you mean the tux isn't here?" Gordon didn't want to yell at the housekeeper—it wasn't her fault. But he only had one tux, and it was supposed to be cleaned and delivered yesterday while he'd been trying to hunt down Eva.

Of course it had been lost.

His uncle's tux had been with his, and it had been lost too.

"We are still searching for them. I have every confidence that we will find them before the service today." The housekeeper hung up the phone, and Gordon pinched the bridge of his nose, trying not to let his anger simmer. Before the service wouldn't be soon enough. He needed it now. Kendra had said she would try to meet him in the kitchen and take him up to talk to Eva. Could he go in his jeans? Because without a tux, he'd be crashing this wedding in business casual.

Lizzy sat at the kitchen counter eating toast and eggs. Chief Rodgers had finally found a place for the children, and he was planning on coming to pick them up. As much as he didn't want to see them go, Gordon also couldn't leave them alone, and juggling the responsibly of stopping this wedding and the children was a lot. A knock sounded at the door, and Sarah and Demitri raced from the living room, through the kitchen, toward the front door.

Chief Rodgers entered as he playfully carried both children over his shoulders. They laughed and squealed in delight. He set them down in the middle of the kitchen and nudged them across the floor toward their game in the living room. "Give me a moment to talk to Gordon here, okay?"

The pair quickly took off for their game.

Lizzy stood up with her plate. "I can tell this is serious. I'll go too."

Stuffing a bite of toast in her mouth, she walked to the couch, and sat, her body angled so she could watch both her siblings and the kitchen while eating her breakfast.

Orlin came out from his room, dressed in a suit. It would work for today in a pinch, but Gordon really needed a tux.

"I expected you to be dressed. If you're going to crash a wedding, you need to look the part." Chief Rodgers eyed Gordon's current getup—plaid flannel pajama pants and a black T-shirt.

"Except my tux is lost." Gordon jerked open the fridge and grabbed a can of soda and offered one to the chief, who declined.

Popping the top, Gordon chugged the carbonated beverage until his throat burned.

"Dude, if you keep that up, you'll interrupt the ceremony with your belch." Lizzy rolled her eyes and continued to eat. "And burping is not attractive."

Gordon set the can down on the counter, his gut churning. She wasn't wrong. Not the interruption he'd hoped for. Definitely not appropriate for a royal wedding.

"Listen, I have a tux." The chief gave Gordon a once-over.

It wouldn't fit. The chief, while as tall as Gordon, had a good number of more pounds to carry around.

"It's old. It might fit you... Accidentally grabbed the wrong one to clean the other day. Martha's been telling me I need to clean out my closet. Perhaps there's someone here who could make it work if it needs some touch-up. It's actually in my car. Walk with me."

Gordon and Orlin stepped out of the apartment and into the parking area at the palace. The chief pulled the tux out of the back of the trunk and handed it to Gordon. "Now that we're alone, I have some problems. I can take the kids with me today on patrols, but the housing situation didn't pan out. Gordon was able to push through some paperwork, so I'm hoping you're willing to keep them through Christmas."

Orlin nodded. "I have some gifts for them because I wanted to make sure they had some to open wherever they ended up. I'm happy for them to be here. If all goes as planned for Gordon, he will be otherwise entertained. I'd enjoy the company. Even long term, since Gordon pushed the paperwork through."

It might have cost him the girl he loved, but at least the children would be well cared for. Positive focus.

Two hours later, Gordon stood outside Eva's apartment in the palace. Kendra had pulled some strings, and the king had told the guards to let him through. Why hadn't he asked about this option sooner? He ran his hand down the tux that had literally been sewn onto his body. Thankfully, the seamstress had been able to work some magic on the tux, and while it wasn't his, it worked.

Gordon knocked. No one answered. He tried again.

Finally, the door opened, and Kendra stood there in a deep red gown, her hair partially styled. She popped her hip to the side and put her hand on it. "It's about time you showed up. But you're too late. She's already started her drive through town. They extended the procession to go by the chapel in the park, so they had to add some time."

Gordon lifted his hand to run it through his hair, and Kendra's grabbed his wrist. "Don't mess up your hair. And what are you wearing?"

"A tux?"

"Is that what you'd call this? No. If you want to stop this wedding, you need to at least look like you're husband material." She yanked him into Eva's apartment.

"They lost my tux."

Kendra dropped his arm and picked up the phone, telling them they needed a tux and some wardrobe assistance in the princess's apartment. Ten minutes later, a bunch of tuxes were wheeled into the apartment, Gordon was redressed, and his hair was styled as Kendra shoved him out of the unit to a waiting maid. "That will do. Now, Maria will take you over to the abbey. Stick close to her and stop Eva from making the biggest mistake of her life."

"This way." The maid, Maria, gestured to follow her. She took Gordon through twists and turns of the castle he'd never been in, before they emerged outside on the plaza near the abbey. Unfortunately, he would still need to cross the plaza packed with well-wishers to get there.

"Thank you, Maria. How do I get inside the abbey when I get there? Do you know where the princess will be?" He turned but the maid had already headed back the direction they'd come from, and she couldn't hear him.

Welp. He'd figure this out himself.

After weaving through the crowd, stepping on people's toes, having unkind remarks thrown at him for trying to get through, he finally stood in front of the abbey. Security stood out front, the red carpet rolled from the double doors at the entrance, down several stairs to the street, where crowds of people stood poised with their phones out, ready to snap a picture of whoever caught their attention.

Gordon checked his watch.

Thirty minutes until the wedding was scheduled to start.

A loud roar from the crowd practically shook the ground. Gordon stepped closer to discover why they cheered. Eva stepped down out of a carriage, a white coat wrapped around her, a long white skirt flowing around her. She wore white gloves, and her crown sparkled in the sunlight. Marco stood next to her, assisting her from the carriage and onto the carpet that led into the church. She greeted the people kindly but worked her way up the stairs quickly.

"Eva!" Gordon yelled, and hurried toward her, but the noise of the crowd drowned him out, and she entered the abbey. The door clanged shut behind her. How was he supposed to get inside?

The security guard at the entrance was unmoving as he approached. "I'd like to speak to Princess Evalina, please."

The guard snorted. "Wouldn't everyone."

"His Majesty the King knows I am here and would like for this meeting to take place." Gordon puffed out his chest, trying to act the confident suitor.

"If that were true, we would know. Do you have an invitation to enter?"

Gordon shook his head. Kendra hadn't mentioned needing an invitation.

The guard grunted and motioned toward the road. "Please, stand with the crowd."

"If you would just ask the king. Tell him Gordon Tarpen is here. Oh! Let me text Kendra. She sent me over here." Gordon took his phone out of his pocket and sent a text to Kendra, followed by one to the king.

"Look, we don't want news reporters inside. They're over there." The guard lifted his chin to an area where the press gathered. At least his reputation preceded him.

"I don't work for the news."

"And I'm not a palace guard."

"Okay, I did use to work for the press, but I quit. Please, just let the king know I'm here."

"Sure. I'll get right on that. Over there." The guard gestured and Gordon had no choice but to step aside. He checked his text messages, but no responses. Ten minutes now. The wedding started in ten minutes.

He couldn't be too late.

There had to be a way in.

SOMEHOW THE COUNTDOWN CLOCK HAD RUN OUT.

There were no more days. No more hours. No more minutes.

No more ways to get out of this.

No more hope of...

Nope.

Eva had decided to do this for her country.

As she stood in the lobby of the abbey, her heart raced and her head spun. She was getting married. The service had already started. Kendra had met her at the church after the procession through the capital. But her friend, as the maid of honor, had already walked down the aisle, looking around and shaking her head. She'd muttered something under her breath but given Eva a hug before she'd started her march down the aisle.

Beyond the closed doors in the sanctuary, the pews were filled, flowers perfumed the air, and security lined the walls and doors almost like decorations themselves.

Everything had come together perfectly—the musicians, the minister, the guests. The dress could have come straight out of a fairy tale, with a fitted bodice and a full, A-line skirt. Eva could hardly believe it had been created within days. The lace and flowers were simple and elegant.

The cascading bouquet filled with red roses, white jasmine, and greenery weighed heavy in her hands. Cliché coloring, but it fit for a Christmas wedding. The florist had done an amazing job, and it smelled divine.

Stringed music floated through the building and then changed when the organist took over, starting the wedding march.

She'd give just about anything to have her father beside her right now. However, the custom in their small country dictated that she walk down the aisle alone, and her father had already been seated.

Marco stepped forward, one hand on the door. He nodded toward Jake, who would open the other door. A double door entrance. "Are you ready, Princess?"

No.

A deep breath, an attempt to calm her racing heart. "As I'll ever be."

Marco studied her for a moment before bowing his head slightly. The wedding coordinator touched her earpiece and then said something into her mic before issuing the final command to allow Eva to enter. "Open the door in five, four, three..."

The doors opened.

Her stomach dropped.

Her hands shook.

She lifted her chin and took one tiny step into the chapel in time with the music.

Two steps.

Three steps.

A few more.

Her timing faltered and she missed a beat.

And another.

The aisle stretched on forever. It had not been this long at the rehearsal.

Alexander stood at the front of the church. Tall. Built. Handsome. A concerned smile plastered on his face. If he met her half-way, they could escape together.

Kendra stood as her attendant. Her face filled with concern.

What had Eva done?

No.

She could do this. For her country. For her people.

Her father stood in the front row. Compassion written across his face, he nodded.

Why couldn't she draw in a normal breath?

She stumbled to the side and grabbed a pew. A collective gasp rippled through the sanctuary and the music stopped. The weight of everyone's intense and puzzled gaze had her gripping the pew tighter, forcing her legs to hold her up. "I'm sorry. I need a moment."

Turning on her heel, Eva rushed from the sanctuary.

She hurried past Marco and Jake, handing one of them her bouquet, and burst through the front doors. People were cheering and waving. Phones pointed her direction, probably recording every move she made.

"Eva!" Gordon? Searching the crowd, she didn't see him. There were so many people. Her imagination had conjured up the man she wanted to see.

She waved to the crowd, lifting her skirts off the ground, and hurried to the side garden of the abbey on the opposite side of the palace. A large hedge surrounded the small garden, protecting it from prying eyes and cameras.

She collapsed on a bench and hugged herself, rocking back and forth. She just needed to breathe.

Inhale.

Exhale.

What was she doing?

A shiver wracked her body, and she hugged herself tighter.

If only that had been Gordon's voice she'd heard. He could swoop in and save the day, like a knight in shining armor. She couldn't think that. She didn't need some prince—or non-citizen in his case—to ride in on a white horse and save the day.

She had decided to do what she needed to do to save her kingdom. To save her role and her place on the throne.

Alexander had promised they were in this together. But even he had appeared a little ill standing waiting for her.

"Oh, Evalina." Her father's deep voice calmed her racing heart as his arms wrapped around her. In his embrace she found security and comfort.

Not to mention warmth. She'd not thought about how cold it would be outside in December. And the cold of the cement bench had worked its way through the many layers of her skirt.

"I'm sorry. I just needed a moment." Eva tried to break free from his hold, but his arms tightened, and he held her firm.

Her father tucked her head under his chin, and she listened to his steady heartbeat. *Thump. Thump. Thump.*

After a few moments, his calm voice spoke. "No, Evalina. No. There is no need to go through with this. You do not have to choose this. My darling girl, you are so much more important to me."

Taking a deep breath, she sat up, and he loosened his arms but didn't let go completely. She studied his face and found no judgment. She closed her eyes and pinched the bridge of her nose.

"No, I can do it. Really. I just...I needed a moment."

Father's hands moved up and down her arms. Slow, methodical movements. "Did you speak with Gordon?"

Her eyes popped open. Why bring him up now? "No."

Her father nodded, like he already knew this, and he glanced to the entrance of the garden. Jake stood there, hands clasped in front of him. Her father mouthed something to his guard, and Jake said something in his earpiece, but he was too far away for Eva to hear. "It's not too late. You do not have to marry Alexander."

Eva's throat tightened. They'd tried everything they could. "I do. For my country. For my future."

"There are other ways around this law. If you love someone else..."

Eva tried to block all thoughts of Gordon. Breaking her father's embrace, she stood and straightened her dress. She wiped her fingers across her cheeks. "He hasn't contacted me. There is no reason to think that is an option."

"That's where you're wrong. He's not been able to reach out because your phone has been off. Your schedule unpredictable. I couldn't even arrange a meeting with you. Neither could Kendra because of the roads yesterday. He has tried. You've been too stubborn to see it, wallowing in your hurt."

Ouch.

"Father, I can't. Please." She hung her head. She'd give anything if Gordon loved her. If he wanted to marry her, but she couldn't take rejection again.

Once had been terrible, twice...would be...more than she could handle.

"I don't want you to regret this. You love him." Father stood behind her.

"I do. But—"

"Then talk to him." Her father spun her around, and Gordon stood next to him. In a full tux, his hair styled perfectly, and a red rose pinned on his lapel.

Logically, Eva knew that oxygen hadn't evaporated, but she couldn't figure out how to draw any into her lungs.

Time seemed to freeze. She could have stood there for seconds or hours. In that time, her father left. When or where he went, she had no idea.

Gordon closed the distance between them. He took one hand and cupped her cheek, letting his hand move down her neck to her shoulder, down her arm until he took her other hand. "Eva, I'm sorry."

His warm hands tightened around hers, and her heart took off at breakneck speed. She'd promised to be faithful to Alexander, and this...this was borderline not okay. "No. No. This isn't right. Alexander..."

"Can wait. Please don't walk down that aisle without hearing me out. Since your wedding announcement, I've tried to reach you. Kendra has even reached out. But even with her help, I couldn't get in contact with you."

His warm, callused hands held hers tight, his thumbs rubbing across the back of her hands.

"Eva, I love you." His deep voice wrapped around her like a warm blanket.

Love?

Gordon loved her?

It didn't seem real. This was a nightmare. A cruel joke before her wedding.

But the constant pressure of his hands, the scrape of his rough skin against hers...it couldn't be a dream. He stepped closer, and a crunch of fabric drew her attention down. Her white wedding dress pushed against his black tux pants.

Her *wedding* dress.

Her groom stood waiting for her at the front of a full sanctuary, and she hid in the garden holding hands with the man she wished to marry.

This couldn't be happening.

"No. No. I can't do this. You don't mean that. I don't want to force you. You were right to push me away."

"No. I wasn't. I love you."

His deep, raspy voice scratched against her resolve. Her vision blurred, but no matter how many times she blinked, she couldn't see clearly. She stepped back and tried to tug her hands free, but he held tight.

"And I want to marry you, Eva. Right now, if you'll have me."

Words didn't form. She didn't know how to respond. She'd wanted this. But breaking her engagement to Alexander at the altar so she could marry someone else? His thumb gently caught the tear and dried her cheek.

"I can't do this."

"Your father says you can. He will fight for us. If you say yes, we can do this. You and me against the world. Forever."

Forever.

The words she'd always wanted to hear but at the completely wrong time. From the right guy...but also the wrong guy. He wasn't her fiancé.

Her throat tightened again and her heart thundered against her ribcage. The wind blew through, chilling her.

Eva. Her name whispered across her heart, and it calmed her racing thoughts. Her God promised what was best for her. He loved her beyond measure, and He gave good gifts. Peace flooded her as she took her hands from Gordon and stepped back. She'd made a promise.

This thing between her and Gordon, it...

If he'd talked to her sooner or even before the ceremony started. But she wouldn't play the what-if game.

But...she hadn't said I do.

Yet.

She hadn't pledged herself to Alexander. And though she loved his fierce loyalty, she didn't love him.

She turned away from Gordon and studied the snow-covered landscape. "I..."

She couldn't answer Gordon. Not when she wore another man's ring on her finger. She had to talk to Alexander. "I need to do something. Will you come to the sanctuary?"

Lord, please. Help him come. Help it not be too late for my happy ending.

Without turning to look at him, she left. Hoping he would follow. Hoping she wasn't making the biggest mistake of her life.

Eva. The name whispered across her heart again and peace settled over her. Her heavenly Father had seen her and called her by name. He knew what her heart longed for. He'd known the desires of her heart, what she needed, and He'd met her in her very own garden.

She just had to talk to Alexander.

GORDON STOOD ALONE AS EVA WALKED AWAY. JUST AS she left the garden, the king came back. Had he witnessed Gordon's humiliation?

Gordon had professed his love, and she'd left.

Rejection? It hurt.

He'd done everything he could. He'd partnered with the king, Kendra, his uncle, anyone he could, and it hadn't worked. He'd laid it all there, quit his job, given it everything he had, and it hadn't been enough.

Eva had walked away.

Come into the sanctuary? Watch her marry someone else? How could he do that? Why would she ask that of him? She'd never been cruel.

Quiet footsteps broke the silence of the garden, and the king stopped next to Gordon, his hand resting on his shoulder. "Don't give up yet, son. She looked too determined for your hope to be lost."

Gordon's eyes stung and he blinked quickly. "She left."

The king offered a comforting squeeze with his hand. "But it's not over yet. Let's go inside as she asked."

Jake fell in step behind the king as the two headed toward the entrance.

He'd rather leave the country than watch Eva marry someone else, but she'd asked him to go inside.

There was nothing else he could do. Nothing else he could say.

But God...

Those two little words rolled through his mind like a bowling ball on a winning streak.

He, Gordon, couldn't do anything else, but God could. The one who he should have asked first was the only one he hadn't really asked.

Lord, I've done what I can. Please work this out. I'm a bit slow on the uptake, but I'm here now for the woman I love. Please don't let it be too late.

Gordon jogged to catch up to Jake and the king before they disappeared into the abbey and he was denied entrance again.

Because whatever happened, he'd put it all on the line. He stayed back, next to Jake as Eva linked her arm in the king's. He kept to the shadows as the doors opened, and Eva walked down the aisle arm in arm with her father to another man.

His stomach might revolt, but she'd asked him here. Eva wouldn't ask him to watch that. She had never been vindictive, so there had to be a reason.

What small hope remained left as Eva placed her hand into Alexander's and the king sat down. Gordon leaned against the wall at the back of the sanctuary.

He'd tried his best, and he'd come up short.

Again.

Sixteen

Alexander squeezed her hand, anchoring Eva in this moment. She stood in front of a large crowd of people, her hand held by the man she'd announced her engagement to, with the man she loved somewhere in this room, she hoped. The pastor had already started his spiel, but he could be speaking in another language, because Eva couldn't focus on his words.

Alexander lifted an eyebrow and mouthed, *Are you okay?*

How could she answer that? Gordon had told her he loved her, and she'd just walked away. Now she stood in front of a church with a different man. Was she ok?

No. Not really. She lifted one shoulder and offered a half smile, because how could she sum that all up with one look? "I'm sorry."

The knots in her stomach tightened. Were her feet sweating in her shoes? The pastor continued to drone on. But then he stopped and asked if anyone objected to this marriage.

Eva glanced around the room, and the people all stared at her with wide, blank smiles. Gordon stood at the back of the church, his hands in his pockets. He'd come. She'd hoped he would, because...

Because she couldn't marry a man she didn't love when Gordon had proposed.

He'd *proposed*.

And she'd walked away because she didn't know how to answer him with another man's ring on her finger.

Well, she had an answer now. Her father said it could work. She had no idea how, but he'd never lied to her before. She'd trust him now.

"I object." Eva's voice rang out through the church.

People started talking and she took the opportunity to drop her voice and step closer to Alexander.

"I'm so sorry. I can't do this. I—" At the back of the sanctuary, Gordon still stood, his hands still buried in his pockets, but his eyes met hers from across the room. The desperation was gone, and hope flamed to life.

She loved him.

She nodded to him, offering what she hoped was a reassuring smile before turning back to Alexander. He held both her hands, and she squeezed them. "I think we both deserve to find love. Don't you?"

Alexander blew out a breath. "Thank you. For standing up for what you want. I should have done so as well."

Eva let go of Alexander's hands and took off the ring. Then she reached for one of his hands, gently placed the ring in his palm. He closed his fist around it, and she squeezed his hand. "This should never have been mine. I'm sorry I didn't see what was right in front of me sooner. You deserve happiness and love. I wish you the best."

Alexander gave her a cocky grin as he nodded toward the back of the room. "Go get him."

Alexander walked away and sat next to Lord Veelsh on the front row.

By now the noise in the room had risen to extreme levels.

People were standing and talking. She couldn't find Gordon among all the movement in the crowd. Was she too late?

"This cannot be happening." A screeching voice filled the room, and Eva didn't need to look to recognize Lord Veelsh's voice. But there was so much noise and chaos, Eva ignored him and scanned the crowd.

Finally, Eva caught a glimpse of the back wall where Gordon had been, but no one stood there now. Marco and Jake had moved to the doors, ready to usher people out. She scanned the room but couldn't find Gordon. Had he left?

No. There was no way he'd left. Many people stood, some sat in stunned silence.

Kendra moved to stand next to Eva. "You finally talked to Gordon."

"Yes." Eva couldn't stop the smile from spreading across her face. Even if she couldn't see Gordon in the crowd, he had to be there somewhere. "Thank you for trying to arrange it sooner."

Kendra grabbed Eva's hand. "I've always got your back."

"And I haven't had yours. I'm sorry. Ale—"

Kendra shook her head. "No. I'm not sure it was meant to be."

Eva let her eyes move toward Alexander, forcing Kendra to follow the subtle motion. "He's watching, and it's not because of me. Go talk to him."

"I don't—"

"You did it for me. Trust me. Go talk to him." Eva squeezed her friend's hand and watched her walk down the steps. Alexander, ever the gentleman, stood and gestured for her to sit next to him.

Eva's father walked toward her. Ever steady, ever calm. Every bit a king. But as he neared Eva, she could see the approval shining from his smile.

"You ready for this?" His deep voice was sure and steady in the sea of voices filling the room.

"As I'll ever be." Eva had never been more confident of any

choice she'd made before. "You've promised I could marry the man I love. I'm trusting you to follow through."

The impish look on her father's face passed quickly before he turned as the king and faced the room. He raised his hand and the room fell quiet.

The silence only lasted a single heartbeat before Lord Veelsh's voice echoed through the room as he made his way up the stairs onto the platform to face off with the king.

Evalina did not step back, though, keeping her ground next to her father. As the crown princess, it was her place.

"The law clearly states that Princess Evalina must be married by her twenty-sixth birthday—tomorrow—or forfeit the throne." Lord Veelsh shook a fist as he spoke.

"I understand the law you are referring to clearly. I also understand that our parliament refuses to bring our country into the twenty-first century and abolish said law." The king spoke calmly, but the edge to his voice clearly rang out his displeasure over the parliament's decision.

Eva lifted her chin. She'd prepared her entire life to stand next to her father. To speak truth. "I have studied and worked for the people of Nevive from the moment I was welcomed into Parliament meetings. My love for this country has never wavered. I respect the laws, and I am willing to do what it takes to meet them. Even if it means marrying by my twenty-sixth birthday."

A wave of murmurs ran through the room as people spoke. Everyone knew her birthday fell on Christmas and she'd just called off her wedding on Christmas Eve.

Lord Veelsh sneered at her before his face morphed into a demeaning expression. "There is no need to scramble for an unwilling groom. We have a qualified leader to take your place."

"No, you don't." Alexander stood, his voice loud and clear. "I refuse to be king. Let this be my official withdrawal from the line of succession."

"You can't do that." Lady Veelsh stood and glared at Alexander. "Think of all we've done to prepare you to fulfill your role."

Alexander's calm expression never wavered. "A role my father never wanted to force on me."

Warmth spread through Eva as she watched Alexander stand up to Lord and Lady Veelsh. When she'd first met him, he'd not wanted to cause any disagreement with them, and today, he'd not only stood against them but done so publicly.

Lord Veelsh made it to Alexander and stood screaming in his face. The man said some truly demeaning words.

Eva hated this moment for Alexander, but he didn't look cowed or overwhelmed. Instead, he remained firm. The man really would have made an excellent king. Just not an excellent husband —for her.

She'd done the right thing, and she'd never been more at peace.

Alexander offered her a quick bow before he turned and walked toward the back of the sanctuary. His cousins followed behind him. The king motioned to security, and the doors were opened for Alexander and closed behind the Veelshes. Eva knew they would not be allowed back in.

As silence fell across the room, Eva drew the attention of the crowd back to the front of the room. "Now, as you're all aware, my birthday is tomorrow, and in order to take the throne, I must be married. I believe you all came for a wedding, and I'd still like that to happen today."

A quiet murmur buzzed through the room, and Eva felt her breath grow shallow. Forcing a deep breath, her heart rate slowed. She had no doubt she'd done the right thing. No doubt about the next words she would say. But as she prepared to speak, she still couldn't find the one man she most wanted to see.

Had he left?

Had he changed his mind?

Had she blown everything by denying him earlier?

But the peace that had filled her from the inside earlier remained. No. He had to be here.

"Gordon?"

BLOOD THUNDERED IN GORDON'S EARS. HAD HE REALLY heard Eva call his name? When she'd objected to her own wedding, he'd stepped into the shadows, trying to stay out of the chaos that had broken out.

Although he'd tried to hope for a positive answer when she'd asked him to come, he had no idea what she'd been up to. This dramatic turn of events was something he hadn't seen coming.

Calling off her wedding in the middle of it? He'd wondered if he'd been dreaming until Alexander had sat down with his ring in hand and chaos had erupted.

Then had she really called his name?

Eva stood at the front of the church with a confident half smile, a relaxed stance. She'd been born for this moment, confidently leading the people of Nevive into a new day. Accepting their ancient laws and showing the world that she loved these people and their customs. But also proving that she would not lose herself in the position.

Gordon had never been more proud of her.

Orlin appeared beside him and elbowed his gut. "Are you going to leave her hanging up there?"

Oops. He hadn't realized how much time had passed, but her confidence had slowly morphed to something a little less certain. Most people wouldn't pick up on the tiny changes, but Gordon had never been most people.

Stepping out from the shadows, he cleared his throat, and every eye in the room fell on him. Yikes. Was this what Eva always felt like? No wonder she'd enjoyed her day of freedom. It hadn't even been ten seconds and already Gordon wanted to loosen his collar.

He didn't.

He rolled his shoulders and lifted his chin, as he'd seen Eva do through the years, and stepped toward her on shaky legs.

As soon as he stood in front of her, it seemed everyone in the room held their breath to see what would happen.

Eva clasped his hands, her voice low. Intimate. He had no doubt that although the entire room waited to hear her, even though lip readers would work to understand what she said, she was speaking strictly for him.

"Gordon, I'm sorry for running earlier. For being afraid. For not saying yes when you asked. I love you. I think I always have. If it's not too late, I would very much like to say yes to your proposal." Eva's thumbs rubbed the back of his hands, and her eyes bore into his. Her lips drew his attention as she smiled. He'd kiss those lips again very soon.

He lifted their joint hands and instead kissed her left ring finger. "I have a ring to put on this finger."

"I object!" A strong feminine voice echoed through the room, and the clergyman seemed to deflate and stepped back to sit on a stool on the side of the platform.

"That man is not a citizen," Lady Galveston said. "He cannot marry the princess. Our law clearly states that the princess must marry either another royal or a citizen of our country. This man is nothing more than a TV personality. And not a very good one at that."

Her words stung. A TV personality? Well, not anymore.

"Ah, yes. I wondered if you would bring this up, Lady Galveston." The king cleared his throat and nodded to security. Jake walked forward with another guard Gordon didn't know. They made their way forward to stand next to Lady Galveston.

"What is the meaning of this?" Lady Galveston moved away from Jake, but the security officer did not seem deterred.

The king stood tall and lifted one eyebrow. "Were you aware, Lady Galveston, that tampering with civilian records is illegal? When I learned that Gordon Tarpen, local TV personality as you put it, did not yet have his citizenship, I decided to look into things. Turns out, he's applied several times, and his paperwork is always mysteriously misplaced, normally at the hands of your son-in-law, who is the head of the department. I had my security do some digging and noticed the Veelshes have been paying you regularly for the past few years. I can't help but wonder if there's a connection."

Gordon's head jerked back, but Eva squeezed his hands. He'd never ever imagined foul play. Maybe he should have looked into the immigration office for that investigative news story after all.

Lady Galveston paled and sputtered. "There is no proof of that, Your Majesty."

"Oh, but there is. Now is not the time to get into the nitty-gritty details, but you can rest assured there is enough evidence to back up my claims." The king gave a single nod to Jake, who took Lady Galveston's elbow and escorted her out of the room.

The king stepped to the center of the church, where the clergyman had previously stood. His strong voice rang out. "The law does state that the princess must marry within certain guidelines. But an addendum added a few years ago states that the current monarch may override any regulations to give his or her blessing. May it be known that Gordon Tarpen has my full approval. I believe he will be a match to our future queen and an excellent husband to my daughter. Not only that, but because outside influences have blocked Gordon's requests for citizenship, I am hereby granting him full citizenship. The paperwork has already been completed and approved by the immigration department."

Gordon's jaw dropped, and he closed it quickly. He didn't need that picture to appear in the news tomorrow. *TV Personality Marries Princess in Shocking Turn of Events.* But citizenship? That was not something Gordon had anticipated. After all the mishaps, all the requests, all the lost paperwork, he'd become a citizen of Nevive.

"Now, if there are not further objections, I believe my daughter would like to get married." The king stepped to the side, but Eva lifted her hand again.

"I'm so thankful for each of you being here. However, as beautiful as this abbey is, I would like to move my wedding to the chapel in the park. One more change today seems minor after everything else that has changed." A chuckle rumbled through the audience.

Eva paused to give them time to settle. "The chapel used to house royal weddings until World War I. It's a much smaller venue, so while I will be re-establishing a time-honoring tradition of a small service, you are welcome to head to the reception now. We will join you after the service for dinner."

The king returned to the center of the platform and nodded. "I like this change."

He turned and spoke to the audience. "Before we leave for the chapel, we will go ahead and sign the paperwork here, making this union official in front of you. Then you may head to the palace for the reception. Reginald, I will turn it over to you." The king turned and gestured for the clergyman.

A bit dazed, Reginald stood and walked to the altar on the platform and took a pen from his inside coat pocket. "Very well. I have the paperwork here."

Reginald handed the pen to Gordon and then pulled out an envelope from behind the altar. He laid the papers inside across the altar.

On each paper, Gordon's name had been printed as the groom. He turned and nodded his thanks to the king.

It had paid off to ask for help. To reach out and rely on other people.

To rely on God.

Gordon set the pen to the first page and signed his name. Then again a few more times. He should take the time to read these documents, but when Eva leaned into his side, he realized it didn't matter. He would literally sign away anything and everything if it meant marrying her.

He finished and handed the pen to Eva, whose fingers skimmed over his hands slowly before taking the pen and signing her own name.

When they finished, the clergyman took the papers, looked them over, and tucked them back in the envelope. He gestured for Eva and Gordon to step forward.

Eva reached for Gordon's hand, and together they stopped at the top of the steps facing the crowd.

"By the law of Nevive, these two are now legally bound together in matrimony. I present to you Her Royal Highness, Princess Evalina Rosalind Marie and His Royal Highness, Prince Gordon Michael Bexley."

Gordon hadn't stopped to think that he'd need to take the royal name, but honestly, he didn't mind. He'd legally married Eva, and now they'd retreat to the beauty of his favorite location and say their vows before God.

The clergyman waited for the applause to subside, then gestured to the king, who stood to the side like a best man. "Now, I believe we are bound for the chapel. Thank you for attending. Your Majesty, we will follow you out."

The king walked to the center of the platform. "We'd like close friends and family to join us. If you were among the group invited to tomorrow's breakfast, please join us at the chapel."

The king went down the steps and exited the sanctuary.

Eva's hand slid around Gordon's elbow. He immediately bent his arm and drew her closer. Her sweet perfume filled his senses, reminding him that this lovely woman loved him. With the slightest pressure on his arm, he started following the king. They walked down the steps and toward their future.

Together.

Seventeen

"I, Evalina Rosalind Marie Bexley, take you, Gordon Michael Tarpen, to be my wedded husband to have and to hold from this day forward. For better or worse."

Honestly, though, Eva couldn't imagine things being worse than thinking she'd marry someone else.

"For richer or poorer."

For themselves and her country. With Gordon by her side, they would all make it through.

"In sickness and in health."

Eva took a deep breath. For the first time since she'd walked away from Gordon at the Renoldses' home, the knots in her stomach had loosened, and her headache had subsided.

"To love and to cherish."

With her entire being. She'd never loved anyone the way she loved Gordon.

"Till death do us part."

May it be years to come, but even if their marriage would be cut short like her parents', she would treasure this time with Gordon.

Gordon repeated the vows to her, his dark eyes never looking away, his speech never faltering.

Someone pinch her.

This was really happening.

They were really getting married.

"Now we will exchange rings." Reginald hesitated, and his statement sounded more like a question.

Oh no! She didn't have a ring for Gordon. Alexander's fingers were so much longer and leaner than Gordon's, the ring might not fit. Even if it worked, did she really want to give Gordon a ring she'd picked out for another man?

Her father cleared his throat and stepped forward with a ring between his thumb and finger. "I had hoped you'd need this today. I took the liberty of making sure it would fit and match yours."

Match hers? Gordon probably didn't have a ring for her either. She hadn't even thought about it.

Gordon reached inside his tux and withdrew a velvet box.

Oh. He did.

Her father set a white gold ring in her hand. The ring had a simple design etched into the band, the royal crest pressed into the top, so the band was wider on one side. Never before had Eva noticed this ring in the vault, but she willingly accepted it. Perfection. Her father had done well choosing. A different one couldn't possibly be better.

Gordon offered her his hand, and she placed the ring on his finger as she once again committed to love him.

When she finished, he opened the velvet box, and Eva inhaled sharply.

Nestled inside?

Her mother's wedding ring. A white gold band with a large oval diamond surrounded by smaller rubies. The band had similar etchings to Gordon's ring.

They matched beautifully.

Her father's eyes shone, as he blinked back his own tears.

Nothing could have symbolized his approval more than the gift of this ring. A ring the country knew and loved. He'd kept it in his room for years, always close by. To give it to her now?

This ring would symbolize more than their love—it would show the world the king approved of the match.

Blinking back her own tears, Eva mouthed a thank-you to her father and turned back to Gordon, extending her left hand.

He cradled it in his own and slid the ring into place. A national symbol not only of her parents' love and commitment but now hers and Gordon's.

The service wrapped up with the words Eva had been waiting for. "You may now kiss the bride."

Eva stepped closer to Gordon. This time, she would let him initiate the kiss. He brought his hands up to frame her face, gently holding her. "You have no idea how many times I replayed our last kiss."

"I might have some idea." The number would be embarrassingly high if it matched how many times she'd thought about it.

"This time I intend to finish it properly." Gordon slowly lowered his head.

He brushed his nose next to hers, tilting her head just so.

Eva's hands lifted and settled on Gordon's lapels as she waited for him to close the distance between them.

"I will kiss you every day from here on out." Gordon's quiet words were a balm to her soul. But he held himself back, his breath warm on her face.

When he still hadn't closed the space between them, Eva gave him a sassy smile. "I'm starting to doubt—"

Gordon cut off her teasing, his lips pressing against hers. Possessive, loving, all-consuming.

Eva's heart rate skyrocketed. Gordon's hands left her face and his arms wrapped around her back, pulling her impossibly close, supporting her.

Kissing Gordon was like Christmas morning. A gift. Filled with joy, excitement, love.

His kiss promised everything he'd vowed a few minutes ago.

She'd always wanted to be seen. Wanted to be loved for who she was, and Gordon offered that in one life-altering kiss.

Never before had she felt more like she'd finally found her spot. Her person. Her place.

Chuckles sounded throughout the chapel, reminding her she had allowed Gordon to turn her legs to Jell-O in front of her father and the few people who had joined them.

Ever so slowly, Gordon ended the kiss. A devilish grin spread across his face, and he quickly pressed his lips to hers again, soft and gentle. She sighed against him as the crowd cheered. It didn't seem to be enough, though, because before she could breathe, his lips were on hers yet again. A quick, fast kiss, before he turned her to face their friends watching this monumental moment.

Orlin sat on the front row, next to her father, Kendra next to him. Beverly sat in the audience with her grandchildren. And Eva's security team were all there. Renee beamed from the back of the room, where she stood next to the frazzled-looking wedding coordinator.

Reginald's voice boomed behind them. "Let me be the first to introduce you to Her Royal Highness Princess of Nevive Evalina and His Royal Highness Prince of Nevive Gordon."

Gordon offered Eva his arm, and she placed her hand into the bend. Even through his tux, he could feel the heat from her touch. Together they stepped down the one step to the front pew where her father sat. He stood as they approached. Gordon bowed, and Eva lowered into a curtsy.

In a surprising move, her father hugged them both. "I couldn't be more pleased with the outcome of today."

Eva and Gordon continued on, and halfway down the aisle, Gordon stopped her, a roguish grin on his face. He pulled her close, dipping her low, and kissing her neck, then her lips.

As he brought her back up, his lips grazed her ear. "Every day, Eva. Every day I will find new ways to kiss you and show you just how much I love you."

"I look forward to it." More than she could ever say.

As they stepped outside, the chill of the winter wind whisked around them. The sun shone brightly, illuminating the outside world like a beacon of golden glitter. The carriage, pulled by a team of horses all dressed with sleighbells on their harnesses, sat in front of the chapel. As the horses shook their heads and stomped their hooves, the bells jingled merrily.

Then the chapel bell tolled.

Eva caught her breath as the rich sound echoed through the park. Deep. Rich. Magnificent.

Just as it should sound after such a joyous occasion.

Her father exited the chapel and clapped her and Gordon's shoulders. "Finally took my turn to see if we could repair the bell. I'd hoped you two would end up here. What better reason to try and repair it?"

Fredrick, the caretaker of the chapel, stood by the carriage as the sounds continued to spill through the town announcing that the princess had a prince.

He bowed as they approached, and her father extended his hand. "Good work, Fredrick. The bell sounds amazing."

"It was the right time, Your Majesty." Fredrick turned toward Eva and Gordon. "I'm so glad to see the chapel filled with love again."

Gordon wrapped his arm around Eva and kissed her forehead. "Me too."

The king cleared his throat. "I know we have to head back to the palace, but at some point, you will want to escape on your own. I've arranged a suite for you. Here's the key. It's not a full honeymoon—you'll have to schedule that later."

She should have grabbed a tissue or a handkerchief this morning. Wrapping her arms around her father, she hugged him. "Thank you for not giving up on me."

He held her tight. "Happy endings are often just the beginning."

Fredrick helped Evalina into the carriage, and then Gordon climbed in behind her and wrapped a blanket over their laps. As they drove away from the chapel, the bell still ringing through the city, Eva realized that the life she'd dreamed wouldn't compare to the life ahead of her. All thanks to the good gifts of her heavenly Father, who saw her and called her by name, even when she wasn't listening.

Who knew that one day as a royal runaway would turn into a lifetime of happiness?

If she'd known, she might have run away sooner. But now, she didn't have many reasons to run.

Because now, she had someone to run to.

Someone to run with.

CHRISTMAS MORNING DAWNED BRIGHT AND BEAUTIFUL, if not a bit nippy. Standing in front of his uncle's apartment door was not where Gordon had planned to be the morning after he married the woman he loved. An armful of gifts that Eva had bought for the children were stacked so high in his arms he couldn't see over them, and he had to peek around the side. Eva had heard about Orlin taking in three children and had wanted to make sure that they had something special for Christmas morning. She'd gone above and beyond.

As Eva bounced on her toes, Gordon wouldn't want it any other way. He'd follow her anywhere she wanted or needed to go today, as her husband.

Eva bit her bottom lip and traced her fingers over the gifts in his arms. "Do you think they'll like these? Will your uncle mind that we're crashing their morning activities?"

Gordon shifted the gifts in his arms, but there was no way to wrap his arm around Eva and hold the gifts, so he tapped his arm against hers. "Uncle Orlin loves tradition. I bet he's made them Christmas pancakes with berries and whipping cream for after they open stockings. I'm not sure if the kids would sleep in, but it's unlikely. It's Christmas morning. Besides, they will love all of this. And you. What's not to love?"

He gave her a quick kiss. Much shorter than he would like, but he pulled back and nodded at the door. "Can you open that?"

Eva shook her head. "We can't just walk in on your uncle."

"Why not? I've been living here for the last few weeks."

"Sorry. I can't just walk in. I'll carry the gifts, and you can walk in."

As if he'd hand her the boxes. "No."

"Then I'll knock." Eva raised her hand and rapped three times on the door.

He could practically hear her saying "Jingle Bells" as she knocked.

Twenty-four hours ago, Gordon was homeless, jobless, and basically hopeless. Now, he had an armful of gifts, a wedding ring on his finger, an apartment in the palace, and the woman he loved to call his wife. Not to mention a new title—Prince. That would take some getting used to.

The door opened, and Uncle Orlin's eyes widened. He immediately bowed. "Your Royal Highness, is everything all right?"

Eva shook her head and extended her hands. "Orlin, we're family now. Please don't be so formal."

Gordon chuckled and shifted the weight of the boxes in his arms. "Will you let us in, Uncle? These gifts are heavy."

Orlin opened the door wide and motioned them in, then he

reached for some of the boxes Gordon carried. "I'm sorry. I wasn't expecting company this morning. It's a bit of a mess."

Setting the boxes down under the Christmas tree next to the ones Orlin had bought, Gordon finally had a chance to look around. Stockings were all on the ground with candy wrappings, oranges, and wrapping paper. Lizzy, Demitri and Sarah stood in their pj's, staring at Eva. Chocolate and whipped cream were smeared across Sarah's face, and she quickly dropped into a clumsy curtsey. "Your Royal Highness? Are you a princess?"

Eva quickly walked through the apartment and dropped down to one knee in front of the little girl. "I am. But you can call me Eva. And you must be Sarah."

Gordon turned toward his uncle and let Eva spend some time with the children. They didn't have long before they had to attend a Christmas brunch and then pass out gifts at the children's hospital. Their day was packed full. "I'm sorry I didn't give you any notice. I didn't realize Eva had planned this until we were pretty much in front of your door."

"You're always welcome here, Gordon." Orlin placed a steady hand on Gordon's shoulder. He looked Gordon over and frowned.

"You can speak your mind, Uncle Orlin."

Orlin let out a cheeky laugh. "You're my prince now—I'm not sure I can."

"I will always be your nephew first." Gordon looked at his uncle, who wore his flannel pj's, his hair mussed as though he hadn't brushed it after waking, merriment dancing in his eyes.

"This is not where I anticipated seeing you this morning."

"Nor me. But Eva has a full day planned. I suppose this is the life I need to adjust to. She so wanted to deliver these gifts in person, and it really only will take a few minutes. Unfortunately, she has to be someplace soon. Besides, as she said, we have the rest of our lives together." And Gordon certainly had plans to celebrate their first Christmas together later. "But speaking of the rest of our lives, were you able to contact Zadock?"

Orlin nodded. "I messaged Marge yesterday, and she coordinated it. I have the painting of the castle in that gift bag by the door."

Gordon turned and saw the holiday bag. Eva had been so captivated with his paintings at the bazaar that Gordon wanted to make sure she had her very own. "You didn't have to wrap it."

"I didn't. That's Marge's handiwork. She insisted it should look like a gift fit for a princess, since that's who it was being given to." Orlin shook his head. "She may be a bit unorthodox, but the woman has an artistic touch."

"Her daughter does too. I imagine that's Jamie's handiwork." Gordon nudged his uncle's elbow.

Eva joined them before his uncle could respond. "Thank you for letting us crash your Christmas morning."

Orlin nodded respectfully again. "Of course, Your Roy—"

"Eva please, Orlin. We're family now." Eva curled her hands around Gordon's arm, and he immediately dropped a kiss on her upturned mouth.

She giggled. "In front of your uncle?"

"In front of the whole world, Eva." Gordon lifted his arm and invited Eva to come closer, which she did, before turning back to his uncle. "I agree, let's not be so formal."

"Very well—"

"Eva," Eva filled in for his uncle and laughed when he struggled to call her by her first name. "It will come in time, I hope."

"If you call me uncle."

Eva stepped forward and kissed his uncle on the cheek. "Merry Christmas, Uncle Orlin. We have to be going."

Gordon grabbed her hand and led her to the front door, picking up the gift bag on the way out. "We'll see ourselves out. Merry Christmas, all!"

Hours later, Eva and Gordon had retired to Eva's apartment—their apartment now—and the beautiful gift sat on the coffee table, where Marco must have had it placed. Eva eyed it and turned questioning eyes back on Gordon. "From your uncle?"

It had been the first quiet moment they'd had together to consider exchanging gifts. Gordon couldn't wait for her to open it up. "It's nothing big, but I wanted to say happy birthday and Merry Christmas."

Eva's breath caught as she glanced back at the bag. Stepping closer to him, she wrapped her arms around his waist and looked up at him. "How did you know we'd be together? I'd given up hope."

"Honestly? I didn't. But I hoped and I prayed, and I asked others for help. Because you were right. I had let pride get in the way. I was so set on doing everything myself, but I learned I cannot do anything without God's help."

Eva ran her hands up Gordon's arms and around his shoulders. "I was worth asking for help over?"

Gordon lowered his head, teasing her with phantom kisses on her cheeks and nose. "You are worth so much more."

Eva's eyes lifted to the ceiling and he discovered that a little bundle of greenery had been hung above them. "Mistletoe?"

A faint blush colored Eva's checks. "I asked the staff if they could hang some in here for us. I've always wanted to kiss under some."

"I think we can make that happen." Gordon's skin burned as Eva lifted on her toes and pressed her lips against his. Fire licked at his skin, and he kissed her until they were both winded.

He kept Eva pressed close as their breathing returned to normal.

"Gordon!" Eva gasped his name as he bent down and picked her up bridal style.

"One surprise for the birthday girl." Gordon crossed the room with Eva in his arms. Then sat on the couch, keeping her in his lap. Carefully reaching over her, he grabbed the gift and handed it to her.

Her fingers brushed over the design on the bag. "Thank you, Gordon. For always seeing me. For reminding me who I am and challenging me."

"Just think, it only took one day of being on the lam to bring us together."

"Maybe I should have run sooner." Lifting the tissue paper out, Eva pulled out a beautifully wrapped package. Jamie had gone above and beyond. Eva's fingers ran along the seam of the paper, carefully opening the package, until she found the painting of the castle. "Oh, it's beautiful. I saw this at the bazaar."

Gordon would always be grateful for the day Eva had gone incognito. "Now we have a reminder of the day that brought us together. I saw you admiring Zadock's work."

"You saw me, even then?" Her voice dropped as she held the picture, a shy smile on her beautiful face.

"I did. Because no matter where you go, or how you dress, I'll know you."

"I had every plan to go back to get that painting." She leaned in, letting her forehead rest against his.

"I know." Closing the distance between them, he tenderly slanted his lips across hers, taking his time. Finding he quite liked this new way of dancing with her. He slowed his movements, reminding her that he would always see her. Always be there for her.

She moved back, a bit breathless. "Thank you for the beautiful gift. Just so you know, if I ever run away again, I'll be taking you with me."

Then she kissed him again.

What's Next?

Can't wait to return to Nevive?
    Sign up for Mandy's newsletter for the latest information.
    www.mandyboerma.com

Acknowledgments

If you're reading this, then thank you. This book has been a journey, and one I've been so happy to go on. With each step of this process, God has been so good to keep moving me forward. And He's called us to give honor where it's due.

So, without further ado—

To Barbara Curtis, Carol Moncado, Sara Turnquist, and Kelly Roy. My deepest thanks in editing and proofreading this book. You have helped to make my story—and me—better. I take full responsibility for any errors left in this book, but I know they are fewer because of you.

To my friends who have encouraged me and supported me through the ups and downs of writing, I can't say thank you enough. Tammy and Sara, you know I wouldn't have finished this without your phone calls, prayers and support. And for rereading my book. Rachel, thank you. Your encouragement is endless and wise. Kariss, your to-do list was beyond helpful. Thank you.

For the always full cup of coffee that has seen me through this process, I have Angela, Trevor, Dylan and Zoe at JoJo's Coffee and Goodness to thank. Your support and encouraging words are worth more than I can say.

Sam. My friend and husband, I love you. Thank you for not rolling your eyes while I dream big and sometimes jump blindly.

For Stella and Johanna, thank you for letting me follow this dream, talk to imaginary people and for laughing at my stories when I needed a pick me up.

And Mom and Dad, thanks for being eager to read my work and encourage me.

Julie. I can't say thanks enough. For the mental check ins, for the peptalks, for the car rides you give my kids, and for the dad faces when I need a laugh.

Steve—you're not here to read this, but your encouragement as I sat at JoJo's and worked will always be appreciated. You are missed everyday.

I saved the most important for last. To my Savior. He's offered encouragement when I was ready to quit and has again taught me more than I was maybe ready to learn. I'm grateful for my God who is always good.

About the Author

Mandy Boerma

Mandy Boerma is an award-winning author of faith-filled contemporary romances. She's been honored with Golden Scroll second place for Romance Novel of the year and third place in the prestigious Selah Awards for her novel *Here With Me*. She writes stories about love, grace, and second chances that resonate with readers seeking hope and happily-ever-afters.

When Mandy isn't tucked away at her favorite coffee shop writing, she's a busy mom on the go. After meeting her own Prince Charming, they began their happy ending in the Florida Panhandle. While romantic sunset walks and sandy toes once filled their days, now carpool lanes, dance lessons, and band practice keep her moving—usually with a cup of coffee in hand and a story in her heart.

For more information or to sign up for Mandy's newsletters visit her at: www.mandyboerma.com